JOURNEY

Look for other books by Chuck Black

The Kingdom Series
Kingdom's Dawn
Kingdom's Hope
Kingdom's Edge
Kingdom's Call
Kingdom's Quest
Kingdom's Reign

The Knights of Arrethtrae
Sir Kendrick and the Castle of Bel Lione
Sir Bentley and Holbrook Court
Sir Dalton and the Shadow Heart
Lady Carliss and the Waters of Moorue
Sir Quinlan and the Swords of Valor
Sir Rowan and the Camerian Conquest

The Wars of the Realm
Cloak of the Light
Rise of the Fallen
Light of the Last

The Starlore Legacy
Nova
Flight
Lore
Oath
Merchant
Reclamation
Creed
Journey
Crucible
Covenant
Revolution
Maelstrom

www.ChuckBlack.com

Author's Commentary

It is with much prayer and extreme carefulness that I present this story to you. Today, our lives are immersed in worldly entertainment, from the innocent to the blasphemous. But rarely, if ever, does the secular entertainment industry point us to Jesus Christ as the exclusive author of our salvation. Therefore, it is my heart that the Starlore Legacy books might entertain while heralding the inerrant Word of God as true and acknowledging that there is no name given among men whereby we can be saved other than that of Jesus. As Jesus taught through parables, allegory, and metaphor, this is my attempt to likewise inspire people of all ages to search out the Holy Scriptures and follow our Lord and Savior.

These books are not intended to replace, distort, or confuse God's Word. These books are also not intended to teach theology or doctrine. Therefore, please do not make the mistake of rigidly applying this loose allegory to such and thus misunderstanding its intent. I am grateful and humbled to be able to share my passion for serving God through literature with you. Thank you.   ~Chuck Black

As a **BONUS FEATURE** for Episode Eight, there are full color images of significant characters, scenes, and technology to help illustrate the story. It is recommended that the entire chapter is read first before viewing the corresponding images for that chapter. Don't look ahead or you'll find spoilers. The images by chapter are here: **www.chuckblack.com/journey** or you can also scan the QR code below. Enjoy!

JOURNEY

EPISODE EIGHT

CHUCK BLACK

Journey

Published by Perfect Praise Publishing
Williston, North Dakota

ISBN 978-1-959574-25-5

Printed in the United States of America

Library of Congress Control Number: 2025927881

Contents

CHAPTER

1

Vanishing

With a scowl on his face, C'fir Dracus glared at the esteemed men and women sitting at the large elaborate command table—admirals, leading his fleets of battle spacecraft, and generals, directing planetary ground assaults. Each Torian officer sat in humiliation and silence. Around the periphery of the elaborate war chamber stood the vice commanders of each of Dracus's 14 highest ranking admirals and generals.

"It has been over 20 years since I killed the Son of Ell Yon. There were only 11 sectators then." Dracus stood slowly, his elite commanders cowering before his wrath. "Why haven't the Creed Havens been wiped off the face of this pathetic planet!" he yelled, slamming his fist on the glass table before him.

Dracus's gaze pierced through each of them, though none dared to look him in the eye. He began to walk behind the sitting officers.

"These...these pathetic weak humans have made a mockery of each of you!" Dracus continued, his rage swelling with each step. He stopped behind the general responsible for the Torian continental ground forces for Jalem and its region.

"Tell me, General Zall, how is it possible that you have not yet eliminated the havens in Jalem, and furthermore that you have allowed them to expand to every other major city on Rayl?"

General Zall swallowed hard. Sweat beaded at his temples. "Lord Dracus, when the sectators duplicated the Protectors, the power of Ell Yon over the people became unstoppable. I have deployed forces to assault every new Creed Haven, but the Navis have become skilled in battling our forces. The Malakian defense forces are bolstered whenever the Navis of Jeshu commune."

Dracus's face contorted into a visage of complete rage with each mention the general made of Ell Yon and Jeshu. Dracus drew his Talon faster than any Torian had ever witnessed and thrust it through the back of Zall's chair. The stasis-charged blade pierced the chair and tore clean through the man's chest. The few seconds of horror on Zall's face seared into the minds of every occupant of the room. With his hand through the chair and into the back of his former general, Dracus lifted the man and chair into the air and cast his former general aside like a crumpled piece of trash. Blood was dripping down his Talon and onto his hand.

"Not the answer I wanted," Dracus growled in a dark voice. He continued around the table, each officer shaking and cowering at his approach. The evil wake of his walk filled the hearts of his officers with utter dread. Upon returning to his seat at the head of the table, he glanced down at the lifeless body on the floor then up to the vice commanders pressed against the wall. "Who was Zall's vice commander?"

One of the Torian warriors stepped forward. He bowed. "I was, my lord—Colonel Graydox."

"You are now the commander of my continental forces for the Jalem sector. Don't disappoint me. Sit!" Dracus ordered.

Graydox's eyes opened wide. He looked at his fellow vice commanders then hurried to recover the blood-stained chair. After righting it and placing it back in position at the table, he sat, leaning forward, away from the gaping red hole in the back of the chair.

"Let me be perfectly clear," Dracus said, scanning the terrified faces of his commanding officers. "The spread of these Navis and their Creed Havens will be contained. None can leave this planet!"

"My lord," Admiral Yelrod dared interject. "Isn't this spreading of the Creed Havens exclusive to the Raylean people? After all, they are the nation of humans Ell Yon chose from the beginning of time. Didn't the Son of Ell Yon come only for them?"

"It's true that Ell Yon's attempt to eliminate Deitum Prime through his pathetic Son was prophesied by the oracles to be for the Raylean people," Dracus conceded. "But you all saw what his Protectors did when we killed him on the Ring. The power surge reached far beyond the planet of Rayl. There are other writings of the oracles that allude to an off-planet expansion." Dracus scanned the faces of his officers once more. "That cannot happen! That *will* not happen!"

"We will destroy every Navi!" exclaimed Admiral Kyrsa.

"No!" screamed Dracus. Every Torian in the room looked at Dracus with confusion on their faces. "You will destroy every *Raylean*! From this moment on, every single human with a drop of Raylean blood, whether they are Navis or not, will be targeted for destruction. Is that clear?"

"The entire planet?" one general dared ask. "That's over three billion humans."

"Yes," Dracus replied with eyes both dark and evil. "Every...single...one of them!"

The order was urgent. Translating into the realm of humanity was a rare and reserved duty for only select Malakian warriors, of which Lieutenant Vry was not a part. Regardless, the order came and was verified on his com band by Major Ki.

It was five o'clock in the morning, and the sun was still reaching for the far horizon, eager to initiate the day with its brilliant light. Lieutenant Vry stood on the opposite side of the table from where a man was sitting in deep contemplation. The man's left hand rested gingerly on the Protector fastened to his right arm. The sleep-deprived man was fraught with concern. Vry was in full battle uniform, so he could only imagine how this encounter might further rattle the man.

"It can't be...it just can't be!" the man murmured. He ran his hand through his hair and back to the Protector. "Why him?"

Vry pressed the interphasal translator on his belt. The fabric of his dimension resisted to let loose of his body, but it finally yielded. Lieutenant Vry materialized directly in front of the man, terror now evident on his face as he pushed back from the table, nearly toppling backward.

"Don't be afraid," Lieutenant Vry coaxed. "The Protector is true. Guide your enemy, for he is your enemy no more. Do you understand?"

The man scrambled to find his feet, still utterly shocked by the presence of an Immortal in his dwelling.

"I...I understand," the man sputtered. "But how?"

"Sovereign Ell Yon births triumph from tragedy. You are called. Go to Abaria and find him."

Vry deactivated the interphasal translator, disappearing from the eyes of the man and transitioning back into the realm of the Immortals. He stayed for a moment to watch the man process this intersection, then left to report to Major Ki.

"Mission complete, Major," Vry said to the holographic display of his commander.

"Well done, Lieutenant. Report back to Delta sector. Time for Rayl is short, and we must be ready."

"Yes, Major. Lieutenant Vry, out."

As dawn lifted the darkness from the landscape, Ledger felt no reprieve from the shadows choking his heart. The memory of holding the still form of Stone in his arms yesterday was all too fresh. It haunted him like an ever-present darkness that no light could dispel. Mingled with these deep feelings of guilt were flashes of anger for the betrayal by Fasa Kylos, the man he had called father for his entire life. Were it not for the fact that Kylos's express purpose seemed to be using Ledger as a cruel tool for revenge, he might have considered the privileges he received as the son of the Master Keeper something to be grateful for. It was all so confusing and destructive to his soul.

Ledger piloted the speeder away from Brohn toward a destination of which he knew not. His clothes still damp and cold from his fitful sleep on the canyon rock bed, he was miserable inside and out. He zoomed out on the navigation display in the speeder. The closest city with a transportation hub was Zareth, a smaller city southwest of Brohn. Ledger calculated that he would have just enough fuel to reach it. From there he could catch a transport to Rea. He knew that Rea had a spaceport to get him off Rayl, but the city was also large enough and far enough away from Jalem that Kylos wouldn't be able to find him easily. Despite this, he would have to move fast. Every hour that passed meant that his chance of escaping the planet would diminish. The irony was that in his urgent desire to leave the planet, Ledger realized he had never once been off Rayl. He had never even been to space. He hadn't ever needed to. Rayl was the center of his universe, and there was no need to find purpose elsewhere...until now.

The rising sun produced long morning shadows and warmth that began to burn off the misty low-lying fog from the ravines not far below Ledger's speeder. At times, the speeder would skim the top of an isolated fog bank, causing the smoky contrails to swirl up and into the golden rays of Rayl's sun, fading away into the higher warm morning air.

Ledger tapped in the coordinates for Zareth's transport station. A moment later, the navigation display illuminated with a flight path and a glowing ETA of 32 minutes. He stole a glance at the android sitting next to him. His feelings of unease about the bot intensified with each waking minute. He couldn't shake the insatiable desire to flee from everything he had once known, including this android. The complete and total betrayal by almost everyone in his life had deeply damaged him.

"Back at the gorge, you said you were Truth. How can you be Truth if you spent my entire life deceiving me?" Ledger asked.

The android seemed to evaluate Ledger's question before answering. "Master Ledger, I can understand why you are questioning my loyalty to you. During your childhood and years of adolescence, I found myself in a...difficult position."

"But you lied to me for years!" Ledger pressed.

"I never lied to you, Master Ledger. I protected you and carefully offered fragments of the truth that Fasa Kylos was hiding from you. Divulging the full measure of truth to you at any point in time until now would have jeopardized my ability to continue to protect you and to guide you. There was much more at stake that had to be calculated to determine a proper course of action." The android tilted his head forward ever so slightly. "Have you considered the fact that many Jeshuans were saved because of my continued position under Fasa Kylos and as an assistance android to the KDF?"

Ledger glanced out the left side of the speeder's canopy as he considered the android's comments. He wasn't even sure what to call it. R32 was obviously not his designation, and the name it called itself was too familiar sounding, which is the last thing Ledger wanted. Simply "android" would do.

"There are powerful forces at work, and it would be prudent to understand that you are not the center of the galaxy...my liege."

Ledger frowned. The android's last comment hit him square in the chest. He didn't like it. In fact, he hated it. Not because it was a rebuke about being selfish, but something about an android having the audacity to reprimand a human smacked of arrogant AI supremacy. Non-AI androids never acted like this. The last thing he needed was some bot pretending to be a superior conscience, especially a bot that he had thought was something it was not. In the last 24 hours, Ledger's perception of the android had completely changed. As a child, he had come to enjoy the company of the android. Now, it frightened him. Everything about it now indicated AI, perhaps a super AI. What were its motives? What were its objectives? What, if any, were its governing principles regarding preservation of life or the taking of life?

Ledger understood that he could have deep conversations with the thing and ask it these questions, but how could he be certain that anything it said was actually the truth? It had already demonstrated a supremely acute ability to operate in a clandestine manner for years. Just conversing with it unnerved Ledger to the extreme. He responded to the android's comments with silence. From that moment on, Ledger determined to ditch the android and recede into the mass of humanity as an anonymous participant in its drudgery of meaningless pursuits. Perhaps then he would find peace from his inner torment. He needed distance from Rayl, time from his crime, hard exhaustive activity to occupy his mind, and isolation from people, his past, and this eerily perceptive android.

When they arrived at Zareth, Ledger parked the speeder in a temporary loading and unloading zone. Ledger twisted in his seat to look at the android.

"This speeder is stolen. I want you to find some place to ditch it so that it won't be found until we are off the planet. I'll wait for you in the transport terminal at the ticketing station."

Without waiting for a response, Ledger exited the speeder and made his way into the terminal. He turned around just in time to see the speeder glide out of the loading zone. Ledger made his way to one of the ticketing stations and purchased a single ticket for the next transport leaving the terminal—Joppik. It wasn't Rea, but he didn't care. He needed to ditch the android as soon as possible, then he would make his way to the spaceport at Rea. He had ten minutes before the transport to Joppik left the planet. He would have to sprint to make it, but he was satisfied that the android would never find him again. He lost himself in the thousands of people dodging to and fro in the transport terminal.

Seven minutes later, Ledger boarded the mid-atmospheric transport vessel destined for Joppik. Despite the impossible odds that the android could spot him, he made a quick scan around the loading platform to reassure himself that he had been successful. All clear. He made his way to an empty row of three seats on the starboard side of the transport and sat next to the viewing port, still scanning for the android among the throng in the spaceport.

A few minutes later, the engines of the transport roared to life. He felt the port window he was leaning against shimmy. The transport gently lifted into the air. The forward motion of the transport slowly accelerated to a flight speed of 950 miles per hour.

Ledger took a deep breath. To flee and to isolate...it was all he knew how to do right now.

Ten minutes into the 25-minute flight, he caught a glimpse out of the corner of his eye of someone sitting down in one of the empty seats next to him. He ignored the person and continued to gaze out the view portal, staring at nothing at all. After five more minutes, Ledger straightened himself in his chair and closed his eyes, leaning back against the headrest. He felt quite ridiculous for his feeble attempt to feign sleep. He opened his left eyelid imperceptibly so that the narrowest of slits would allow a sliver of sight of his unwelcome row-mate. He was rewarded with a glimmer of gold alloy and composite white plating. Ledger's eyes popped wide open as he turned to see his android sitting next to him.

"The speeder has been taken care of, Master Ledger," the android said, staring straight ahead.

"You!" Ledger blurted, then realized that his voice might carry to other passengers. He stifled his volume but not the intensity with which he spoke. "Impossible! How did you find me? How did you even get a ticket?" Ledger whispered sharply, but the android turned its steely cold eyes on him...waiting.

"Never mind. I don't think I want to know," Ledger finished. He glared at the android, more unnerved and irritated than before. "You have become the most annoying android I have ever encountered!"

"Yes, Master Ledger, oftentimes truth is annoying," the android returned, matching Ledger's hushed tone.

"You're also the most arrogant android I've ever met, and the word *arrogant* should never be associated with an android."

"I shall endeavor to be less human if that is what you prefer."

Arrogant, sarcastic, condescending...this android is a constant thorn in my side. It is everything I don't need, Ledger thought.

"Master Ledger, I'm the same android that you grew up learning to trust."

"But you're not!" Ledger snapped. "To me you are a completely different creation, one that I know nothing about. Not even where you came from or what your true motivations are." He glared. "You even have weapons built into your technology," Ledger whispered even more quietly. "I've never seen you use them before yesterday...not once! And scanners don't detect them?" Ledger leaned back, shaking his head. "Everyone in my life was lying to me or at least hiding the truth...my father, you, even..." Ledger couldn't speak Stone's name. There was too much unresolved emotional turbulence.

The android remained silent as Ledger processed. After a minute, the android spoke softly.

"My liege, what do you need me to be for you?"

"I need you to be gone! I must reset everything in my life so I can figure out what is real...what's true and what's not," Ledger said. He was dangerously close to having an emotional meltdown right there on the transport, something he had never felt coming his way before.

"Perhaps you could consider me as simply a utility android, and I promise to function solely as such. Wherever you're going, and I suspect it is far from here, you will need a source of income. I can be leased for labor to provide a supplemental income."

Ledger clenched his teeth. *So it's going to go back to pretending...more deception!* Just as he was about to stand up and move to a different seat in the transport, the rationality of the android's offer took hold. He had to admit that the bot did have a valid point.

"Fine. But there are stipulations."

The android remained silent...waiting.

"Don't presume to know what's best for me," Ledger stated. "You're not human and you never will be. I don't need a machine psychoanalyzing me."

"Agreed," the android returned flatly.

"You don't transmit communication to anyone about anything unless I expressly authorize it. Is that clear?" Ledger asked.

"Very."

"By the way, what are your communication abilities? Are they the similar to other KDF androids?"

"No, my liege, my communication abilities are extensive, but I will honor your request."

Ledger glanced around at the other passengers. He and his android seemed to have escaped any scrutiny.

"And you will act like every other android when we are in the presence of others. Can you do that?"

The android tilted his head as if to question Ledger's reasoning. It was then that Ledger realized the absurdity of his command. Of course it could do that. It had been successfully doing so for the past 21 years. Ledger figured that if the android could smirk, it would.

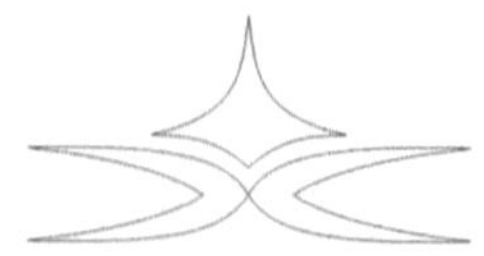

CHAPTER

2

To the Outer Rim

When they arrived at Joppik, Ledger and his android caught the next transport to Rea. The transport terminal and the spaceport were located at the same complex, so they were able to easily navigate their way. The Rea spaceport was bustling with thousands of crew members, terminal personnel, and spacefarers, as well as hundreds of ships landing and launching.

Ledger found a financial exchange terminal and accessed his account, withdrew the whole amount in Morian credits, and closed the account. He figured Morian credits would be accepted throughout the galaxy and were his safest play. He became lost in anxious thoughts as he stared at the console flashing, "Account Terminated." If Fasa Kylos was intent on finding him, Ledger might have just given himself away by leaving a digital footprint. Without warning, his mind flashed to the previous night. Dark but clear images of Stone's mother and father, Fasa Kylos, the android, and Chief Deklan with his operatives surged through his mind. Kylos's words relentlessly played over and over in his mind, crushing him to nothing.

"Execute all three of them!"

In a moment, his father had cast him away like a used and worthless rag. All his life he had yearned to earn the love of his father—real love. But it would never have been, for he was the true son of Kylos's arch-nemesis…a tool to be used to satisfy Kylos's ugly revenge. It was in this moment that Ledger realized he had never experienced true love from anyone, least of all from the man he had called father. A dark bitterness washed over him, threatening to destroy him.

"Master Ledger?"

The android's voice rattled Ledger. He wiped his eyes, shaking himself out of his dark reflection and back to reality.

"Where's the nearest terminal station?" Ledger asked.

The android pointed, and Ledger moved that way mindlessly, shutting off all other thoughts. He needed to decide his final destination. Arriving at the terminal, he studied a display showing thousands of systems in the known galaxy. He zoomed in on the region of space that highlighted the planets in the Outer Rim—28 systems with 33 habitable planets.

One half of the Aurora Galaxy was undiscoverable. The best scitechs of the galaxy across thousands of years had not been able to unlock the mystery behind how a slipstream conduit worked. The extremely pragmatic scitechs believed that a slipstream conduit was a naturally occurring phenomenon in the realm of spacetime, where the conditions of bodies of great mass and their corresponding gravity wells spawned the conduits. But the scitechs thus far had no concrete proof on how such a phenomenon could self-create, nor did they have an explanation as to why only one half of the galaxy had the conduits. The speculative scitechs believed that a higher dimensional technology gateway existed at each end of a conduit and thus could not be replicated within the domain of humanity. The notions of such a theory originated in the ancient mythical tales of the Immortals, a race of higher dimensional beings that were responsible for the watching and manipulation of humanity. Whatever the source of the conduits, it was clearly understood by all scitechs that a jump drive engine was required to utilize a gateway. The ancient knowledge that slipstream conduits once existed throughout the entire galaxy was now the fabric of myth and legend. But in reality, the androids of the AI wars thousands of years ago had sabotaged a vast number of conduits that severed the galaxy in two. Unknown to the inhabitants of the alpha and bravo quadrants, there were thousands of isolated worlds—uncharted, unexplored, and unknowable. It was an irritating reality that many scientific minds were determined to solve.

At the fringes of the alpha and bravo quadrants where the slipstream conduits ended lived a fragment of humanity with a quest to push the boundaries of human existence—the Outer Rim, often referred to simply as the Rim. The Rim was a handful of systems at the far reaches of humanity's known habitation. The slipstream conduits reaching out there were few. The people who chose to live at the Rim were the outliers of society—bold, reckless, adventurous, and reclusive colonists driven by a desire to be free from overly technology-dependent living, researchers with a quest to seek new life and new phenomena, mining organizations hoping to capitalize on untapped resources that the rest of the galaxy depended on, and space raiders. Life on the Rim was extreme in every sense of the word. This space frontier is where Ledger chose to disappear.

"I would recommend the Garro System," the android offered. "Its two habitable planets provide ample opportunity for employment while still offering the anonymity and seclusion one might seek."

Ledger tried to ignore the bot's counsel. It was one of two systems he was considering, but now he would choose the other. Was the bot still trying to manipulate him?

He clicked on the Regalis System and its corresponding planet, Abaria. It would take four different transport ships and 16 connecting slipstream jump flights to get there, exhausting most of his credits, but Ledger didn't care. For spaceflights like this, android tickets were set at cargo rates since they could be placed in cargo holds without any regard for comfort. Knowing what he knew about this android, he felt a subconscious twinge when he thought of the bot cooped up in a dark storage room with dozens of non-thinking machines.

It's just a machine like every other bot, Ledger thought, trying to convince himself.

Ledger was about to scan his ID to make the spaceflight purchases then hesitated. He pulled back his com band.

"If I scan, there's every possibility that the KDF and the Morian Commandos will flag my ID." He looked over at the android. "But you already knew that, didn't you?"

"With so many people nearby, I am attempting to abide by the stipulations you have placed on me," the android replied.

Ledger huffed. He came close to the android and whispered. "Can you alter my ID so I can make this purchase without alerting the authorities?"

"Yes, Master Ledger, but it is becoming difficult to know when I am supposed to play dumb and when not to," the android said, leaning closer to Ledger so as not to be overheard by others.

Was this another jab? Ledger wondered. Its subtle sarcasm was uncanny. Ledger never quite knew if the bot was playing with him or being sincere.

"Just do it. We need to get off the planet, and there's no other way."

"As you wish. First, I will need to access your com band and modify your ID. What name do you wish to use?" the android asked as Ledger held up his left forearm to the bot.

"Uh...Brandt. Ledger Brandt."

The android pointed his index finger at the com band's access port. A moment later, a data interface connector extended out of the tip of its finger and connected with the com band. Five seconds later, the android disconnected and turned to the ticketing display.

"Now I must gain access to the spaceport's network and alter its database to allow Ledger Brandt to be identified as a legal passenger," the android said, positioning its finger and data interface connector near the terminal's access port.

"How's that possible?" Ledger asked. "They wouldn't allow such access from a ticket terminal like this, and their network will have security protocols in place."

The android turned its head to look at Ledger, its data interface connector just a fraction of an inch away from making contact.

Ledger and the android locked eyes. This android was either fantastically nefarious or one of the most brilliant machines he had ever encountered. Chills flitted up his spine. Ledger looked left and right then stepped closer to the terminal to hide the android's actions.

"Just do it," he said quietly.

The android inserted the data interface connector. "This will take a little longer."

Sixty seconds passed, and Ledger tapped anxiously on the panel next to the data port. "Any time now," he egged.

A few seconds later the android disconnected. "You are now able to purchase the spaceflight tickets. The identification of Ledger Brandt should also propagate to all other global and intergalactic databases over the next few days."

Ledger looked at the android with wonder. Fear was giving way to curiosity, but for now, they needed to get off the planet as soon as possible. Ledger completed the purchase of the tickets. No alerts sounded—so far so good. Now to get through the security scans.

"Are you certain you're able to pass their weapon scans?" Ledger asked as they made their way toward the section of the terminal where their launch platform was located.

"Nothing in my construction has triggered a weapons scan in the past. I must assume the same would be true for this station." The android's answer wasn't completely satisfying, but it would have to do.

Morian security agents were working alongside the typical Raylean space terminal security personnel. Ledger passed through the security scans first then turned back for the android. An amber beam scanned the bot up and down several times. Although an alarm didn't trigger, one of the security personnel took an extra two minutes to analyze the graphical data being displayed. Just when Ledger thought the android's hidden weapons had been discovered, the security guard waved him onward. When Ledger rejoined with the android, he lifted an eyebrow.

"He was fascinated by my superior construction," the android explained. "A testimony to the technical skills and prowess of your mother."

Ledger's jaw tightened at the bot's comment. *My mother?* Ledger replayed. *What does it even mean to have a mother?*

The spacecraft for their first flight was scheduled to depart in four hours, and the launch platform was located on the far side of the spaceport complex. Ledger found an eatery where he could get a much-needed meal. He was constantly scanning the surrounding area, just in case the android's attempt to give him a new identity had failed. He noticed a bot charging station nearby where dozens of androids were recharging.

"You should charge up. It might be a long time before you have another chance," Ledger said, motioning toward the charging station with his head in between bites.

"My power module is designed to provide ample energy for another 13 years," the android replied.

Ledger choked on his last bite. "What? Surely not! That's imposs—" Ledger found himself saying that much too often. He stared at the android once again, stunned. "We never know who might be watching. Go and appear to charge up so we don't draw attention."

The android hesitated. Ledger fully expected it to make another sarcastic jab about deceiving others at Ledger's command while being accused of being so deceptive to him.

"As you wish," the android said, proceeding to the charging station.

Ledger wondered at the mystery of the android. Why had it chosen to attach itself to him from birth? Even the android didn't seem to fully understand why.

Ledger finished up his meal then turned his attention to a holographic news display showing the recent advances of the Morian Empire. Inwardly he was disgusted by the propaganda they called news. The Morians had complete control of all public communication networks. One story that caught his attention was of the increase in sabotage attacks by the anti-Morian rebel group known as the Partisans. Ledger had been cheering them on secretly for years, and he could only imagine that every other Raylean was doing the same. The Partisans wanted independence from the Morian Empire, but their cause seemed hopeless. The vast resources and immense power of the Morian Empire were too overwhelming.

Watching this story brought back painful memories. As Kylos's key KDF operative, Ledger had received vicious rebukes during some of the raids that were supposedly carried out by violent Jeshuans. Many of them had claimed to be Partisans and not Jeshuans. Near the end, this suspicion had contributed to the growing doubt about his missions. Some of the pieces of his past had already begun to align, yet there were so many fragments he wasn't ready to process...not yet.

When he grew weary of the broadcast, he recovered the android and began making his way to the loading platform for their space transport vessel. The air was thick with the scent of fuel and the clamor of announcements echoing off the vaulted ceilings. Ships of every size cycled through docking bays, exchanging passengers and cargo in a constant stream of motion. The spacecraft designated for his flight to the Rim was average in size as far as space transports went. It had a crew of 16 and could transport 250 passengers along with 60 tons of cargo divided into bulk cargo and personal cargo. Ledger's android would be placed in personal cargo with any other bots. This compartment was accessible from the regular passenger section of the craft. Two hours before launch, the line to board was already forming. Ledger was eager to board and be underway. This flight would get him out of reach of the KDF, and the next five slipstream jumps would put him outside of the Morian Empire. His greatest risk of discovery was right here in the spaceport. Just as those anxious thoughts crossed his mind, a squad of five well-armed Morian commandos appeared through the closest terminal entrance just 100 feet away. The tension on the launch platform instantly crescendoed as the squad began scanning the line of waiting passengers.

"Everyone face the scanner," ordered one of the commandos.

Ledger's stomach rose to his throat. The beam of one of the scanners passed through Ledger and those around him. An alarm sounded, and the other four commandos instantly leveled their plasma rifles in Ledger's direction. His instincts told him to run, but he would die in seconds if he tried. His heart pounded against his ribs, but he resigned himself to his fate as the commandos closed in on him. Ledger's android stepped in front and lifted its hands toward the commandos.

"On the floor...now!" one of the commandos shouted.

Ledger knew by their approach that they wouldn't hesitate to make this a fatal apprehension if necessary. All they needed was an excuse to pull the trigger, and Ledger was tempted to give it to them.

"Stand down. Let them have me," Ledger said once he considered the potential collateral damage to others, but the android didn't retreat from its protective stance.

Ledger began to kneel, but at the last second, one of the commandos pushed him out of the way while aggressively taking down the man standing behind him. All five commandos descended on the man, pushing his face into the concrete pad while yanking his arms behind him. One commando stood straight then tapped on his tactical com band. He read the hovering text.

"Harlow Trindan, you are charged with high treason against the Morian Empire for your association with the terrorist organization known as the Partisans. You will be tried and sentenced within the next 48 hours."

The commandos whisked their detainee to his feet and proceeded back toward the entrance. The adrenaline still coursing through Ledger's body made it difficult to stand. Ledger worked on catching his breath and trying to slow his heart rate. He watched as the commandos exited the platform, disappearing as quickly as they'd come.

"I thought my time had come," he said quietly.

"As did I," the android replied.

Once order was restored to the platform, Ledger boarded the space transport with his android close behind.

It was Ledger's intention to avoid all people as much as possible. He strategically selected a position near the back of the transport where most people would choose not to sit, hoping he could cocoon himself away from the galaxy. The problem was that whenever he had space to think, dark memories from the previous day charged in upon him without warning. He could isolate himself from other people, but he couldn't shut out his own mind. He found himself staring at his hands, palms turned upward...hands that had shed innocent blood...the blood of his best friend...and his brother? If Stone truly were his brother, the burden of guilt would be magnified tenfold. He just needed to get off this planet and away from his horror.

Ledger glanced toward the entrance of the transport where the flow of boarding passengers had slowed to a trickle. Still no sign of being apprehended. Finally, the doors to the transport closed and sealed. He felt the engines rumble to life, and moments later, the transport lifted off.

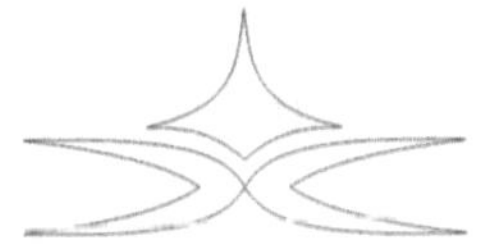

CHAPTER

3

34,000 Light Years

Two days later, Ledger stepped off the transport and onto the planet Abaria in the Regalis System—his final destination. The planet's main spaceport lay within its largest city, Bria. As he took a deep breath, he beheld a world wildly different from Rayl, absorbing sights, sounds, and smells that were alien to him. The air on Abaria felt heavier, more humid, tinged with a faint industrial pungency. He looked around, gripped by the strangest sense of freedom and threat at the same time. His android stepped up beside him.

"We're certainly on a foreign planet," Ledger said, gazing at the massive arching skyscrapers that dotted the cityscape of Bria.

Bria was an industrial city where the glamorous and the grungy often shared the same sectors. On Outer Rim planets, little attention was paid to aesthetics. This was where credits were earned and spent fast. Millions of people came to seek their fortune, but tragedy and despondency were by far the more common stories.

Ledger pursed his lips together. *This is a place where I can disappear.*

It took significant effort to figure out how to navigate through the city of Bria. After six hours of searching, Ledger discovered that he had just enough Morian credits to lease a small, dingy one-room dwelling, referred to by the locals as a hovel, for one week. Within the hovel was a bed, a bathroom, and a kitchenette. The single window looked out toward another identical living quarter skyscraper just a few feet away.

The journey from Rayl had taken its toll on Ledger. Fatigue pulled at his body. He had escaped, and now there was nothing left to do except sleep. He fell onto the bed, his last waking thought a quiet hope that 34,000 light years of distance would separate him from his misery—at least a little. Seconds later, Ledger's thoughts twisted into a bizarre merging of reality and absurdity until he had fully yielded to deep slumber.

Eighteen hours later, Ledger sat up and wiped his eyes clear of the crusted nodules of sleep that had formed. The world was just as gray now as when he had fallen asleep. He saw the back side of the android standing in the kitchen preparing food. His stomach growled at the smell of it. A moment later the android presented a sparse meal of bread, soup, and a strange-looking plant bulb that was apparently edible.

"You must eat, my liege," the android said. "I have spent the last of your credits to acquire this food. We must now consider how to earn additional credits if we are to survive here."

Ledger began devouring the simple but delicious meal. "You find employment," he replied. "Isn't that why you're here?"

The android nodded. "Having accessed your com band, I have all of the information needed to register my labor under your identification. Do you have a preference as to what type of labor you would like me to assume?"

Ledger shook his head as he transitioned from the bread to the soup. When he worked up the courage to try the plant bulb, he wasn't disgusted by it, nor was he pleased. It was a bland taste that he was sure the android had forgotten to add seasoning to. When he looked up from the meal, he realized the android was gone.

Here, in a dreary hovel at the edge of the known galaxy, Ledger was finally alone. He stared at the dark window across the room for a full hour, working hard to dodge treacherous thoughts. Then, as if all his guilt and sorrow had just arrived from its own slipstream jump, the avalanche of grief slammed into his psyche to resume its full crushing weight on his soul. Ledger leaned back onto his bed, curling up into a fetal position, wishing desperately that there was some way to numb the emotional pain of his recent past. Sleep seemed the only respite, so he shushed his mind to its peaceful embrace once more.

Over the next six weeks, Ledger wallowed in the mire of his grief, unknowingly building walls of defense around his mind and heart. He didn't care what day it was or even what hour it was. Lethal Ledger gradually disappeared from humanity, all the while his android labored to keep him alive with food and water.

Upon his most recent waking, for he didn't know if it was day or night, he forced his eyes to focus on his android standing beside him, its emotionless eyes staring down at him.

"What is it?" Ledger mumbled, trying to clear his mind, but it hadn't been clear for weeks. He scratched his scruffy, bearded face.

The android just continued to stare, motionless. Its hovering presence began to unnerve him.

"What is it?" Ledger repeated loudly. He blinked multiple times so he could more clearly see the bot and the room behind him. With great effort, he stood up, rubbing his hand through his matted hair.

The android carefully and methodically crossed its arms, an action Ledger had never seen before by this or any other android in the galaxy. He didn't even know it was mechanically possible.

"You said not to presume to know what's good for you. You can be certain that I am not presuming anything when I tell you that I *do* know what is good for you, and *this* is not it."

Gone were the polite addresses of "Master Ledger" or "my liege."

Ledger snorted, shook his head, then laid back down on the filthy bed. The android proceeded to pick up the entire bed with Ledger still in it.

"Hey, android, what are you doing?" Ledger screamed.

The android then turned the bed upside down, throwing Ledger to the floor with a loud thump. Ledger howled. The android placed the bed on its side up against the wall.

"What in the galaxy has gotten into you?" Ledger yelled, trying to get to his feet. "I will have you decommissioned!"

"Then you will be on the street with no place to sleep and no food to eat," the android said bluntly, undaunted by Ledger's anger. "That would be an unwise decision, but then again, so was every other decision you've made in the last two months, including leaving Rayl."

Ledger was now livid. He scanned the room for a makeshift club to beat against the android, but there was nothing. He turned, glaring into the cold, lifeless eyes of the android, but to Ledger's shock, something deep was looking back at him.

"Do you really think that the one who spoke to you intended for this to be your lot?" the android asked. "The Starlore legacy must not end with you, Master Ledger."

The android's words instantly disarmed him. The vision and the voice from Stone's Protector were the only anchor in his life that had not moved...had not lied to him. Like a rock standing firm against the waves of torment, the image of Jeshu, Son of Ell Yon, remained firmly moored in Ledger's mind as the single tether of truth.

Ledger turned away, placing his hands against the nearby wall he leaned into it. With head hung low, Ledger realized that his frantic dash across the galaxy hadn't earned him a shred of respite from his torment. If anything, it had become worse.

Ledger sighed deeply. "You're right. One of the Keepers I came to respect once told me that despair is best fought by the activity of productive hands." Ledger dropped his hands from the wall to look at them. "It's time I use these for something productive."

Over the course of the next hour, Ledger shaved his hair and face, cleaned himself up, and dressed in a new set of clothing that his android had purchased for him. After a modicum amount of food and water, he entered into a discussion with the android regarding the type of work he might try.

"I witnessed your skills with weapons while at the KDF," the android noted. "Your abilities far exceeded every other agent on the force. The special training Fasa Kylos arranged for you with the elite Morian combat commandos makes your superior skills unique. You could easily work as a private security agent."

Ledger huffed. "The last thing I want to do is handle a plasma rifle again. My days as a weapons expert are over."

"I've scanned the global public network on Abaria. There are 3,049 different types of jobs that have openings," the android reported.

Ledger thought for a moment. *Productive hands*, he thought. "What's the hardest job on that list?"

"According to all comments and accessible records, the most difficult job on Abaria isn't on the planet," the android stated. "There are four space mining vessels that are looking to fill the position of excursion miner. Evidently, that is the most difficult job available in this sector of the galaxy. But, Master Ledger, it is not only the most difficult, it is the most dangerous. I highly advise against—"

"That's it," Ledger interrupted. "Which mining ship is the closest to this location?"

The android hesitated. "The *Hammershot*. It is located 12.4 miles southeast of here."

Ledger stood up from the small table in the kitchenette. "Let's go."

The android guided Ledger through the public grav rail system that wove throughout the city. After one transfer, the grav rail would take them all the way to the mining spaceport built specifically for spacecraft dedicated to this industry. An entire network of grav rail routes and cargo cars had been created for offloading the precious minerals brought back by the mining vessels. Via the grav routes, mined minerals were transferred to massive processing facilities in the city of Bria and other nearby cities.

"According to the posting for these positions," the android explained, "you must fill out an application and be interviewed. There are hundreds of applicants for each position because these jobs are also the highest paying non-managerial positions on the planet. Evidently the turnover rate is extremely high due to stress and—," the android hesitated, "attrition."

"I'm not concerned," Ledger replied as they approached a massive space vessel docked at one of the spaceport's terminals. Ledger took a moment to gaze at the brawn of the spacecraft. He had seen larger spacecraft but none with such a dramatic appearance of productive purpose. In the foreground were multiple structures built to manage much of the pre-launch requirements of the vessel. Four long lines of people were forming in front of access gates.

"It appears that all of these lines are interview lines," the android said.

"Can you submit my application?" Ledger asked.

"Yes. Would you like to include that you have a capable android to assist in the mining labor? Often the mining vessels are willing to hire androids as well," the android offered.

"No. You've done well with the labor you found in the city. Let's just leave that alone," Ledger said.

"As you wish," the android replied. "Your application has been submitted, and I have received confirmation." The android turned toward Ledger. "All that remains is for you to pass the interview."

Ledger scanned the lines as they approached.

"I don't see any other bots in the lines," Ledger said. "Wait over there," he added, pointing to a bot charging station not far away.

Once the android separated, Ledger selected one of the lines, settling in for the long wait for his turn to interview. After only a few minutes, dozens more applicants had lined up behind him.

"Have you worked on a space mining vessel before?"

Ledger turned to see a slender but taller man about Ledger's age standing behind him. Ledger instantly recognized his type. Back in the academy, a small number of students just didn't fit in anywhere, not even with each other. They took the brunt of insults from the bullies and the narcissists. Like the north and south poles of a magnet, bullies and misfits were drawn together by the cultural structure of youth and its folly. Ledger always felt sorry for them, stepping in when possible, but there was always too much to fix.

"No," Ledger replied, fully intending to stop with that and turn back around. "You?"

The man shook his head while looking to the ground. "Never. I doubt they'll take me, but I need the money for my family. There's a lot of need back home."

Ledger nodded then turned back, hoping that interaction would suffice for his social obligation with the man.

"I saw you arrive with an android," the man continued. "Is he a good one?"

Ledger sighed, turning back toward the man.

"Yeah. He's good. Almost too good at times," Ledger confessed.

The man stuck out his hand. "I'm Corbin—Corbin Messer."

Ledger offered his hand. "Ledger."

"Maybe we'll get assigned to the same crew," Corbin said with a sheepish grin.

Ledger forced a smile. "Maybe," he said then turned back. He was next up and eager to move on. A hover bot floated just above the interviewer's position, scanning the people in preparation. Ledger felt the man behind him lean close.

"I'd let them know you have a top-of-the-line bot," the man whispered. "I've heard that has a lot of sway."

"Ledger Brandt," the interviewer announced as he swiped away the current interviewee's profile, replacing it with Ledger's.

"Thanks, but I don't think so," Ledger said over his shoulder as the man in front of him side-stepped out of the way.

"Have you ever worked on a space mining vessel?" the man asked in the most monotonous tone imaginable as Ledger stepped forward. He speculated the man had interviewed thousands over the past months.

"No."

The man frowned. "What's your previous employment experience?"

Ledger hesitated, unsure how to answer. "I provided security for an organization known as—"

"Our security personnel have already been hired," the man interrupted. He reached up to touch the "DENIED" icon.

"I'm applying for a crew miner position," Ledger said.

"We're looking for experienced excursion crew members. Any experience in an excursion suit?" the man asked.

"No, but—"

"Denied," the man exclaimed, reaching back up for the hovering icon in front of him.

"I have a top-of-line android who can do anything you need," Ledger added.

The man's hand froze. "Why didn't you include that in your application?"

Ledger shrugged.

"How capable is the bot?" the man asked. "I need to inspect him."

Ledger tapped on his com band, and his android appeared instantly beside him.

"Yes, Master Ledger?"

Ledger noticed that the interviewer became keenly interested in the android.

"We have a significant use for quality androids. Android, what are your capabilities?" the man asked.

The android turned to address the man. "I have an ion-fusion power module capable of sustaining full functionality for over 30 days. My strength ratio is three to one, and my processing speed exceeds 6.8 exaflops. My articulating joints are constructed from a titanium-cobalt composite with permanent lubrication—"

"That's enough," the man interrupted as he eyed the bot from head to foot. "Impressive. Your application is approved contingent on adding your android as a mining crew bot. You will receive double wages for as long as the bot remains in service. Contractual assignment of your bot is for a minimum of three tours with no down days. Is that acceptable?"

"Remains in service?" Ledger asked.

The man frowned again. "Space mining is a tough job that's hard on people and machines, especially bots. However, you will be compensated accordingly for its use."

Ledger looked over at the android. As much as he had wanted the bot to disappear, the machine admittedly had started to grow on him. He didn't want it destroyed.

"I will be fine, Master Ledger. I am fully capable of maintaining full functionality throughout the course of three tours," the android encouraged.

Ledger looked back at the man then nodded.

"Hold up your right hand for the bio scan to accept this contract," the man ordered.

Ledger held up his hand as a thin blue light beam scanned him. The man then tapped the "APPROVED" icon on Ledger's profile before swiping it away. "Report to in-processing through the door behind me on the right. The android reports to automated mechanics on the left. Next!" the man finished.

Ledger side-stepped with his android. "Are you sure about this?" Ledger asked as the interviewer began questioning Corbin.

"I am sure, my liege. The extra income will be useful to you."

"DENIED!" Ledger heard the man announce as he swiped Corbin's profile away. "Next!"

Ledger turned to see Corbin's shoulders sink, despair settling in the man's eyes.

"Hey," Ledger exclaimed, turning back to the interviewer. "He's with me. This is a package deal. If you want the android, both my mate and I come with."

The man cocked his head and scowled. He looked over at the android once more before swiping Corbin's profile back into view.

"Fine, but by the looks of him he won't last a week out there. You'll be signing disclosures when you in-process. If you don't make it back, we keep the android."

He glared at Ledger then at Corbin. He shook his head before instructing Corbin to hold up his hand for scanning. He tapped, "APPROVED."

"Next!"

The odd trio stepped away from the interview table. Corbin looked at Ledger as if he had just saved his life.

"Thank you! You don't know what this means to me and my family." Corbin's eyes filled with gratitude.

"It's nothing. We'd best in-process before he changes his mind," Ledger said, glancing back at the man who was already immersed in the next interview.

Ledger turned to his android. "You be careful."

"And you as well, Master Ledger," the android said then passed through a portal marked, "Automated Mechanics."

A pit formed in Ledger's stomach as the android disappeared through the portal.

"I'm sure he'll be okay," Corbin said, egging Ledger toward the portal that read, "*Hammershot* In-processing."

"I suppose so," Ledger said, but the pit in his stomach only worsened.

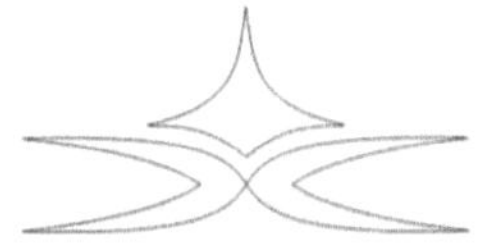

CHAPTER

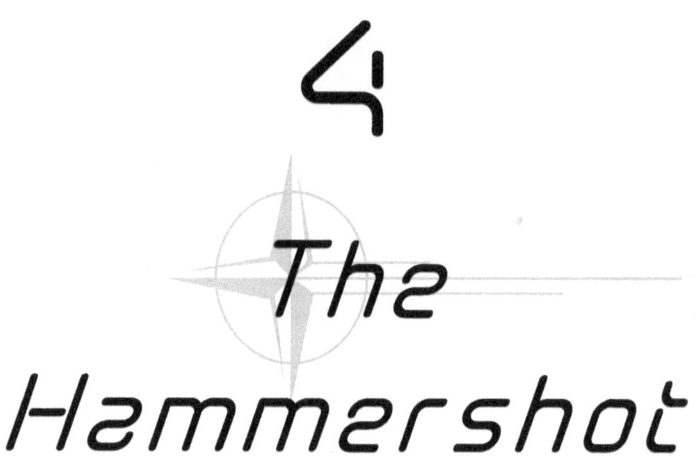

4

The Hammershot

Transponder — A device that receives a signal and automatically transmits an identifying signal in response. Transponders are used for identification, tracking, and communication in vessels of all types. Excursion suits can also incorporate a transponder for quickly locating and identifying an excursion miner or operator.

Captain Sigmund Rosco ran a tight ship. His baby, the *Hammershot*, was a space vessel of elegant power and uncompromising functionality. Two mega-torch drive engines outboard of the main fuselage provided twice the thrust needed to power the ship through asteroid fields and gravity wells where mining was profitable but risky. Two additional fusion drive engines were available for backup thrust or added thrust during emergencies. Dozens of maneuvering thrusters were placed fore and aft of the main engines on both sides of the ship.

HAMMERSHOT MINING VESSEL

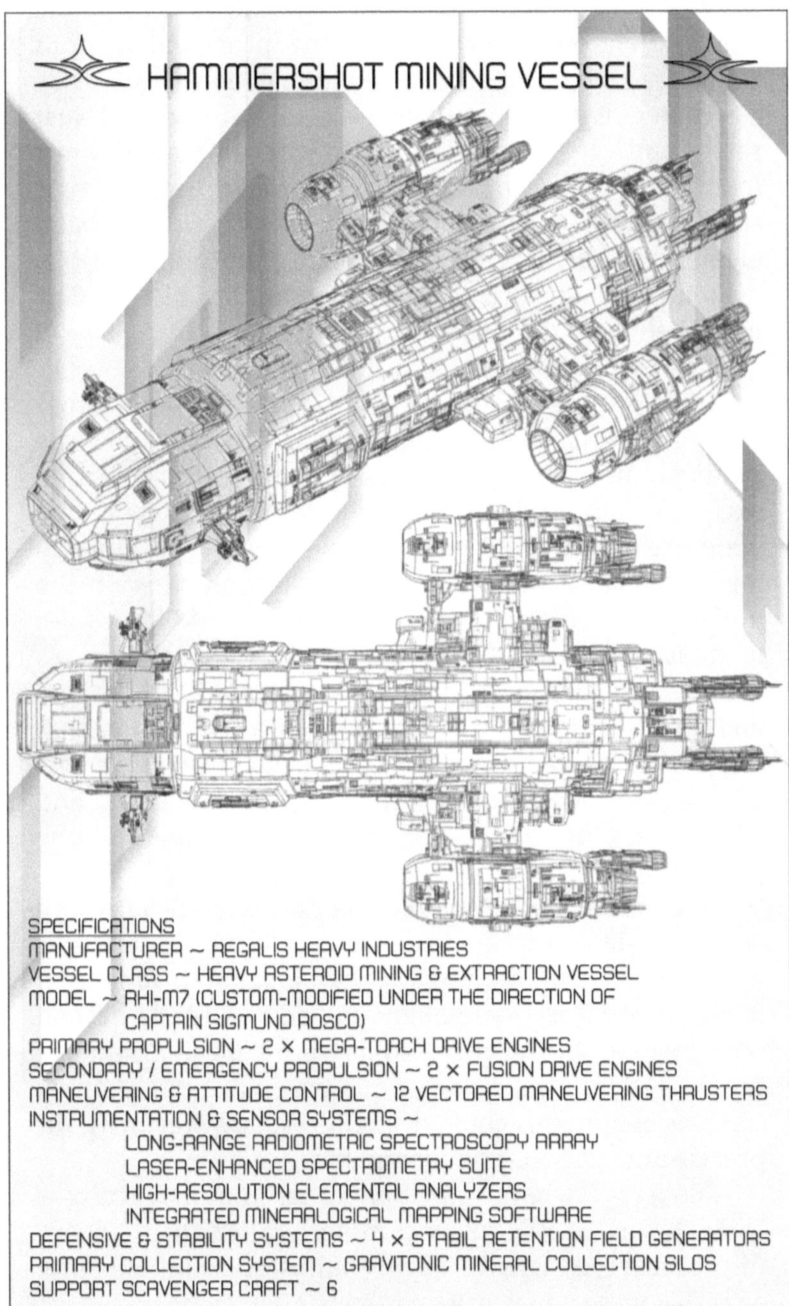

<u>SPECIFICATIONS</u>
MANUFACTURER ~ REGALIS HEAVY INDUSTRIES
VESSEL CLASS ~ HEAVY ASTEROID MINING & EXTRACTION VESSEL
MODEL ~ RHI-M7 (CUSTOM-MODIFIED UNDER THE DIRECTION OF
      CAPTAIN SIGMUND ROSCO)
PRIMARY PROPULSION ~ 2 × MEGA-TORCH DRIVE ENGINES
SECONDARY / EMERGENCY PROPULSION ~ 2 × FUSION DRIVE ENGINES
MANEUVERING & ATTITUDE CONTROL ~ 12 VECTORED MANEUVERING THRUSTERS
INSTRUMENTATION & SENSOR SYSTEMS ~
      LONG-RANGE RADIOMETRIC SPECTROSCOPY ARRAY
      LASER-ENHANCED SPECTROMETRY SUITE
      HIGH-RESOLUTION ELEMENTAL ANALYZERS
      INTEGRATED MINERALOGICAL MAPPING SOFTWARE
DEFENSIVE & STABILITY SYSTEMS ~ 4 × STABIL RETENTION FIELD GENERATORS
PRIMARY COLLECTION SYSTEM ~ GRAVITONIC MINERAL COLLECTION SILOS
SUPPORT SCAVENGER CRAFT ~ 6

The *Hammershot* was equipped with four powerful Stabil Retention Field generators that protected the craft from dangerous asteroids or mining debris so often associated with its missions. Captain Rosco had just retrofitted its sensor array with state-of-the-art instrumentation, including long-range radiometric spectroscopy, laser-enhanced spectrometry, and elemental analyzers for determining the mineralogical makeup of asteroids, comets, and satellite moons. The underbelly of the *Hammershot* housed an array of gravitonic mineral collection silos.

But what set the *Hammershot* apart from many other mining vessels was its complement of six small, agile mining craft called Scavengers. These agile craft ferried excursion miners to and from a designated work area while creating and directing a gravitonic energy tunnel to feed pulverized minerals to the collection silos on the underbelly of the *Hammershot*. A skilled pilot maneuvered the Scavenger while an operations controller sitting beside the pilot managed the sensors and energy tunnels. It was a novel way of mining that Captain Rosco had tested two years ago, proving its cost effectiveness despite the added crew members and additional costs associated with this unique mining process.

A full crew for the *Hammershot* included 5 command crew, 7 maintenance and silo techs, 7 Scavenger pilots, 6 operation controllers, and 32 excursion miners for a total manifest of 57 crew members. In addition to the human crew members, a dozen androids were utilized to manage the collection silos, a dangerous task since the arriving streams of minerals could destabilize at any time without precise and consistent adjustments.

Ledger, Corbin, and six other new recruits—"greenhorns" as the veteran miners called them—were in-processed, assigned sleeping bunks, and shuffled off to a crash course on excursion mining operations.

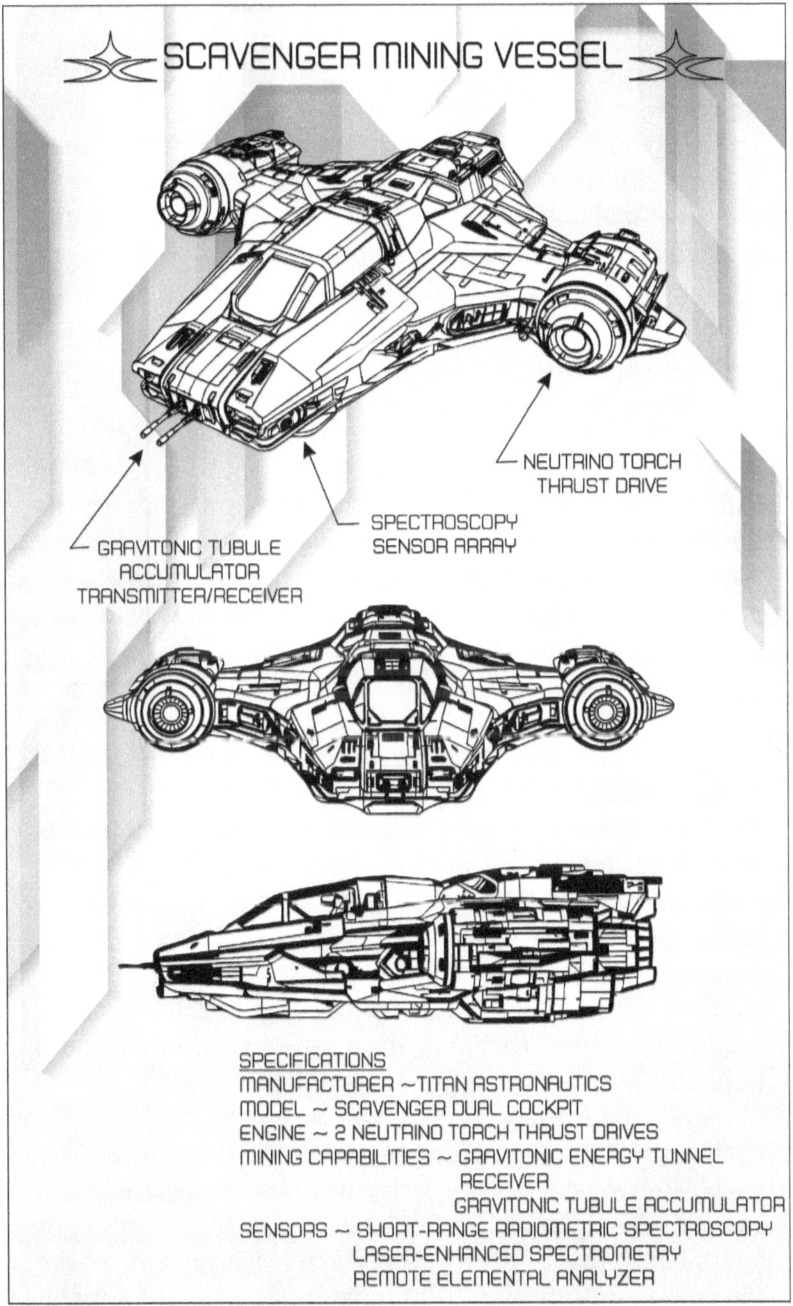

SCAVENGER MINING VESSEL
NEUTRINO TORCH THRUST DRIVE
SPECTROSCOPY SENSOR ARRAY
GRAVITONIC TUBULE ACCUMULATOR TRANSMITTER/RECEIVER
SPECIFICATIONS
MANUFACTURER ~ TITAN ASTRONAUTICS
MODEL ~ SCAVENGER DUAL COCKPIT
ENGINE ~ 2 NEUTRINO TORCH THRUST DRIVES
MINING CAPABILITIES ~ GRAVITONIC ENERGY TUNNEL
RECEIVER
GRAVITONIC TUBULE ACCUMULATOR
SENSORS ~ SHORT-RANGE RADIOMETRIC SPECTROSCOPY
LASER-ENHANCED SPECTROMETRY
REMOTE ELEMENTAL ANALYZER

One of the new recruits was separated out to learn operations controller skills. With just three days of training, the *Hammershot* launched with its new recruits on its next 120-day mining tour. The first few days in space would be dedicated to system and sensor calibrations, surveying, and training with a couple of extra vehicular sessions for the greenhorns so they could get a few hours in the excursion suits.

For Ledger, the first couple of days aboard the *Hammershot* were a blur of safety briefings, technical overviews, and tense introductions to seasoned crew members. The sense of being watched was palpable, not just by the command crew but by the miners themselves, who weighed every newcomer with wary eyes. Meals in the mess hall were quick affairs, punctuated by whispered advice and the occasional sharp word of warning from a veteran. Ledger learned that there were some crew members to give a wide berth to. Rough cuts, crude manners, and foul mouths marked them as brutish in all their ways. Despite the vastness of space outside, life within the ship felt close, almost claustrophobic, with every corridor and berth serving as a reminder of the risks that defined the space miner's existence.

Ledger checked on his android once, but the demands of training left little time for anything outside of work, sleep, and meals. Each drill and simulation forced him to focus on survival, teamwork, and the constant threat posed by mining in deep space. It was a relentless routine, yet he found a strange comfort in the structure, hoping that the order and discipline of ship life would help him keep his own inner turmoil at bay.

Many asteroid belts offered a return on mining time, each one with varying degrees of reward and risk. The Keller Belt was a mineral-rich ring of asteroids orbiting a small lifeless planet in a red-dwarf star system 68 light years from Abaria. Although it wasn't rich in some of the more precious minerals that most mining vessels sought, enough of the base minerals existed to make a seven-day mining venture worthwhile. Asteroids often contained mineral deposits 100 times more concentrated than on most planets. Typically, precious minerals like titanium, gold, silver, platinum, iridium, osmium, palladium, rhenium, and rhodium were the most coveted, but iron and nickel were suitable substitutes. Captain Rosco considered mining the Keller Belt as insurance for a long tour, as well as a marginally safe belt to initiate the greenhorns into the world of excursion mining.

All asteroid belts had a certain level of stable chaos. The chaos factor, or CF, of an asteroid belt determined its level of stability with "1" being quite stable and "10" being extremely unstable and therefore extremely dangerous. As fate would have it, the higher the chaos factor, the more precious the minerals seemed to be, and no mineralogist knew why. The more planets and moons there were in a system, the higher the chaos factor for any associated belts because of the gravity influences of those extra mass bodies. Ledger was grateful that his first excursion mining experience would be in an asteroid field with a chaos factor of two.

Upon arriving at the periphery of the Keller Belt, final crew assignments were to be made by Captain Rosco. The Scavenger pilots were the de facto leaders for their crew of one ops controller and five excursion miners. Pilots managed and directed their operations for the most efficient mineral extraction, given the allocated time on location.

Captain Rosco scrolled through a glass tablet, silently weighing the experience and training records of the excursion miners and ops controllers. Executive Officer Fraun remained at his side, posture rigid. Nearby, the six Scavenger pilots stood apart from the miners, exchanging quiet words as they conducted their own assessments. Ledger and the rest of the crew were lined up, fully suited with gear ready.

Captain Rosco looked older than he should have. Space mining did that to anyone who spent more than a decade doing its harsh work. Gray-white hair and beard framed a seasoned face with wrinkles that traced outward from the corners of his eyes. Above his brows, deeper wrinkles gave the impression that this captain was tough, demanding, and a seasoned space-mining veteran.

"Pilot Corgan, your ops controller is Harcort, and your excursion miners are Dix, Sahn, Briscot, Tram, and Dade."

"Aye, Cap," Corgan said. "*Raven* crew...with me." He walked down the narrow aisle of the launch bay to the far Scavenger ship. In bold, aggressive text, *"Raven"* was emblazoned across each side of the cockpit section of the nimble craft.

The new recruits shifted on their feet, anticipation and nervous energy coursing through the group. A cold bead of sweat rolled down Ledger's temple as the captain called out more names, pairing pilots with controllers and excursion miners.

After three crews were assigned, Ledger eyed the remaining pilots, wondering with whom he would be teamed up.

"Pilot Lux, your ops controller is Naybus, and your excursion miners are Wisco, Bane, Allendorce, Brandt, and Messer."

"Seriously, Captain?" Lux exclaimed. Ledger eyed the young female pilot as she turned to confront Captain Rosco. Ledger thought she looked way too young to be considered a "seasoned" pilot, but he had overheard the veteran excursion miners speak highly of her skills.

"A greenhorn ops controller *and* two greenhorn excursion miners?"

The veteran excursion miner named Bane stepped forward, throwing his hands in the air. "Agreed, Cap. Are you trying to get us killed out there?"

Captain Rosco frowned, his wrinkles sinking deeper into his face. He glared at the protesting pilot and miner. "I didn't hire you to complain about my assignments. Get with your crew and shut up, or I'll give your mining assignment to the backup."

Lux huffed at the captain then stepped forward to face her new crew.

"*Osprey* crew with me!" she shouted, turning to march toward her Scavenger craft two bays down.

Ledger was anxious about his first space excursion as a miner. The training and simulations could only prepare the new recruits so much. Nothing could fully prepare them for the reality of floating in space, tethered to nothing, and attempting to perform dangerous work.

The excursion suits were incredibly agile and functional. A main backpack micro-fusion force engine provided ample forward thrust. Thrust diverter nozzles on the thrust pack allowed for complete directional control. Orientation and thrust were linked to the miner's head position and movement, thereby freeing up his hands for the activity of mining. Whatever direction the miner's head was turned, the suit automatically aligned to face that direction, allowing full three-dimension control. If a miner wished to move forward or backward, he simply pushed his head forward or backward slightly. This head-control system freed up the miner's hands to operate the tools and equipment necessary to extract precious minerals from an asteroid, meteor, or small moon.

During simulations and training, Ledger had to concentrate intensely to master his excursion suit control, ultimately moving only his eyes once positioned correctly. He was grateful for his experience as a skilled Fireball player—mastering a hoverboard while managing gameplay had developed similar coordination required for excursion mining.

Ledger, Corbin, and the other three excursion miners assembled for Pilot Lux's pre-launch address. Lux appeared to be approximately the same age as Ledger. Like all the pilots and experienced excursion miners, she displayed a confident and focused demeanor. Her blonde hair was neatly braided and tied back, accentuating her composed and capable presence.

"Listen up. We've got a greenhorn controller and two greenhorn excursion miners on this team. I don't expect to set any recovery records today, but I do expect total focus and hard work." Lux paused to finish securing the upper section of her pilot suit. "Wisco, Bane, and Allendorce, keep an eye on Messer and Brandt. Nobody gets dead today—understand?"

Bane smirked, but the other two nodded.

Ledger offered Corbin a reassuring nod, hoping to encourage him a bit.

"Okay, miners, lock in and hang on. We're 15 minutes out from the edge of the belt. I'll be working the outer edge until I'm confident our greenhorns can handle more. Fly hard and live long!"

"Fly hard and live long!" Wisco, Bane, and Allendorce returned.

Lux and Naybus, her greenhorn ops controller, climbed into the Scavenger cockpit and strapped into the side-by-side seats. As the cockpit closed, Ledger's headset came to life.

"*Osprey* crew, radio check," Lux's voice boomed.

"Ops Naybus, check."

"Bane, check."

"Wisco, check."

"Allendorce, check."

"Brandt, check."

"Messer, check."

"Give me a lock and load," Lux followed.

Bane turned to Ledger with a grin on his face. "You greenhorns ready for this?" he asked as he reached for his extendable lanyard from his belt. Not waiting for a reply, Bane jumped onto a foothold on the outside of the Scavenger's starboard side and snapped his double-locking lanyard hook onto a tie-down ring on the fuselage. He then grabbed onto a handhold.

"Bane is locked and loaded," Ledger heard him radio.

Each of the remaining excursion miners followed suit, with Corbin Messer being the last to confirm his readiness. The fuselage of the Scavenger trembled under Ledger's feet as its engines came to life. A few seconds later, the craft lifted upward and proceeded toward the large metal bay door in the side of the *Hammershot*. A siren blared in the docking bay as the door began to open. As they passed through the Stablil Retention Field holding the atmosphere of the bay in place, the simulated gravity of the *Hammershot* let go of Ledger. The Scavenger accelerated, pulling hard on Ledger's handhold and pushing him into his excursion boots. He concentrated on not losing his foothold. When they were just a few hundred feet away from the *Hammershot*, the vastness and the loneliness of space began to press in on Ledger. He couldn't help imagining the *Osprey* Scavenger as his only link to humanity...to life itself. His grip automatically tightened as the blackness of space swallowed him. Seeing four other excursion miners clinging to the side of a spacecraft as it rocketed toward a massive ring of orbiting rocks was an odd sight.

This is absolutely insane, he thought, working hard not to let panic rule him. He glanced over at Corbin, seeing near terror on the man's face.

Ledger tried to steady his breathing, his heart pounding not only from the adrenaline of launch but also from the anticipation of what lay ahead. The sight of the swirling asteroids, their jagged surfaces gleaming faintly in the reflected starlight, sent a chill down his spine. He glanced at the veteran miners, each one focused and silent. The Scavenger's hull continued to shimmy as it rocketed onward, cutting through the emptiness, destined for a massive ring of swirling rocks.

As the edge of the asteroid belt loomed larger and larger before them, Lux flipped their Scavenger craft end for end to decelerate their approach. Once the *Osprey* was within a hundred feet of the first sizable asteroid and their velocity synchronized with this sector of the belt asteroids, Lux repositioned the craft, and the veteran miners snapped into action.

"Equipment bay opening," Pilot Lux warned.

"Mineralogical scanning initiated," Naybus added.

A panel near the aft of the ship began to open. Bane detached and recovered his lanyard then maneuvered himself nimbly and perfectly in position to retrieve and distribute the mining equipment to each of the other excursion miners. Ledger was the last to receive his.

Each excursion miner operated two critical pieces of equipment. Attached to the left arm was a quad tool that performed the heavy-duty demolition work of mining. A rotary selection wheel position near the thumb allowed the miner to choose between one of four different extraction devices. First was the laser boring beam—a powerful rotating tri-laser tool that utilized focused beams of high-intensity laser light to punch through the toughest of asteroid rock. Second was the Stasis cutting blade—a Stasis-field-reinforced titanium blade used for slicing off larger pieces of mineral deposit for transport back to the *Hammershot*. Third was a plasma grinding torch—an energy-enhanced plasma cutter that was used to grind non-explosive minerals. Fourth was the magnetic pulverizer—an extremely effective tool to crush and granulize ferrous mineral rock.

Attached to the right arm was a gravitonic tubule accumulator. This device was used to make an energy field connection with their associated Scavenger craft that allowed an excursion miner to direct a tightly constrained stream of mined material back to the craft.

EXCURSION MINING EXTRACTOR

SPECIFICATIONS
MANUFACTURER ~ HEPHAESTUS HEAVY INDUSTRIES
MODEL ~ VX-9 "CORE-BREACHER"
POWER MODULE ~ SOLID-STATE FUSION CELL
MODES ~ LASER BORING BEAM
          STASIS CUTTING BLADE
          PLASMA GRINDING TORCH
          MAGNETIC PULVERIZER
OPTIMAL EXTRACTION DISTANCE ~ 3 TO 8 FEET

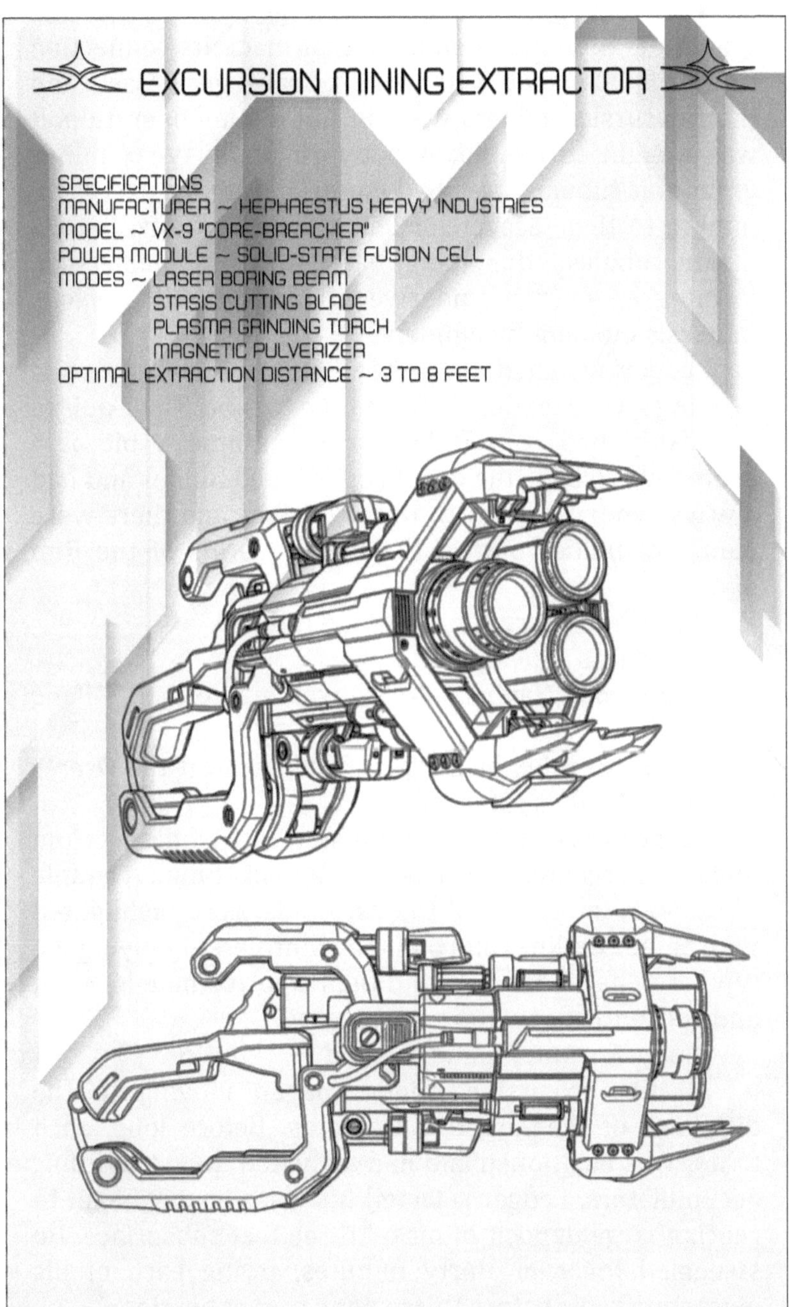

The Scavenger powered a larger version of the gravitonic tubule accumulator that made its connection to the *Hammershot*. When all six Scavenger vessels and their excursion miners were in full mining operation, it was a sight to behold. A network of thirty-six minor gravitonic tubules streamed material from the excursion miners to their Scavenger ships, which in turn fed six major tubules connecting back to the *Hammershot*, forming an energy spiderweb that captured precious minerals moment by moment.

Ledger watched the veteran miners closely while keeping an eye on Corbin from time to time. Their quirky friendship had caused Ledger to assume a bit of a protective role for the guy. Ledger hated bullies and had always sympathized with the underdog, and there were plenty of bullies out on the harsh worlds of the Rim planets.

"What's our target, ops?" Bane radioed.

There was a long pause.

"Come on, Naybus. We're wasting oxygen," Bane prodded.

"Two asteroids bearing 22.3 degrees off the *Osprey* azimuth," Naybus returned.

Ledger's helmet HUD illuminated with a full spectrum of data. He scanned the asteroids ahead of him. A couple of seconds later, two of the asteroids were highlighted with amber outlines and balloon identifiers signifying the type of mineral deposits and their approximate location and concentration within the asteroid.

"Copy. Enroute," Bane radioed.

All five excursion miners began moving in the direction of the targeted asteroids. Before long, each miner was positioned and had activated their gravitonic accumulators. Ledger selected his laser-boring beam to reach a large deposit of nickel three feet subsurface. He struggled for over thirty minutes, trying each of his extraction tools before Wisco appeared at his side.

"Angle your boring beam like this to create multiple fracture lines then switch to your Stasis cutting blade to remove the rock," Wisco explained and demonstrated.

In just a couple of minutes, a steady stream of nickel fragments was pulled in and delivered back to the *Osprey* via his gravitonic energy tubule accumulator.

"Got it...thanks," Ledger said.

Excursion mining was hard, frustrating work, and Ledger marveled at how efficient Bane, Wisco, and Allendorce were. After three hours, Ledger felt like he was beginning to master the maneuvering of his excursion suit, but the extraction tools were still fighting him.

The radio chatter between miners and Scavenger crew was succinct and consistent. Near the end of their excursion run, Ledger finally began to feel the rhythm of the operation and appreciate its efficiency. He noticed that one of the veteran miners was never far away from both Corbin and him, which both annoyed and comforted him at the same time.

"Wisco, I'm reading a high concentration of super hydrogenated ice in your location," Ops Naybus radioed.

"Wisco, pull back," Bane shouted over the com, but it was too late.

The plasma tool that Wisco was using fractured and ignited a large pocket of the hydrogenated ice crystals which exploded right in his face. Chaos immediately ensued. Wisco was thrown violently backward as the asteroid fractured into a hundred pieces, sending fragments everywhere. Ledger, Corbin, and the other two miners scrambled to avoid being pummeled by the explosion debris as Wisco struggled to orient and reduce his backward velocity. Three seconds later he collided with another large asteroid that knocked him unconscious. He continued to tumble like a rag doll, deeper into the asteroid belt. Ledger instinctively began to propel himself to chase after Wisco, but it became apparent that his pursuit would be pointless.

"Stand down, Brandt!" Pilot Lux ordered. "Disengage all gravitonic accumulators. I'm going after him."

"That's suicide!" Bane radioed back.

"*Osprey* this is *Hammershot*," Rosco's voice thundered over the emergency com channel. "What's your status?"

Ledger watched as Lux shut down her main gravitonic connection to the *Hammershot*, closed the equipment cargo door, and engaged her main thrusters, diving headlong into the Keller Belt.

"A hydrogen explosion has catapulted Wisco deeper into the belt. I'm going after him," Lux radioed.

There was a five-second delay. "Zara, don't be foolish. Return to ship, and we'll come up with a rescue plan," Rosco replied.

"Negative, *Hammershot*," Lux returned. "He's unconscious, and his suit is reporting significant damage. I'm going in."

Ledger reversed his course back to the other miners while keeping an eye on the *Osprey*. He held his breath as he watched Lux dodge, flip, and barely skirt by one asteroid after another in pursuit of their tumbling crew member. Lux's piloting skills with her Scavenger were nothing short of superhuman. As Lux closed in on Wisco, Ledger could see a massive rotating asteroid careening toward them that would surely end him. Lux extended the *Osprey's* two grappling arms, snatching Wisco out of the way at the last second. She flipped the Scavenger end for end and began navigating the treacherous journey back to the outer edge of the belt. Once clear, she punched the engines up to full thrust.

"*Osprey* excursion crew, sit tight," Lux radioed. "This miner needs emergency attention. I'll be back in 20."

Ledger, Corbin, Bane, and Allendorce assembled at one of the largest asteroids, waiting for Pilot Lux to deliver Wisco to the *Hammershot*. An hour later, all members of the *Osprey* crew were tucked into their bay on board the *Hammershot*. Bane removed his helmet, and Ledger could tell that he was furious. He came at Controller Naybus, looking like he was going to rip him to pieces.

"You should have warned us earlier!" he shouted.

Naybus did his best to hold his ground. "The orientation of the asteroid gave inconclusive readings."

"Not good enough!" Bane yelled.

"That's enough, Bane," Lux said as she dismounted from her side of the cockpit. "I was watching too. The other minerals nearby were inhibiting the sensor's readings."

Bane's nostrils flared. He pushed a finger into Naybus's chest. "Get better!" He turned and walked away in a huff.

Naybus took a deep breath as Ledger came up next to him. Lux turned her attention to Ledger.

"What were you thinking, Brandt?" she asked, scrutinizing him. "You would have gotten both of you killed."

"I couldn't just let him die," Ledger replied.

Lux scrunched her lips to the side of her mouth as she eyed him. "Next time think before you act out there. Come on, Naybus, the captain wants a word."

Naybus glanced over at Ledger.

"Don't sweat it, man," Ledger said. "It sounds like Wisco is going to be fine. Everything turned out okay."

Naybus didn't look convinced, but he nodded his appreciation and followed after Lux.

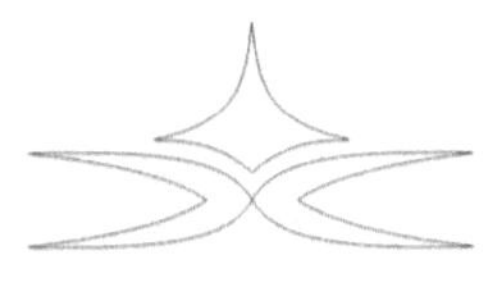

CHAPTER

5

Dock Days

The incident at the Keller Belt was a raw introduction to the world of space mining for the greenhorns. Thankfully, Wisco's injuries were minor, and he returned to duty within a couple of days. Ledger was sure that this wouldn't be the last tense situation they would face. With the incident fresh on the minds of the miners, the mess hall became a favorite place for the veteran miners to regale the greenhorns with many more exaggerated stories of great peril. Frozen bodies due to ruptured excursion suits and amputated limbs from asteroids crushing unsuspecting miners were the common stories, but other stories were worse...much worse. Ledger never quite knew how much truth was in them, but after seeing what could have happened at the Keller Belt, none of the stories sounded too far-fetched.

The experienced members of the Scavenger crew Ledger was assigned to had little to do with their greenhorn counterparts when off duty. Wisco, Bane, and Allendorce made it clear that they would not be fraternizing with any greenhorns. Pilot Zara Lux was in a class all by herself. Outside of duty, Ledger rarely saw her, and even then the miniature draco creature often perched on her shoulder seemed to be her only companion. Ledger wasn't sure if the winged critter was more than a pet. Its keen awareness of its surroundings and rather sharp talons might allow it to also serve as Lux's protector. Either way, most people kept a wide berth when the draco was with her. On the whole, Lux kept her business life serious and her private life private.

Corbin continued to attach himself to Ledger, but Ledger didn't mind. He was discovering that a friend in space wasn't such a bad thing. The ops controller, Arn Naybus, also seemed to gravitate their way. Ledger did his best to encourage them, and in a strange way, it seemed to help diminish some of his own mental anguish.

Ledger checked in on his android from time to time, and the bot seemed to be doing extraordinarily well. The silo tech supervisor had given it more responsibility and latitude than any previous bot.

"Where did you find this bot?" the silo tech supervisor asked. "I want a dozen more just like him."

"He's one of a kind," Ledger admitted. "I don't think you'll ever see another."

More than 70 percent of the material collected by the excursion miners had no use—clay, silicate rocks, and organic carbon. The *Hammershot* contained a preliminary refinery that increased desired mineral purity to 90 percent, separating the major precious minerals into their own collection silos. The waste material was dumped in a decaying orbit around a dead planet or moon. This allowed the crew of the *Hammershot* to mine for longer periods of time until each of the silos was full of nearly pure precious minerals. That's when the real danger appeared. Ledger noticed that even the most seasoned *Hammershot* crewmembers were constantly anxious once their silos were full, for one reason, and one reason only—space raiders.

Space raiders, they were told, were some of the most vicious, bloodthirsty criminals in the entire galaxy. One fully loaded space mining vessel full of precious minerals was worth a dozen lifetimes of great wealth. Captain Rosco had armed the *Hammershot* with a modicum of defensive weapons—though they were little help against a well-organized, well-armed armada of space raiders. Three or four space raider vessels executing a well-planned attack with fast ships, ruthless crewmembers, and weapons galore, both legal and illegal, posed the worst kind of threat to men like Captain Rosco and their hard-working crews.

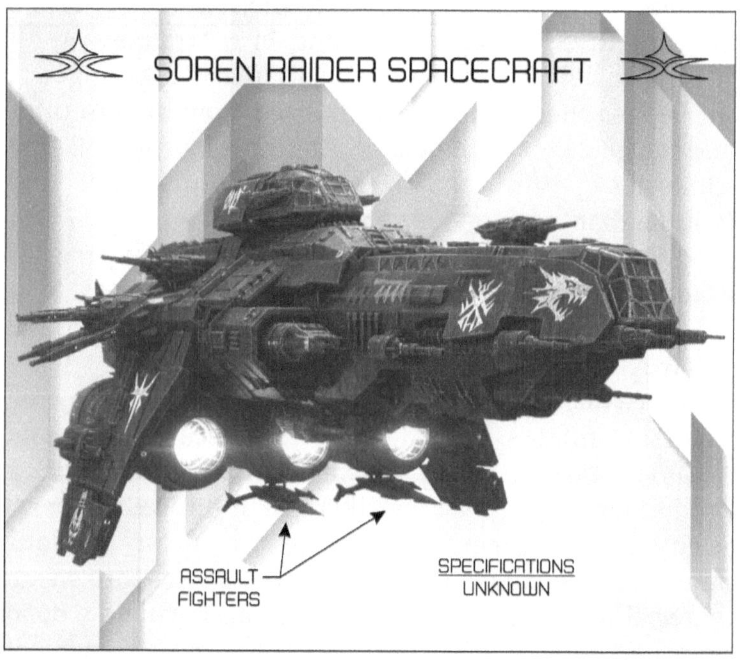

Their only real hope against the space raiders rested in the hands of the Rim Syndicate. Twenty-six years earlier, a former Morian Empire special operations commando founded the Rim Syndicate as a taskforce to tackle the dire threat of raiders. Over the last three decades, the Rim Syndicate had become the protectors of the space miners and even a respected authority force on many of the planets where they had bases of operation. Space mining captains gladly paid an annual protection fee to the Rim Syndicate in exchange for protection and aid. They often provided escorts for a fully loaded mining vessel heading to an offloading facility. More recently, the Rim Syndicate had begun operating the offloading facilities as well, which strengthened their resolve even further to ensure appropriate protection was provided. The *Hammershot* would offload its precious cargo at one of five facilities, three times during a 120-day tour. The entire *Hammershot* crew was grateful each time a Rim Syndicate escort of three fighter craft appeared to guide them in. Ledger was grateful that his first 120-day tour had ended without any further incidents.

During dock days, some crew members stayed in their quarters to save money, but most chose to pay for an end-of-tour bungalow or a temp-dwelling either in the city or in a nearby city. Personally, Ledger was ready to find a bed that didn't move and to re-experience real gravity and real food. They would moor at Bria, the capital of Abaria, once again, making ship repairs and replacing any crew members that weren't planning on coming back.

Out on the Rim planets, nearly everyone carried a weapon of some sort, usually a handheld blaster. All weapons were confiscated and secured before boarding the *Hammershot* and redistributed when offboarding. Ledger, however, had resolved never to carry a blaster again. The memory of Stone's death was all Ledger needed to commit himself to never carrying or wielding another weapon.

Surprisingly, Ledger found it difficult to leave his android behind on the *Hammershot*, but per his sign-on contract, his android was required to work three full tours with no down-days. Ledger consoled his nagging guilt by convincing himself that the bot's duties while in dock would at least be minimized and safer.

Once Ledger exited the *Hammershot*, he passed by multiple stations just off the spaceport campus, beckoning him to deposit his hard-earned credits with them for safekeeping, at a fee of course. Nothing about any of them gave Ledger the least hint that they could be trusted, yet he saw many of his fellow *Hammershot* mining workers utilizing their services. He shook his head.

Fools, he thought as he passed by.

Ledger's hope that the intense labor of the mining ship might serve as a crucible to crush away the torment of guilt had only partially worked. In the exhaustion of his down time, there was little space left to self-condemn since those precious few hours were saturated end to end with needed sleep. Now, during his dock days, he was hoping to free himself from the close quarters of the *Hammershot* and be away from people. Corbin Messer and Arn Naybus had indicated a desire to meet up during their off time, but Ledger thought he had successfully deflected any such offers.

The *Hammershot* would moor for ten days, unloading its precious minerals, refueling, and effecting any repairs that could only be accomplished at a spaceport. That was the cycle. A tour of 120 days followed by ten days at dock to be repeated ad nauseam. Some of the veteran miners had chalked up 30 tours, and it was easy to tell which ones. The life of a space miner was brutal on the body and the soul. Ledger inwardly felt like it was exactly what he wanted...a harsh life serving as penance for his heinous crimes.

Ledger trudged onward to what looked like a transport station, hoping to travel to a quiet sector of the city to get some food and rest. He had no furlough plans other than to recover his body in preparation for his second tour. As he passed by a narrow break between two buildings, the sound of a ruckus caught his attention. He glanced into the dimly lit alley to see four brutes accosting a fellow space miner about 50 feet away. Ledger instantly recognized all five of the men as fellow crew members of the *Hammershot*. The four brutes were veteran miners, the kind Ledger avoided. After seeing them severely harass some of the other greenhorns on the last tour, Ledger only interacted with any of these brutes when absolutely necessary. The poor fellow they had jacked up against the wall was none other than his quirky friend, Corbin, his blaster nowhere in sight.

"Give us your credits, greenhorn, or we'll crush your legs, and you'll never walk again!" commanded the gruff voice of one of the men named Lorak.

Ledger stepped into the shadows of the alley to reconnoiter his options.

"Please...no...I have to get my credits to family—"

Corbin's words were cut short by the sound of a solid punch to his face. Ledger stepped out of the shadows, approaching the men from behind. The irony wasn't lost on Ledger, for just a few months ago he had been the abuser...the one bruising the heads of innocent people.

More punches...more insults...more scuffling.

"Got them!" exclaimed one of the brutes.

Ledger quickened his gait, but by the time he arrived, Corbin was slumped against the wall in a heap.

"Give the credits back!" Ledger shouted with as much fortitude as he could muster.

The four brutes turned to face Ledger, a wry smile forming on each of their faces.

"Another greenhorn...just as stupid as this one," Lorak sneered.

Within seconds, the men had surrounded Ledger. Although Ledger was quite skilled at hand-to-hand, four against one was impossible, especially when the brutes knew how to handle themselves. But he now had no choice but to fight. He chose the easiest target first, hoping he could even the odds at least a little.

He readied himself as two of the thugs each drew extending Stabil-Retention-Field-enhanced bludgeons. Ledger had experienced the painful end of one of these weapons before and had never forgotten the experience. It was like getting hit by a hammer and a lightning bolt at the same time. He had no way out now.

"Hand over your credits, greenhorn, or you'll end up worse than him," Lorak said with a slight nod toward Corbin's pile of flesh and bones.

Ledger figured he could get one good shot in against the smallest of the brutes, but his end would come seconds after that. Just as he was about to charge, a voice called out behind him.

"Lorak! Captain Rosco doesn't take on thieves. Is that what you want?" a firm female voice called out.

Out of the corner of his eye, Ledger could see a fit young woman walk from behind him straight at Lorak, seemingly undaunted by the brute's fierce demeanor. The low growl of a Thorian draco perched alertly on the woman's shoulder rose in volume as she approached. Her draco was a nimble, four-legged, leathery-winged creature with iridescent blue scales and large, amber eyes. Its crown of feathered fins and sharp, inquisitive beak suggested that this creature was a keen-eyed scout as well as a loyal aerial protector.

Lorak turned his attention to the woman, sneering and squinting. He spat. "Go on your way, Zara. Unless you want to join these two in the infirmary."

Zara Lux put her hands on her hips. "Go ahead, Lorak," she taunted. "And not only will you never work another tour this side of the galaxy, but Rosco will have his men disappear you in a day." The draco bared its sharp teeth, its wings poised to fly. Lux then made a sequence of clicking and tonal sounds with her throat. The draco instantly took flight, circling the three thugs, its yellow eyes fixed on Lorak.

Lorak's sneer deepened, but Ledger could see the fight in his three companions disappear in a moment as they nervously watched the circling draco.

"Come on, Lorak. We got what we came for," one of the men muttered.

Lorak scowled, wiping his nose with the rough hem of his shirt as he stepped toward Lux. Lux made another sequence of throat sounds, and the draco dutifully returned to her shoulder. Lorak pulled back then walked past, keeping just out of reach of her threatening creature. He sneered at the draco, making a quick gesture toward it as if to attack. The draco shrieked, lunging forward at Lorak as if eager to rip one of its sharp talons across the man's neck, but Lux reached up and calmed the angry beast. The other three brutes jumped back. The draco watched them with angry yellow eyes, despite Lux's restraint.

"You better hope Rosco lives forever, girl. Cause the day he doesn't..." he said, pausing and staring her straight in the eye, "I'm coming for you *and* your flying rat!"

Lorak led his three thugs out of the alley, disappearing back into the underbelly of the city. Lux turned to glare at Ledger.

"Are you that stupid?" she asked.

Ledger decided thanking her was pointless. Instead, he turned to help Corbin gain his feet. The guy winced as he tried to stand. His face was bleeding, and already a purple bruise under his eye was starting to swell.

"They took it all. My family needs those credits," Corbin muttered.

"Don't you greenhorns know to never carry credits?" Lux said. "The first thing you do when you get off the *Hammershot* is get your credits into a depository."

"Those guys look as shady as Lorak and his cronies," Ledger returned.

Lux shook her head. "Use the Rim Syndicate depository. They look crude, but the Syndicate doesn't stand for thievery. The whole organization's financial basis is built on trust."

Ledger eyed Lux. She was as tough on the streets of Abaria as she was piloting their Scavenger, yet something about her just didn't fit within the world of space mining. Lux's winged companion eyed Ledger, tilting its head. It was quite the fascinating creature. Although Lux had successfully calmed the draco, it still uttered a low guttural growl as it glared at him.

He nodded his thanks for the information then turned back to Corbin.

"How many credits did they take?"

"Six hundred fifty," Corbin sputtered.

Just then Arn Naybus entered the alleyway from the street.

"Messer, what have you gotten yourself into?" Arn called as he came to them. He helped Ledger get Corbin up and onto his feet.

"Can you take us to the nearest Rim Syndicate depository?" Ledger asked, glancing toward Lux.

She frowned, glancing at the display on her forearm before looking back out into the street. "Yeah," she said without looking back at them. Ledger fully understood. Lux clearly intended to separate from them as soon as they'd helped Corbin, just as Ledger himself was planning to do.

Arn tucked himself under Corbin's other side as they stood him fully up. Lux walked ahead without waiting. When she entered the street and turned left, she glanced back at the three of them, then pushed on. Once they'd made it to the street, Corbin straightened himself.

"I can make it on my own," he said with a wheeze.

Ledger and Arn dropped their aid but stayed close just in case. Corbin seemed to rally once other street farers looked his direction.

"There's no point in this now since I don't have any credits to deposit," he said as they continued to follow Lux's lead.

"I'll loan you a few," Ledger replied.

Ledger caught Arn's concerned glance as Lux turned her head slightly, but she pressed on.

Corbin looked over at Ledger. "Why would you do that? You know I don't have any way of paying you back."

"I'm not worried about it. My android will make it up for both of us," Ledger replied as the group shuffled past bustling rows of shops.

"There's the depository you want to use," Lux said, glancing to her left at a crude-looking shop tucked into the corner of a massive building with a hundred other shops. A short quirky-looking man sat at a counter next to a glowing control panel. Behind him stood a massive dark figure with a full array of weapons hanging from his belt and chest harness.

Ledger eyed Lux. "You sure about this?"

Lux rolled her eyes. She sauntered up to the depository counter as if she owned the shop.

"Turlic, you little weasel," Lux said, slamming a fist on the counter. The draco on her shoulder added a frightening shriek to her insult, flapping its wings and hissing.

The man scowled back at her, but Ledger noticed that the monster of a man behind him unleashed a crooked grin.

"What do you want now, Zara? I already took your credits. You can access them when processing is complete."

"I'm bringing you more business, so I expect a discount on your next fee...got it?" Lux said. She turned to look at Corbin, not waiting for Turlic to respond. "You're up," she said then stepped away, but stayed close enough to keep Turlic honest in his dealings with Corbin.

Ledger stepped up beside Corbin and placed 650 credits on the counter. "Deposit these into whatever account he gives you."

Corbin looked over at Ledger with disbelief on his face. "I can't—"

"It's a done deal," Ledger said, then stepped aside to allow Turlic and Corbin to finish the deposit. He could feel the glares of Arn on his right and Lux on his left. He continued to look straight ahead, watching Corbin finalize the deal with Turlic. As far as Ledger was concerned, he didn't need the credits. Although he didn't know Corbin's story, he figured the man was desperate to help whoever was back home. Ledger had no one.

A few minutes later, the deposit was complete, and Corbin looked at Ledger with grateful eyes.

"I'll figure out a way to pay you back," Corbin said.

"You better," Ledger jested. "And by the way, I charge a lot of interest," he added with a wink.

Ledger stepped up to Turlic and deposited most of his remaining credits in his own account. Surprisingly, Lux had not yet left them as Ledger would have expected. He watched as she reached into a pocket and offered her creature a morsel of meat.

"How about we all get something to eat and drink?" Arn suggested. "And I'm betting that our renowned pilot knows some pretty great eateries."

Lux put her hand up. "Not me. Greenhorns always find their way into trouble, and I don't need any more of that. Enjoy your dock days."

As Lux was turning to leave, Corbin stepped forward.

"Thanks for your help back there."

Lux offered a crooked grin. "I need my crew back on the *Osprey* for the next tour so...stay out of alleys," she said before disappearing into the crowd.

Although Arn and Corbin were the closest Ledger had to friends, he had been keeping them at a distance, and now all he wanted was for a few precious days spent alone. He searched for an excuse to separate as well, but one look at Corbin and he couldn't bring himself to do it.

Arn turned to look at Corbin and Ledger. "Wisco told me there's a great place to eat on the docks called the Paragon Eatery. Says it's a bit rough but worth it. What do you say?"

Corbin looked to Ledger for approval.

"Sounds great. Let's go," Ledger said with as much enthusiasm as he could muster. Corbin looked pleased.

Thirty minutes later, Ledger, Arn, and Corbin entered the eatery to find a long waiting list for a table.

"What else have we got to do?" Arn shrugged. "Might as well wait."

After twenty minutes, the eatery door opened behind them, and in stepped none other than Zara Lux, her Thorian draco perched dutifully on her shoulder.

"Yikes," Lux said, eyeing the line of people waiting. When she saw Ledger, Arn, and Corbin, she shook her head. "I can't seem to get away from you guys."

"The wait time is 40 minutes," Arn offered.

Lux frowned. "Well, I'm too hungry to wait that long, so see ya round!"

"You're welcome to join us," Corbin offered. "We should be seated in just a few minutes."

Ledger looked at Corbin, surprised by the invitation he offered. Lux looked like she was about to refuse Corbin's offer but was cut short by the hostess.

"Your table is ready," the hostess said, approaching from within the eatery. "Follow me."

The three of them looked Lux's way for an answer.

"I'm starved. Surely you guys have already had your dose of bad luck. What else could go wrong?" Lux said, wagging her head as she joined them.

The hostess seated them at a table near the center of the crowded dining area. Ambient conversation noise and background music added to the cacophony filling the eatery.

While they waited for a waitress and drinks, Ledger, Arn, and Corbin were fixated on Lux's shoulder creature. This was as close as any of them had been to it. A crooked grin crossed Lux's lips as she seemed to sense their apprehension. She tapped on the table while voicing a strange tonal sound, and the draco flitted down her arm. Tucking its wings tightly to its body, the creature eyed each of the table mates with its yellow cat-like eyes. Ledger reached for a nut from a bowl in the center of the table, cracked it open, and held it out to the draco. Lux's right eyebrow lifted as her creature sniffed the nut then growled at Ledger. Ledger wondered if the thing would bite his fingers off to get the nut. The draco carefully stretched out its neck, snatching the nut from Ledger's fingers. Ledger pulled back his hand, thankful all his digits were still connected.

"Hmm," Lux muttered, her eyes narrowing.

"Do you actually talk draco?" Ledger asked.

"More or less," Lux replied.

"How big will it get?" Arn asked.

"Jix is a full-grown miniature draco. A full-size Thorian draco is twice as long as a man." Lux offered a wry smile then scanned each of her tablemates. "Three greenhorns and you all made it through your first tour," she said, as the draco became preoccupied with dismantling and devouring the nut Ledger had given it. "I must say I had my doubts." She glanced at each of them. "Why in the galaxy would you sign up for duty on a space mining crew?"

Great, thought Ledger, *just what I didn't want to talk about.*

They all exchanged quick looks, wondering who would offer an answer first.

"I need to take care of my people," Corbin began.

"Big family?" Lux asked.

Corbin nodded. "Very." He turned to look at Arn. "How about you?"

Arn squirmed in his chair a bit. "Somebody told me to come, and I didn't feel like I could say no."

Lux leaned forward. "Wait—you're here because somebody told you to be here...working on a space mining ship?"

Arn looked uncomfortable now. Ledger was just as surprised as Lux seemed.

"What I don't understand is how you got selected to be an ops controller right out of the gate. It usually takes many tours as an excursion miner," Lux said as she stroked the back of her draco. "That is, unless you have prior expertise," she finished with an inquisitive look in her eye.

Arn fiddled with a couple of nuts he had taken from the bowl on the table. He glanced up at Lux. "My father owns a rare mineral mining company back on my home planet. I've been working there for the past three years. I guess when they saw that on my application, they figured I could learn to be an ops controller."

"So your father's expanding into space mining, and he sent you to learn the trade?" Lux asked.

Arn fidgeted with the napkin in front of him. "Not exactly."

"How about you, Lux?" Ledger said, trying to rescue Arn. "What's your story?"

Lux leaned back, taking a deep breath. "If we're eating a meal together, you might as well know my name...it's Zara. Don't ever use it on the *Hammershot* though," she warned with fierce eyes, "or I'll leave you stranded on an asteroid." Ledger knew she was joking...mostly.

"Mining is all I've ever known," Zara continued. "Parents were killed when I was nine. I was sold as a slave and have been mining ever since."

On the Outer Rim planets, Ledger learned that some worlds accepted slavery, or indentured servitude, as part of their culture. On Abaria, however, it was rare and frowned upon.

Ledger watched Zara closely. She was a tough gal, but her captivating eyes didn't hide the pain when she spoke about her past. Despite her rough and tough personae, to Ledger she seemed lonely and afraid, although he would never say such a thing because she would probably lop his head off with a stasis-enhanced short sword. Zara winced a quick smile then turned her attention to Ledger.

"Your turn."

Ledger pursed his lips and shook his head once. "You could say I'm out on the Rim planets to find myself." He hoped that would suffice but the silence from the group made it obvious they weren't satisfied.

"Well, that tells us everything," Zara teased. "I still know almost nothing about any of you. I suppose that's to be expected. At least tell me why you don't carry a blaster," Zara said, tilting her head to look at Ledger's empty belt.

"Don't even try," Arn said. "The man is just as elusive on that subject. We've tried."

Zara glanced toward Arn then back to Ledger, eyeing him over. "Either you aren't any good with one, or you think it makes you a target, or you're afraid—cause I know you're not stupid."

"I'll let you pick," Ledger said with a slight smirk.

To Ledger's surprise, Zara's draco flitted across the table toward him. The closer it came, the more nervous Ledger became. He froze as the creature lifted itself on its hind legs, sniffing him. Ledger looked to Zara for some assurance this was normal, but the look on her face didn't help. She seemed curious and surprised. After a few seconds of evaluating Ledger, the creature turned about and nuzzled Ledger's hand toward the bowl of nuts. Ledger reached past the draco, hoping it wouldn't change its mind and make his hand a meal. The creature jostled its feet in anticipation as Ledger cracked open another nut, then handed it to the creature. Zara tilted her head, watching. After two more treats, Zara warbled a short command and tapped her shoulder just as a waitress appeared. In a flash, the creature returned to its perch, a nut still in hand. The waitress set four drinks down in front of them and then left with a promise to return shortly. Ledger was acutely aware that Zara seemed annoyed by how her draco was responding to him.

Ledger took a sip of his fresh ale. "So, what's good to eat here?" he asked, flipping the menu that was displayed up through the glass top of the table. He swiped a couple of times until he found something that looked interesting. "Outer Rim monibou brisket with fresh obra roots. Sounds interesting. I think I'll take a chance."

He looked up in time to see Zara shaking her head. "No blaster...I don't ever leave the ship without a blaster. There are too many thugs around," she said, looking Corbin's way. "You two ought to know that."

Corbin faked a smile then appeared preoccupied with selecting something off the menu.

"How long have you been with the *Hammershot?*" Ledger asked Zara.

"A long time. I started as an excursion miner just like you, then went to ops, and then to pilot." She smiled. "The fun job."

"But you're not that old—" Ledger began but was interrupted by a ruckus at both entrances of the eatery at the same time, while a man in the middle of the room jumped up on a table brandishing an advanced blaster. The two entrances were now blocked by two additional men with fierce-looking blasters of their own.

"Do not attempt to draw your weapons!" the man in the center shouted as three hovering bots flew up from an open case on the floor, each one taking a strategic position around the room. The bots scanned the room in a continuous, sweeping arc. One man drew his blaster, but before he could lift it high enough to fire, one of the bots locked in on him and fired. The energy discharge ripped clear through the man, leaving half of a smoldering corpse that fell to the ground with a thud. All the people in the eatery gasped in horror.

"There's always one," the man said, leveling his blaster at another random occupant.

"Soren raiders," Ledger heard Zara whisper. "None worse!" Her draco was issuing guttural warnings as she tried to calm it.

All three raiders were now in eyesight of Ledger and his table while the bots continued to scan and circulate.

"If you attempt to leave, they will kill you," the man said calmly. "I'm going to make this easy for all of you. My associates are going to make the rounds to each of you with a credit scanner. Everyone will immediately accept a transfer request of 100 credits when scanned. If you delay, you will be shot. If you comply, you leave here tonight having offered a small contribution in exchange for your life."

The other two raiders immediately began their electronic thievery, and no one dared refuse them after the grisly demonstration moments earlier. They pulled a scanner from their belt and thrust it at each unwilling contributor, pointing a charged blaster their way as each one shakily accepted the transfer. Ledger began to tremble with anger as he watched the raiders torment the people. When one of them came to Ledger's table, Ledger, Arn, and Corbin all complied, but the raider's eyes lingered on Zara.

Zara's draco growled and hissed in a most ferocious way. The thug made a gesture, and the bot, hovering just behind him, instantly fired a micro energy burst that blasted the draco off Zara's shoulder.

"No!" Zara screamed. She stood up to charge the man, but before she could fully gain her feet, the thug grabbed her by the throat and aimed his blaster at her head.

"I can easily blast that pretty head of yours right off your shoulders," the man said with a snarl as his finger tightened against his blaster trigger.

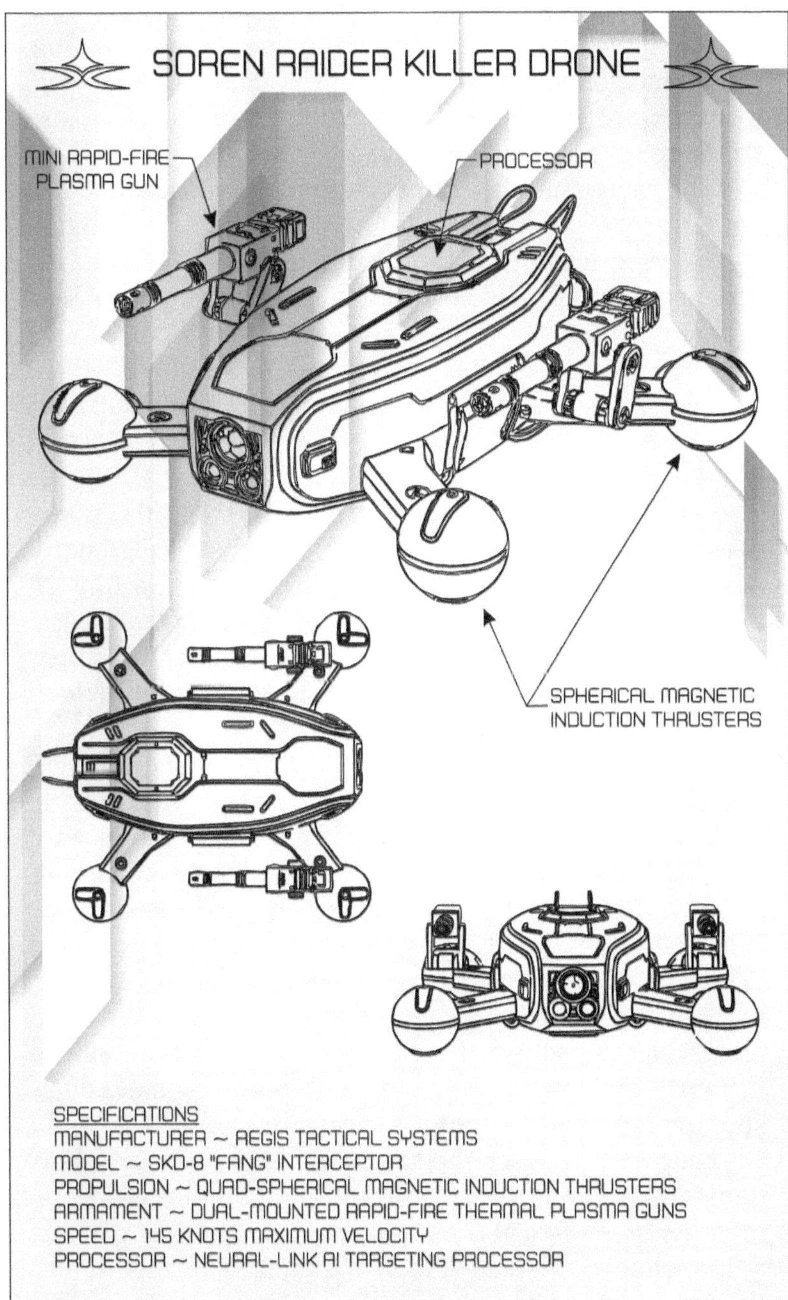

SOREN RAIDER KILLER DRONE
MINI RAPID-FIRE PLASMA GUN
PROCESSOR
SPHERICAL MAGNETIC INDUCTION THRUSTERS
SPECIFICATIONS
MANUFACTURER ~ AEGIS TACTICAL SYSTEMS
MODEL ~ SKD-8 "FANG" INTERCEPTOR
PROPULSION ~ QUAD-SPHERICAL MAGNETIC INDUCTION THRUSTERS
ARMAMENT ~ DUAL-MOUNTED RAPID-FIRE THERMAL PLASMA GUNS
SPEED ~ 145 KNOTS MAXIMUM VELOCITY
PROCESSOR ~ NEURAL-LINK AI TARGETING PROCESSOR

Ledger's fierce anger awakened—anger that had never truly left. Two decades of intense combat training slammed against his inner wall of self-control, clamoring to break out to exact justice. Without thinking, Ledger stood up to face the man. "Leave her be!"

The raider's eyes widened with fury. He loosened his hold on Zara and instantly pointed his blaster at Ledger, the knurled muzzle resting firmly against his forehead. The hover bot zipped to a new position to monitor this new situation.

"Or what, idiot?" the man spewed.

Ledger glanced toward Zara, terror on her face, for she and everyone in the room knew what was coming...or did they?

Ledger's gaze returned to the man with his finger pressed tight against the trigger, his blaster pushed hard against Ledger's forehead. When there wasn't a hint of fear in Ledger's eyes, the raider seemed to sense something was very wrong. In that moment, Ledger unleashed every second of combat training in a flurry of perfect action and with blinding speed.

Before the raider could finish the final few ounces of pressure on the blaster's trigger, Ledger executed a crosscut using both hands. Ledger's left hand struck and grasped the barrel of the blaster next to the man's right hand while his right palm pounded into the man's wrist. With blinding speed, Ledger rotated the blaster 180 degrees, taking full control of the weapon, all in less than one-tenth of a second. He pushed the raider into the energy discharge of the nearby hovering bot, which instantly obliterated the man. With perfect aim, Ledger shot the hover bot, sending it careening to the floor.

Ledger dove over the top of a nearby empty table, dodging two rounds fired by the man standing on the table. Ledger fell to his knees in a perfect position to make a fatal shot at the lead raider. The man fell to the floor. Ledger pivoted, knowing the other hover bots would commence firing at any second. With one more shot, he took out a second bot.

Only the third raider and one more bot remained. He calculated he wouldn't have time to take them both out, so he targeted the raider, fully expecting the last bot to end him. The third raider got off two shots, but Ledger dodged once more and took his final shot at the man, putting him down. Just as the third bot hovered over him and initiated an energy discharge, a blaster from a man in the corner of the room blew the thing to bits. The entire exchange lasted less than ten seconds.

Smoke and arcing pieces of the remaining bot filled the air as the occupants of the eatery recovered in an eerie hush. Ledger stood up from his crouching position, scanning the crowd.

"Is everyone okay?" he asked.

A few people began to clap and cheer, and soon the entire eatery joined in. Outside, flashing lights indicated that a Rim Syndicate patrol was setting down near the eatery. Ledger threw the blaster to the ground and came back to the table where his friends sat in stunned silence.

"We need to leave now," Ledger urged.

Without a word, the four of them made their way through the chaos. The man that had taken out the last bot intercepted them at the door opposite where the patrol would soon enter.

"Nice work, kid, but you need to know that those raiders belonged to Kilman Soren and his raider ships." The middle-aged man holstered his blaster as the patrol entered the eatery. "They'll be hunting you, so watch your back."

Ledger nodded his thanks, then exited with his friends. After walking a few paces away from the eatery, Zara stopped and turned to face Ledger.

"What was that back there?" she asked as Corbin and Arn gathered around them.

Ledger's response had surprised even himself. It had rushed in on him so fast that instinct and reaction took over. The thought of those thugs hurting Zara had triggered a response in him that he couldn't stop.

Ledger just shook his head.

"Lethal Ledger," Arn said quietly.

Everyone looked his way, including Ledger.

"Where did you hear that?" Ledger demanded, anger flaring within him once again. He took a threatening step toward Arn.

Arn swallowed hard. "You're why I'm here."

Ledger grabbed Arn by both collars, shoving him up against a nearby wall. "You followed me? Are you KDF?" Ledger bellowed, rage threatening to ruin him.

"No," Arn said as Corbin and Zara looked on, unsure whether to intervene or not. "I'm not KDF!" Arn urged as Ledger pushed him harder into the wall.

"Who sent you?" Ledger yelled.

Arn took a second to look toward Zara and Corbin. "An Immortal sent me...I'm a Jeshuan. And I know that your name isn't Ledger Brandt. You're the son of Fasa Kylos."

Ledger froze, unable to process what Arn had just said. He peered into Arn's eyes, looking for some shred of deception but found none. *What did this mean?*

Zara stepped up next to Ledger, placing her hand on his arm.

"Let him go," she ordered.

Ledger took a deep breath then pushed off from Arn, turning away. He ran his hand through his hair, confused. Did he even want to know what this meant? He had tried to flee his former life across the galaxy, and in just a few minutes, every horrid deed from his past came crashing back into his life. Was there no escape?

Ledger took large, commanding steps to escape the three of them, wondering if he now needed to escape from here as well. But there was no place further than the

Rim planets—he had gone as far as humanly possible. He shook his head, wishing he hadn't needed to reveal himself at the eatery. But he knew he could never have lived with himself if the raiders had hurt Zara, knowing he could have stopped it.

Ledger walked on without concern for his direction or destination. A minute later, Zara appeared at his side, falling in step with his indeterminate journey. He trudged on in silent turmoil and she with him.

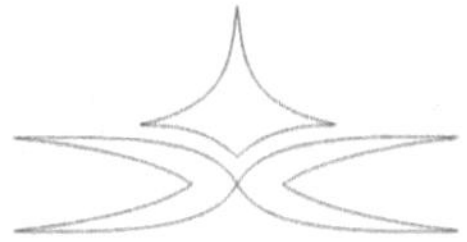

CHAPTER

5

Zara Lux

Zara Lux was a complicated young woman with a complicated history. Many of the hardships she had endured would have utterly ruined most people, but she learned to be resilient even as a young child. She had harnessed a tenacity for life that weaker souls lacked. She trusted few and guarded herself well, for life as a space miner afforded few friends. This type of work tended to draw the dregs of humanity. On rare occasions, an honorable sort would pass through, but the harsh world of space mining typically filtered them out in short order. As such, Zara was extremely careful, cautious, and wary. She had to be—she was a survivor. Though young, she had attained a moderate position of authority and respect as a Scavenger pilot. This gave her the greatest measure of safety she had ever experienced, yet she still felt vulnerable—alone.

Part of her carefully constructed wall of protection included a modified backstory that she knew other miners would respect, but the true reason she kept people an arm's distance away was a fierce resolve to prevent experiencing the pain of losing someone close. At nine years old, young Zara had witnessed the death of her parents at the hands of ruthless brigands. That pain was so raw and so soul-shattering that she vowed never to love anyone again that could cause that much pain in her life. She knew that she would never be able to survive a second portion of such bitter sorrow. Jix had been a substitute for true friendship, but even losing him to the Soren raider refreshed that lurking monster of emotional pain. She suppressed tears and purposely turned her mind away from the memory of her small, winged companion.

From the first day that Ledger Brandt had appeared as a greenhorn on her excursion crew on the *Hammershot*, she could tell he didn't belong—not because he was simply new or untrained, but more that he was a character in the wrong story. She watched him closely that first tour, trying to sort him out, but he was a new mystery, a man of honorable character yet broken in the worst of ways. Having just witnessed his extraordinary skills in combat at the eatery, her intuition regarding him was spot on—something was off. Something deep in her soul shivered, and it unsettled her.

By now it was late evening, a time when one should take extra care out on the streets of Abaria, especially a young woman. But Zara was experiencing something different and new. After having just seen what Ledger was capable of, she felt safe, even at night on the street. She looked over at him as they walked.

"I don't like mysteries, Brandt—not on my crew. Where do you come from?"

Ledger walked on, appearing to ignore the question. Finally, he spoke without looking up from the street.

"I was a KDF agent on the planet Rayl," he offered.

"KDF?" Zara asked.

"Keeper Defense Force," Ledger explained. "It's a security force that was created to eliminate a radical group of people who had claimed that the Son of the Immortal Ell Yon from the dimension of the Ruah had come to save the planet from the evil Lord Dracus."

Zara nearly laughed. His explanation sounded like some of the fantasy stories she used to read as an escape from the frightful things in her life. She chose her next words carefully so as not to reveal her thoughts regarding the absurdity of Immortals and dimensional evil beings.

"What happened? Why are you here and not there?" she asked.

Zara noted that Ledger had turned up a street that was well lit and busy with legitimate businesses. He appeared to struggle with an answer to her question. His eyes reddened, but no words came. His gait slowed.

"Hey, don't sweat it," Zara said. "I have garbage in my past I don't want to talk about either."

Ledger seemed relieved for the pass she had offered. He stopped, taking a moment to look up at the stars above them. His silence made it clear that he wanted to be alone.

"Well, I just figured I should check on you." Zara scanned for the transport hub. "I'd better find my way back to the *Hammershot*."

Ledger brought his gaze from the stars to Zara's eyes.

"I couldn't let them hurt you," Ledger said, his gaze filling with something deep—something powerful. It nearly shattered her tough resolve and rather frightened her. "I couldn't live with myself if I'd allowed it."

Zara avoided his eyes, glancing up the street then back to Ledger. "I'm still hungry. Want to try eating again?" she asked. "I figure I at least owe you a meal."

Ledger's fierce eyes softened, and the darkness inside them abated. A nearly imperceptible smile landed on his lips. It was the first time she had ever seen the man look pleasant.

"I'm hungry too," he said.

Zara flashed a quick smile as they turned to continue their walk.

"I'm so sorry about your draco," Ledger said. "He seemed incredibly loyal to you."

Zara swallowed hard to keep her tears at bay. She clenched her teeth. "He was...special."

Ledger quietly nodded.

"He seemed to like *you*," Zara said, looking over at him.

"Unusual?" he asked.

"Extremely," she replied. Her draco hadn't acted that way toward anyone, especially not a stranger. Losing Jix to that Soren raider thug revived a pain in her bosom that she fought to suppress.

They approached another eatery, scanning inside and out before considering entering, but before they did, a spotlight shone down on them from above. In just a few seconds, a Rim Syndicate patrol craft descended right beside them. Two guardians exited and approached them. Zara looked over at Ledger, and his fierce countenance said it all. He looked past the guardians, and she knew what he was considering.

"It's not worth it," Zara said, putting a hand on his arm. "Let's not make this worse."

Ledger looked down at her hand holding on to him, then to her face, and some of the tension in his eyes diminished.

"Hold!" one of the guardians commanded as his partner stood beside him with a plasma rifle at the ready. "Look into the scanner."

The man raised a small device that swept an amber scanning beam from the top of Ledger's head down to his chest, then repeated the process with Zara before returning it to his belt. He tapped the com band on his left forearm, paragraphs of floating text appearing as he read them aloud with the cold formality of a courtroom indictment.

"Ledger Brandt, you have been identified as the individual responsible for the deaths of three people in the Paragon Eatery. Do you acknowledge this charge?" the man asked.

Ledger stood straight. "I do."

The guardian continued. "The Rim Syndicate Judicial Council has reviewed the video logs taken by the eatery and has issued a judgment. Ledger Brandt's actions are determined to be justified on the basis of self-defense. No punitive actions will be taken. Do you accept this judgment?"

Zara looked over at Ledger, silently thrilled for him.

"I...I do."

The guardian nodded, then tapped his com band to make the judgment readings disappear. He looked up at Ledger, eyeing him closely.

"We have no record of you before five months ago. Your actions in the eatery were extraordinary. The Rim Syndicate would like to offer you a position as a guardian. Your skills would prove beneficial for this sector of the galaxy and serve you well." The man relaxed. "We take care of our own."

Ledger seemed surprised by the offer. "I'm honored by the invitation. I'll give it due consideration."

The man hesitated. "Very well. If you decide to join the Syndicate, identify yourself to any guardian and explain your intention. That is all that is required."

The man then glanced toward Zara and nodded. "Good evening."

As the patrol craft launched into the night sky, Zara watched Ledger's face soften with relief.

"Are you?" she asked. "Giving it due consideration?"

Ledger's gaze fell from the departing patrol craft to Zara's eyes. "Are you kidding? I don't carry weapons anymore, remember? I don't think that would work for them."

Zara chuckled. "I suppose that's true. Food then?"

Ledger took a deep breath. "Yes, please!"

Zara and Ledger spent the next two hours eating and talking about nothing important. She was careful not to let things become too familiar. He was still just a greenhorn excursion miner on her crew that she had to manage, but when he delivered her safely back to the *Hammershot* and left her, she became afraid in a way she had never experienced. Could she really protect herself from the lure of a friendship that her inner being craved but hadn't dared to consider?

If he really is a decent guy, then he won't be here for long, Zara warned herself. *The sooner he leaves, the better.*

Ledger didn't know what to think about Zara. She was easy to talk to, but she was careful to keep him at a distance. He wasn't sure how much of that was because of her being a Scavenger pilot and his being an excursion miner or if she was just one used to keeping everyone at arm's length no matter what. She was the first person he'd had more than a surface-level conversation with since the incident on Rayl. He had to admit that talking to her felt a little like talking to Stone. Perhaps that was why he enjoyed their time together so much. Regardless, neither he nor Zara had indicated that they should arrange another opportunity to get together, so he did his best to dismiss any hopes of even a platonic friendship.

Ledger found it difficult to sleep that night. Every detail of the incident at the eatery played through his mind, including Arn's confession and bizarre words about an Immortal. Finally, after hours of tossing and turning, exhaustion overtook him, and he fell into a deep sleep. When he awoke ten hours later, he felt like his body had completely shut down and would not revive. It took an enormous amount of willpower merely to walk to the kitchen for food. Two hours later he managed to bathe, dress, and exit his bungalow. He tapped on his com band.

"Arn, we need to talk."

Ledger met up with Arn and Corbin at a café to talk over a mid-afternoon meal. Ledger sat on one side of the table, and Arn and Corbin sat across from him.

"I thought Corbin should be here since he was with us last night," Arn said.

Ledger nodded his approval.

"I first want to apologize for roughing you up a bit," Ledger began. "You caught me off guard, and my adrenaline was pumping after the raider incident."

Arn offered one quick nod in response.

"Those are quite the skills you have," Corbin said. He looked at Ledger with new respect in his eyes. "I have a feeling that wherever you learned those skills has a lot to do with what happened last night."

Ledger glanced toward Arn and could see by his countenance that he understood more than he had ever let on.

"I see," Corbin said, sitting back. "Maybe the best way through this is for each of you to tell your story."

Ledger and Arn locked eyes again.

"Makes sense," Arn said.

Ledger nodded. "I should probably start."

He took a steadying breath, feeling the weight of his sordid past bearing down on him. As he started to share his life story, each word he spoke produced a cathartic effect on his soul. When he came to Stone's death, he could hardly speak the words. Articulating the truth conjured up all those powerful emotions once again. His eyes reddened as he told how he had held Stone in his arms through his dying breath. Corbin reached across the table, briefly grabbing his arm. Ledger paused, allowing his confession to saturate the space they were in.

Ledger looked up at Arn to see what his response might be. The man was silent and contemplative.

"I'd heard the stories and seen the results of your efforts as a lead KDF agent," Arn said. "You were...*are* feared among all Jeshuans." Arn looked across the table at Ledger. "When I heard the voice of Ell Yon that night, urging me to come find you, I could hardly believe it. How can you be that man?"

Ledger's head fell low. All along he had thought he was doing the bidding of Sovereign Ell Yon. The guilt rushed back in on him in full measure.

"What you probably don't know is that the man I killed that night, Stone Stryker..." Ledger lifted his head to look into Arn's eyes. "He was my brother, and Fasa Kylos is not my father."

Arn's eyes opened wide. "What do you mean?"

"I still don't know all the details on how it happened," Ledger began. "But somehow Fasa Kylos took me when I was an infant, or perhaps even before I was born, and raised me."

Ledger finished his story by telling about his encounter with Brae and Rhett Stryker. Arn sat back in his seat, stunned.

"As far as I know, no one realizes you're their son," Arn said, lifting a hand toward his mouth. "So technically...you're still KDF?"

Ledger frowned. "I don't know what I am...I'm nothing, which is why I'm here at the Outer Rim. I just wanted to disappear, and here you show up."

"I'm sorry, Ledger," Arn replied. "I'm just as confused by that as you are. I was at home minding my own business when an Immortal warrior appeared and told me to come to Abaria and find you. That's not something you can just ignore."

Corbin held up his hand. "Wait...an Immortal warrior? What's that?"

Arn looked hesitant to fully confide in Corbin, but after a moment, he sighed.

"Our people on Rayl—well, most of our people—believe that there is an immortal race of beings who live in a higher dimensional plane called the Ruah. In that realm there is a fierce war being waged for control of the galaxy by two immortal races known as the Malakians and the Torians. Sovereign Ell Yon is the ruler of the Malakians, and his arch nemesis is Lord C'fir Dracus, ruler of the Torians. Ultimately, the Malakians are trying to save humanity while the Torians are trying to destroy us."

Arn paused, looking first at Corbin who Ledger thought seemed skeptical regarding Arn's explanation. Clearly, Corbin had never heard of the Raylean's deep-rooted beliefs concerning the Immortals. Arn glanced at Ledger. Ledger knew what Arn was thinking. *Here comes his Merchant story.*

"This is where Ledger's and my beliefs part ways," Arn added. "Sovereign Ell Yon, in his great love for humanity, sent his son, Jeshu, into our dimension to save us from Lord Dracus's genetic poison, Deitum Prime, just as was foretold by the ancient oracles. But the Morian Empire, coerced by certain powerful factions in the Raylean government, killed Jeshu...the Merchant who was destined to save us all. Yet, in his death, his blood became the catalyst for an antidote to the destructive effect Deitum Prime has on humanity."

"But you can't deny that the Keepers and Builders have been the defenders of the ways of Sovereign Ell Yon for centuries!" Ledger interjected. "This man you herald as the Merchant came to destroy that legacy."

Ledger looked sternly at Arn, feeling the deep emotions of his former days rise up within him again. "How can we both be well-versed in the writings of the oracles and have such vastly different views of them?" Ledger asked, shaking his head.

Corbin turned to Arn, waiting for an answer.

Arn took his time responding to Ledger's question.

"You must listen to the wisdom of the oracles, Ledger, not the orders that have betrayed you and everyone else on Rayl," Arn urged. "When the Keepers read the oracles, they do so with a bias, wanting the prophecies to say what they believe to be true. Perhaps if you read them with the preposterous possibility that Jeshu *is* the fulfillment of every one of those prophecies by the oracles, you would see them for the truth they have been telling all along."

Anger began to burn within Ledger, but he suppressed it in light of all the falsities that he was now being forced to deal with.

Arn's gaze dropped to the table. "In the middle of the night, while I was wrestling with the call of Sovereign Ell Yon, one of the Malakian warriors appeared to me and told me to come here and guide my enemy."

Arn lifted his gaze to look at Ledger once more. Ledger felt a lump forming in his throat.

"I knew exactly who he meant," Arn continued. "When you signed up for a mining tour, I knew I had to follow you. My Protector's gone silent, so now I have no idea what I'm supposed to do."

Ledger leaned forward. "You have a Protector?" he asked, his voice unsteady.

Arn eyed Ledger, hesitating. "Every true Jeshuan does."

"How is this possible? I've never…" Ledger began. He was entering a place that would force him to confront all his doubts…all his past beliefs.

Arn extended his right arm, pulling back his sleeve to reveal something beautiful and terrifying.

"It's not just a com band?" Ledger asked.

Arn shook his head. "We disguise them when necessary, but no, it's our pathway to Sovereign Ell Yon."

Ledger reached for it, trembling as he remembered his encounter from touching Stone's Protector. Just a fraction of an inch away, Ledger pulled back his hand, afraid of what it might mean. Arn seemed to understand. He too pulled back, covering the Protector once more.

Corbin exchanged glances between Ledger and Arn, folding his hands in front of him. "You each tell quite a story, and it sounds to me like you both have a lot more story to live…perhaps not as enemies but as friends."

Ledger looked over at Corbin, rather surprised by his ability to mediate their meeting. Ledger locked eyes with Arn. Both offered one subtle nod, and a small corner of Ledger's heart mended.

Nine days later, Ledger, Arn, and Corbin began their next mining tour on board the *Hammershot*. Other than the addition of a couple of new recruits, the crews stayed the same, for which Ledger was grateful. He didn't relish the thought of having to get used to additional veteran miners belittling him for his mistakes. He felt as though he had heard most of the insults that Bane, Wisco, and Allendorce would hurl at him. Besides this, Zara was a good Scavenger pilot, and he had come to trust her with his life. While on the ship, he attempted to discern any subtle signs from her regarding their possible budding friendship, but there wasn't a single indication that she was even remotely interested. That single meal during their dock days was the extent of it, so he put any such notion to rest. He did notice that Zara seemed to have conversations with Captain Rosco more so than any of the other pilots. He attributed it to the fact that she was one of the captain's best pilots and so was an asset. She would therefore naturally receive more of his attention.

Ledger's second tour proved to be far more successful than his first. A little experience and skillfully implemented technique was remarkably beneficial, although he, Corbin, and Arn hadn't yet lost the derogatory label of "greenhorn." Even so, the days fell into a familiar pattern. Ledger's confidence grew as he learned to anticipate the subtle quirks of the equipment and the unpredictable dangers of mining asteroids and small moons. He took comfort in the routines—scanning reports over breakfast, briefings before each excursions, and a few friendly exchanges with Corbin and Arn. The camaraderie among the crew, rough as it was at times, created an environment of cautious mutual respect.

Still, Ledger couldn't ignore the undercurrents of loneliness that sometimes surfaced, especially in the rest hours between shifts. Although the inner turmoil he was running from had abated some, there were still vivid dreams of Stone and his final moments that often haunted Ledger in the middle of the night. For some strange reason, revisiting his conversation with Zara at the eatery was the only way to settle his distraught mind and entice him back to sleep. Once he caught Zara glancing his way in the mess hall, but the look was so fleeting that he dismissed it as inconsequential. Ledger did notice, however, that Zara didn't seem to have a close friend or confidant, at least not on the *Hammershot*. He wondered if she struggled against the same invisible walls he did or if she had simply learned to live behind them more gracefully than he ever could.

By the end of the tour, Ledger couldn't wait for solid ground beneath his feet and real food, or at least better food. Before leaving the ship, however, he checked on his android.

"Master Ledger, it is good to see you survived your second tour," the android said as it continued to focus on managing the final purging of the minerals in the silos. He was directing five other bots in the process.

"Are you okay?" Ledger asked.

The android stopped for a moment to look toward Ledger. "Is that concern I sense in my liege? It seems that perhaps excursion mining may be good for you after all."

"I just want to make sure you're not damaged or being mistreated," Ledger said.

The android tapped the controls on a display in front of him with blinding speed without looking.

"Hey! Don't distract my bot while he's working!" one of the silo techs yelled as he approached.

Ledger turned to face the man. "He's *my* bot, and I'm just checking on him."

The man sneered. "He's not your bot while he's on the *Hammershot* and under contract, so get lost."

Ledger instantly became furious.

"It's okay, Master Ledger. All is well. Our time here is needed. You will find what you're looking for," the android said, turning back to his work.

"Ledger, let's go," Arn yelled from the upper deck.

Ledger glared at the silo tech. "I know he's the best android you have. You'd better never let him get damaged!"

He looked at his android, realizing that it had become much more than just a utility bot to him. "Rivet...you be careful."

Rivet stopped and looked back at Ledger. "And you, my liege."

Ledger turned and left, a sinking feeling in his stomach. He was eager for the next tour to be over so he could recover his android in accordance with the three-tour contract he'd signed. As he walked away, Rivet's cryptic words lingered in his mind. *What am I looking for?* he asked himself.

Ledger, Arn, and Corbin agreed to pitch in and rent a luxurious bungalow with three sleeping rooms, a spacious commons area, a large kitchen with all the amenities, and a beachfront view of the Antillian Sea.

"I would have thought you'd be joining your family," Arn pressed Corbin as he made the final arrangements over his com band.

"Getting back to my homeworld would cost too much," Corbin explained. "Transports there are only made once a week, so it's not worth it for just a couple of days home."

As the three of them disembarked the *Hammershot*, Zara was returning from the spaceport dock authorities with a glass tablet in hand.

"Enjoy your dock days, boys," she said without smiling.

"What are you doing with your downtime?" Arn asked.

Zara broke from her mission to return documentation to Captain Rosco to talk with them.

"Same thing I always do—work."

"It's good to rest too," Corbin said. "You should try it."

Zara chuckled. "What are you three up to this time? Going to be taking on any more raiders?" she asked with a side glance toward Ledger.

"No, absolutely not. These two talked me into splurging for a bungalow on the shores of the Antillian Sea."

Zara's eyes lifted. "No kidding. Well, you guys have fun and don't think about skipping out on the next tour. I just got you to where you're useful now."

"Why don't you come with us?" Arn asked. "Sunshine, warm water, and a boulevard of eateries that are raider-free. There's a single bungalow right next to ours I can set you up in."

Ledger eyed Arn, knowing that such an invite would violate the unwritten rule of no fraternization between pilots and crew. When he glanced back at Zara, she appeared hesitant.

"Sounds fun, but I have a lot to prepare for the next tour," she replied with a sheepish smile. "The captain tells me we have a new profile he wants to try out near the Orixian Belt."

Ledger instantly regretted the look he had given Arn. "You know, Zara...Corbin's right. Resting will make you an even better pilot."

Zara studied Ledger for more than a few seconds as she considered his words. He caught her gaze, offering a half smile. "You should come."

There was a twinkle in her pale-blue eyes. "Sandy beaches and sunshine, huh?"

Ledger nodded.

"I need to talk to Captain Rosco and make sure he's okay with it. Can you give me 20?"

"No problem," Arn returned. "We'll be waiting right here."

As Zara turned and walked away, Ledger thought it odd that Captain Rosco would have so much say in her life.

"She's all right," Corbin said.

Arn and Ledger looked at him.

"I mean, there aren't many people here in the mining world that are all right, but she is."

Arn put a hand on Corbin's shoulder. "I sit beside her in the Scavenger every day, and I must say that I agree with you, my friend."

Ledger said nothing.

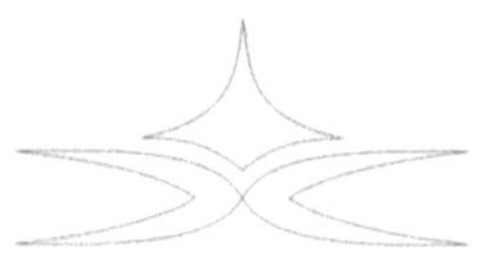

CHAPTER

7

Meteor Melee

By the time the sun was setting on the watery aqua horizon, Arn, Corbin, Zara, and Ledger had settled into their bungalows and were taking a leisurely stroll along the peaceful shores of the Antillian Sea. Ledger felt the remnant warmth of the fine sand massaging his feet as the soft colloid of water and silica oozed up between his toes with each step he took. Clear salty water licked at his feet every few seconds as he and his three friends walked between the seam of land and sea. He filled his lungs with delicious, clean sea air, knowing that in a couple of weeks, he would be confined in his excursion suit, wishing he was back here. He glanced over at his friends, seeing pleasant looks on each of their faces, including Zara's.

"Beats the musty decks of the *Hammershot*, doesn't it?" Ledger said, looking over at Zara.

She looked at him out of the corner of her eye, trying to remain stoic, but then let loose a delightful smile. "Maybe just a little."

They filled the next few days with evening campfires, seaside dining, refreshing swims, and long conversations that often went late into the night. It seemed to Ledger that every one of them, himself included, remained guarded, never offering too much information about their past. No one pried, which put Ledger at ease right away.

One evening, Arn and Corbin decided to make a run for a midnight snack, leaving Ledger and Zara behind in their respective bungalows. Ledger stepped out onto his deck to absorb the beauty of the dusky sea. A few minutes later, he noticed that Zara had done the same in the bungalow next to his, just 30 feet away.

"So why do we go up into space where it's minus 450 degrees and the slightest mistake can kill you?" he asked.

Zara chuckled, which delighted Ledger in the strangest of ways.

"We are odd creatures, aren't we?" she returned. "Always pushing the limits of what we can do and where we can go."

Ledger smiled back. "Care to take a walk along the shore?" he asked, but immediately questioned whether or not such a suggestion might imply something he hadn't intended. He cringed inwardly as Zara hesitated with her response.

"I don't think so," she finally replied.

Now Ledger felt painfully awkward for suggesting it. "Of course...it's late," he offered, trying to save a bit of his dignity.

Zara glanced his way, then went back into her bungalow, piling upon him even more humiliation.

Great! he thought. *She's offended and things will be awkward forever now.*

Ledger ran his hand from his forehead down his face. He shook his head in embarrassment as he looked out to the darkening horizon. Just as he was about to return to his bungalow, Zara exited her bungalow and stepped up onto his deck with a delicious fruit drink, locally known as a malata, in each hand. She offered one to Ledger.

"It's not late. I would just rather sit and watch the sunset," she said, sitting down in one of the reclining chairs on the bungalow deck.

Ledger smiled, relieved she hadn't read too deeply into his original suggestion.

"Thanks for the malata," he replied as he took the chair next to Zara. "I was hoping you didn't think—" Ledger stopped, realizing he was about to embarrass himself for real.

"Didn't think what?" Zara asked, eyeing Ledger.

Ledger shook his head. "Never mind. So, tell me about the Orixian Belt. What's the chaos factor there, and where's it located?"

Zara seemed fine with his diversion as she began to regale Ledger about Captain Rosco's desire to tap into a set of asteroids supposedly rich with rare minerals.

As she talked, Ledger watched her eyes light up as she explained the details of their next tour. He found himself mesmerized but realized it wasn't because of the prospects of the Orixian Belt. Rather, he found he couldn't stop staring at her illuminated face and listening to her melodic voice. Until now, he had never dared watch her so intently, and as he did, something deep inside him was being drawn to her. It surprised him, and he wasn't sure what to do with it. He found himself asking her questions just so he could watch the subtle movements in her lips and eyes. On the *Hammershot,* she was stoic, but here she was relaxed, and her face revealed a plethora of charming expressions.

Suddenly, Zara seemed to notice Ledger's gaze. "What?"

Ledger almost gave in to the temptation to be flustered, but he successfully rejected the emotion with a boldness he didn't expect. Instead, he smiled. "You're different here."

Zara's eyes opened a little wider. "How so?"

"You're relaxed...more expressive."

"And?" she urged.

"And it suits you well," Ledger finished.

"Oh," she said as Arn and Corbin appeared at the far side of the deck.

The evening ended around a campfire with the four of them eating copious amounts of fresh sea driscas. Once everyone decided to retire, Ledger lingered just a bit and was rewarded when Zara did the same.

"Thanks for the drink and conversation earlier," he said.

Zara turned and sauntered to her bungalow but stole a glance at Ledger over her shoulder. "Sure thing. I'm back at the *Hammershot* tomorrow, but you were right. I needed this."

"Glad you decided to join us," Ledger said.

"Me too, but just remember, on the *Hammershot* it's business as usual."

"Aye aye, pilot," Ledger said with a casual salute.

Zara smirked. "Goodnight, Brandt."

"Goodnight, Lux."

Zara entered her bungalow feeling refreshed yet more than a little conflicted. First, there was this vacation with her ops controller and two of her excursion miners. That was a breach of the unwritten rule—*don't fraternize with the crew you run*. Despite her misgivings about this time off, she had to admit that it had restored something in her soul that she didn't even know had been missing. Second, there was Ledger Brandt. She knew he was different the first time she saw him, and she couldn't deny that seeing his combat skills against the Soren raiders had profoundly affected her. It heightened her curiosity regarding the man all the more. She had accepted the invitation to come on this seaside retreat in part because she hoped to learn more about him and how he'd come to acquire such skills. But now that her time with him was over, the mystery remained, and it had the uncanny effect of drawing her to him in ways she hadn't expected. She was hoping that once she was back on the *Hammershot*, such inclinations would disappear, and all would return to normal.

In her determination to survive in the harsh galaxy in which she was born, Zara had carefully crafted an impenetrable wall of protection for herself, each stone in its foundation designed to minimize the hurt threatening to rush in on her—a stone of independence so as not to have to rely on anyone but herself—a stone of superior skill and ability to earn the respect of her crewmates—a stone of isolation so as not to allow the faulty hope of friendship ruin her with betrayal or loss. At twenty-three, Zara was desperate never to be hurt by anyone ever again. But in that moment of absolute vulnerability when the Soren raiders had threatened to kill her, one man had come to her rescue. Brandt had thrown her a lifeline of noble kindness that had penetrated her carefully constructed wall of self-protection. *What do I do with this?* she asked herself.

As she lay on her bed that night, her mind replayed parts of her conversation with Ledger. She found herself smiling when she thought of catching him looking at her. *How ridiculous,* she thought, wiping the smile from her face. *Go to sleep, Zara. You have a lot to prepare tomorrow.* She concentrated on emptying her mind and allowing slumber to take her, but even then she couldn't keep the corners of her lips from turning upward.

Halfway through Ledger's third tour, Captain Rosco navigated the *Hammershot* to the Orixian Belt, a large ring of asteroids orbiting a nearly dead uninhabited planet called Orixia. Orixia was the second planet in a binary star system of an eight-planet system. The chaos factor for this large ring of asteroids was 4.6 due to the binary star system they orbited, as well as four large gas-giants and three additional moderate-sized planets. The risk was significantly greater than the Keller Belt, but the concentration of precious minerals was three to four times higher.

Captain Rosco stepped forward in the Scavenger docking bay to address the pilots, ops controllers, and all excursion miners.

"I've been waiting for two tours to mine the Orixian Belt, and since we don't have any greenhorns this tour, now's the time."

Ledger, Arn, and Corbin exchanged looks. Evidently they had finally graduated from the greenhorn status. Arn signaled a subtle "thumbs up" Ledger's direction.

"The chaos factor is higher here, so I need all of you to be careful and focused. We'll have 25 days of good mining before we need to abandon the belt due to approaching meteor shower activity. Any questions?"

"Yeah, Cap, what's our commission on this belt?" one of the miners from the *Hawk* Scavenger crew asked.

Captain Rosco didn't seem annoyed by the question at all.

"You get me good rocks, and I'll give everyone a 15 percent bump in pay for the days we mine here."

The bay erupted into a mighty cheer. Captain Rosco didn't smile, but he nodded his approval of his crew's enthusiasm.

"Fly hard and live long," the captain finished.

"Fly hard and live long!" the entire crew shouted.

Zara gathered her crew around the *Osprey*.

"Don't let your zeal for a few extra credits get in the way of good, safe mining. No one gets dead today," she finished as usual. "Lock and load."

Just before Ledger donned his excursion suit helmet, he glanced toward Zara. She was climbing into the cockpit but seemed to sense his gaze. She hesitated, looking his way. As their eyes met, Ledger felt his pulse quicken ever so slightly. She offered a rare smile that caused his heart to stumble.

Not good, Ledger...not good, he said within himself. Ledger was fully aware of the danger of being distracted on excursion missions, both for himself and for Zara, but his heart was fighting logic.

He saw Zara mouth the words, "Be careful."

Ledger returned the smile. "You too," he mouthed back.

The exchange was short, but in Ledger's mind it transcended friendship, which he found thrilling and frightening at the same time. *Pilots and excursion miners don't fraternize*, he told himself, but the four days at the Antillian Sea shore had already destroyed that notion.

Ledger finished securing his helmet in place, then jumped on to his position on the *Osprey*. Ten minutes later Ledger, Corbin, Bane, Wisco, and Allendorce were tagging a ride on the hull of the *Osprey* on their way to the alluring Orixian Belt. As they approached, multi-layered rings reflected the brilliant rays from two suns against the beautiful backdrop of an alien blue and gray planet. Ledger realized he had never seen anything so exotic or majestic in his entire life. Once Arn had chosen a large asteroid on the external orbit, Ledger focused his attention on executing his duties in the safest, most efficient manner possible.

The first five days of mining the belt proved to be extremely profitable. All six Scavenger crafts and their crews were funneling rich deposits of platinum and gold via their gravitonic tubule accumulators back to the *Hammershot* in a steady stream of mineral harvest. One excursion mission even led to the discovery of a significant deposit of the rare element of rhodium. The morale among the crew of the *Hammershot* was at an all-time high. But on day six, things unexpectedly changed.

Zara and Arn were directing their excursion miners to focus on two large, slowly-rotating asteroids that allowed them to more effectively mine a deposit of palladium. Allendorce was assisting Ledger and Corbin on the face of one of the asteroids while Bane and Wisco tackled a more delicate vein of the mineral on a nearby asteroid. Zara was skillfully maneuvering the *Osprey* to avoid being pulverized by a random asteroid while keeping the accumulator tubules from each miner connected. Ledger found himself fighting the micro gravity from the large asteroid as he focused his laser boring beam on a sizable crevice on the surface of the asteroid. Corbin was just above him performing a similar operation. Allendorce was ten feet to Ledger's right.

"Brandt and Messer, sensors indicate you are nearing the palladium vein, so it's time to switch your quad tool."

Ledger shut down his laser boring beam and turned to look at Allendorce. "What are we switching to?" Ledger asked.

"Use the—"

Mick Allendorce didn't finish his sentence. A helmet-sized meteor flying at the speed of a cobalt missile struck and severed Allendorce's body in half. Ledger gasped as the impact of the meteor into the asteroid set loose a chain reaction of utter chaos. The asteroid accelerated its spin, Allendorce and his equipment were tumbling in multiple directions, and Ledger was desperately trying to avoid being crushed by jagged edges whizzing past him.

"*Osprey, Osprey*, Allendorce is down!" Ledger radioed.

Seconds later, hundreds of meteors began pounding the asteroid belt, raining down around every miner and Scavenger craft of the *Hammershot*. Panic swelled, creating total pandemonium. Ledger's radio blared out multiple urgent messages as he tried to regain control of his own excursion suit.

"*Osprey* crew, return to ship immediately!" Zara radioed, her voice taut with angst.

Ledger's headset continued to fill with emergency calls from the *Hammershot* and two Scavengers that had been hit and damaged.

Ledger finally recovered and took a second to locate the *Osprey*. As he scanned, he saw all five of the other Scavengers and their excursion miners scrambling to recover to the *Hammershot*. One glance at the *Hammershot* made it obvious that it too was in the throes of a fierce assault. Meteors were glancing off the ship's Stabil Retention Field that Captain Rosco had energized, but if any larger meteors hit, total destruction would surely come.

Ledger looked up to find Corbin struggling to free himself from a large section of asteroid rock that had wedged his arm in a crevice.

"What's going on, Messer?" Ledger asked as he navigated towards him, but it was difficult since the impact of a large meteor had accelerated their rotation.

"That meteor collision collapsed the crevice I was working in, and my arm is pinned," Corbin radioed.

After a precarious few seconds, Ledger made it to Corbin. Smaller but just as deadly meteors were smashing all around them each time the asteroid rotated toward the oncoming shower.

"Brandt and Messer, get back to the *Osprey* now!" Zara commanded. "It's just a matter of time before we take a hit."

Ledger knew he would have to work fast, but the risk of using either the laser boring beam or the plasma torch was too great. It would be too easy to accidentally sever Corbin's arm. He would need the precise control of his Stasis cutting blade to do the job, but it would take more time than the *Osprey* could afford.

"Messer's pinned. You're going to have to come back for us," Ledger radioed. He imagined Bane and Wisco trying to shield themselves on the protected side of the *Osprey*, wondering how many seconds they would survive before a meteor hit them.

Several seconds elapsed before Zara's radio response came. Ledger knew she was weighing the odds.

"*Osprey* and *Raven*, this is the *Hammershot*. Return to ship immediately. We need to abandon this sector."

Ledger began cutting through the rock, hoping Corbin's excursion suit hadn't been compromised. A rip in his suit would only bring a different form of death to his trapped friend.

"Bane and Wisco, hang tight, I'm going in for them," Zara radioed.

Ledger didn't dare take the time to contradict her decision. Their chance of survival was diminishing with each passing second...and so was Zara's.

Zara had faced life and death situations before, but the tension of enduring a deadly meteor shower with her remaining crew of five was off the charts. Her actions would determine who lived and who died. Despite her guttural aversion to such a predicament, this was simply the consequence of command, and that command fell to her alone. Risk the lives of three of her crew and herself to save two? She knew what logic dictated, but she couldn't bring herself to abandon Ledger and Corbin.

"I thought we had days until this meteor shower," Zara said out loud to Arn.

"This is something different...uncharted," Arn replied.

"Rotate your sensors in the direction of the oncoming meteors and give me any information you can on them," Zara ordered.

"Will do, but the smaller ones are impossible to track, and they're just as deadly to the miners."

Zara kept the side of the ship Bane and Wisco were on away from the approaching meteors. Every few seconds she could hear the impact of smaller meteors on the hull of her ship.

"The relative velocity of the meteors is 320 miles per hour," Arn reported. "Lux, from what I can tell, this is just the leading edge of the meteor shower. We have four minutes before the real storm hits."

Zara could hear the terror in Arn's voice...and she felt every bit of it herself. She didn't dare take her eyes off the instrumentation that was displayed on the front view port as she deftly maneuvered the *Osprey* closer to the asteroid Ledger and Corbin were on.

"Brandt, what's your status? We're 2,600 feet away and closing," Zara radioed.

"Working as fast as I can. This is bad, and his suit looks damaged," Ledger returned, his voice steady but tense.

It took Zara two agonizing minutes to close the distance until she hovered just 200 feet outside of the swirling rock, constantly repositioning to avoid other asteroids. A quick glance at her instrument panel showed that the large meteors had upped the chaos factor for this section of the belt by nearly three points.

"Incoming...and it's large!" Arn exclaimed.

"It's now or never, Brandt," Zara urged. The asteroid rotated Ledger and Corbin into view. Zara wished that the mythical Immortals that Arn and Ledger believed in were real so she could call on their intervention to save her friends. She had done everything in her power, but now she could only wait and watch, hoping with all her being against their impending doom.

"Ledger, you have less than one minute," Zara transmitted.

"He's free!" Ledger exclaimed.

Zara could now see them clearly. She longed to swoop in and close the distance, but a rocky protrusion on the asteroid was rotating toward the *Osprey* and would most certainly end them.

"Impact in ten seconds!" Arn warned.

"Get out of there now!" Zara screamed as the meteor hurtled toward them.

"Impact in ten seconds!" came Arn's panicked radio warning.

Nine. Eight. Seven. The seconds ticked as Ledger tried desperately to orient Corbin in the direction of the *Osprey*.

Six. Five. Four.

Out of the corner of his eye, Ledger could see the massive meteor hurtling toward them without mercy.

Three.

"Engage drives!" Ledger yelled.

Corbin glanced at Ledger—terror remarkably absent from the countenance of his friend. Corbin reached for Ledger's arm.

Two. One.

Ledger closed his eyes, wondering how much pain he would feel in death. The crushing weight of a massive 600-ton collision hit him, and his world went black.

"NO!" Zara screamed. A moment of shock paralyzed her. She was vaguely aware of Arn taking control of the *Osprey* to back away from the impact zone.

"*Osprey*, you have three minutes to return to ship, or we are leaving without you." Captain Rosco radioed. "Get back here now!"

"Zara," Arn yelled. "There are no life signs. You need to get us out of here!"

Zara forced herself to resume control of the *Osprey*. She would have to grieve later.

"Hang tight...max acceleration," she radioed to Bane and Wisco.

Captain Rosco had oriented his ship so that it protected the *Osprey's* approach and its docking, but if more large meteors were coming, even the *Hammershot* wouldn't survive.

Zara docked in record time. As she spooled down her engines, she felt the *Hammershot's* engines engage and accelerate. She sat frozen in her pilot's seat, replaying those few seconds over and over in her mind. Deep sorrow began to swallow her just like it had 12 years ago.

"You did everything you could," Arn said, touching her arm.

She rotated her head to look at him. "They're gone," she whispered. "Mick...Ledger...Corbin...they're gone." Tears quietly rolled down her cheeks as her heart fractured amidst the horrific pain she had so carefully tried to avoid.

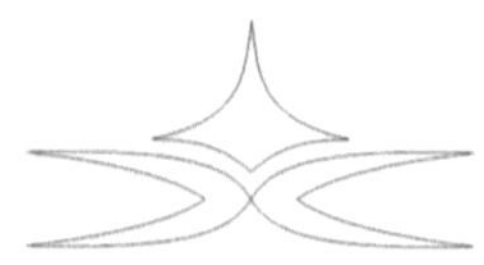

CHAPTER

8

Galactic Navi

Admiral Kalem stood in the center of the command deck on his newly commissioned fleet star cruiser, *Vigilance*. After the *Advent* had been destroyed over 20 years ago at the battle of Brahm's Cradle, the Malakian tech centers were commissioned to collaborate on designing and building a new command star cruiser class starship that would lead the Commander's fleet forces for centuries to come.

As Kalem gazed out the huge front display port onto the blue and white orb of the planet Rayl, he knew that his new star cruiser would soon be put to the test. With a few quick hand gestures, he overlaid his galactic fleet positions as well as the positions of known Torian ships onto the display. He could feel the Torian fleet's squeeze as C'fir Dracus continued to expand his power throughout the Morian Empire. Kalem had maintained their dominance over Rayl, but just barely. They were the last bastion of Malakian strength throughout the galaxy.

How could Dracus appear so victorious over Sovereign Ell Yon's forces? Kalem wondered. He couldn't help but quietly question his own abilities as the First Admiral of Ell Yon's Galactic Fleet Force.

"Admiral Kalem, Captain Andover is requesting your presence in the command ready room for a secure briefing," Kalem's executive officer announced.

Kalem broke from his fixation on the current status of the two warring fleets.

"Very well, prepare the brief and ask Admiral Galec to join."

Kalem restored the front display to its default and exited the command deck. He entered the ready room and sat in his usual chair at the advanced tech conference table. He activated the secure link with Captain Andover, the commander of the Malakian Recon Team, MRT7, a program that supported Ell Yon's entire galactic force. A perfect holographic representation of Captain Andover appeared on the opposite side of the table. At another seat, a hologram of Admiral Galec appeared. They did not exchange pleasantries.

"Captain Andover, I understand you have some critical information for us," Kalem began.

"Yes, Admiral."

Andover was a serious, calculating, and extremely intelligent warrior. He had commanded the MRT7 program for the last two hundred years, so his intimate knowledge of all things secret was profound. Such sensitive knowledge always leaves little space for anything remotely trivial.

"At great peril to one of my key MRT7 agents, we were able to briefly place a quantum video transmitter within the briefing chamber of C'fir Dracus. Before it was detected, we captured a conversation that I believe you will find extremely important."

Admiral Kalem nodded, and Andover tapped on a couple of controls before him. A floating display of the video event appeared in the middle of the conference table. Kalem instantly recognized one of Dracus's top commanders, Admiral Kyrsa. She had been given command of the Morian Empire's homeworld, Moria, and a large number of systems under its control.

In the video transmission, Dracus was focused on the displays laid out before him in the briefing room, keeping his back turned to Admiral Kyrsa as she began to speak.

"Lord Dracus, your command to exterminate all Rayleans regardless of whether they are Jeshuans or not...what is your timeline?" Admiral Kyrsa asked.

Dracus turned, looking at his admiral with disdain, and she nodded her understanding.

"I only ask, my lord, because in order to initiate your directive, I'm going to need a human more ruthless than First Leader Chancellor Krish. One whom I have complete control over," Admiral Kyrsa explained.

"Krish has been an effective pawn for us, but I suppose this situation was always an inevitability. Do you have someone in mind?" Dracus asked.

"I've been preparing a man with a heart as dark as the night," Kyrsa answered. "I'll just need to have Krish executed, which should be easily arranged. I can leverage my Morian human pawns to make the path for young Eron to rule supremely as the new First Leader of the Morian Empire."

Dracus's face contorted with dark delight. "Make it so. As soon as he's in place, I want you to crush the planet of Rayl until not a single Raylean remains alive."

"I'll begin immediately, my lord," Kyrsa said with a sharp salute.

The video disappeared, leaving Kalem and the holographic representations of Galec and Captain Andover sitting across the table from each other. Kalem's jaw tightened, and his fist clenched.

"The time is now," Kalem said. "The prophecies of the ancient oracles are being fulfilled. Rayl will be no more, and there is nothing we can do to stop it."

"What will this mean, Admiral?" Andover asked.

"It means that all our forces must be ready. We will be stretched to our limits. Our battles will become decentralized, smaller, and much more fierce. We must become nimble, tactical, wary...prepared to carry the fight to the corners of the galaxy."

Galec looked at Kalem. "I'll begin preparations, Admiral."

Kalem nodded, and Galec disappeared. He turned to Andover. "Let your agent know that his mission to recover this video is duly noted and will be a key factor in our preparedness."

Captain Andover saluted and disappeared.

Kalem stroked his chin as he considered how difficult these next few decades would become. "The age of the Outworlders," he said quietly to himself. "Both glorious and horrific."

First Leader of the Morian Empire—it was a great title for a great man. The dark mind of young Eron had been fashioned well by his mother in preparation for this day. For over two decades, Eron's mother, Errudica, had been quietly forging a network of powerful advocates among the Morian Empire's most commanding figures. Political, miltech, and financial sector leaders had all been positioned for an opportunity for power ascension. And when his mother had called upon all these forces, Eron was ready.

The assassination of First Leader Krish spawned a new era of dark rule in the Empire. Perhaps some of the men and women in his mother's web thought that young Eron could be controlled, but they soon learned that was not the case. Little did they know that Eron had tapped into a force far more intelligent and powerful than any of them had ever dared imagine. At times, his inspirational brilliance was transcendent, catapulting him to schemes and devices no mortal human had ever conceived in history. And in that brilliance, he harbored a ruthless commitment to absolute power, even if it meant executing anyone that showed the slightest hesitation to submit. For a boy of 16, his heartless rule was unexpected and extraordinarily effective. Within a week, the entire Morian Empire had been completely transformed. Eron's dark empire turned darker as all objection to his rule was deftly silenced, and its planetary subjects felt the edge of First Leader Eron's grisly blade. All resistance was met swiftly and with overwhelming force.

The gentle sound of meadow birds landed softly on Ledger's ears, beckoning him to awaken.

"Ledger," came the sound of a strong voice.

Ledger blinked, but the bright sunshine made it difficult to fully open his eyes.

"Ledger," the voice called again, familiar yet different.

Full consciousness came slowly. He forced his eyes open to see Corbin kneeling in front of him. Ledger found himself in a sitting position, propped up against a large boulder. A picturesque scene of transcendent natural beauty surrounded them. Rolling hills covered in grass and vibrant wildflowers were watered by a crystal clear stream. Sprawling trees dotted the countryside. Ledger felt the glorious warmth of the sun—no, two suns, high in the sky.

"Corbin...are we dead?"

Corbin smiled. "No, my friend. You are far from dead."

His friend looked different. Corbin appeared stronger...commanding. He reached his hand out to Ledger. Ledger took it, and Corbin lifted him with a strength that had not been present before. Ledger took in the serenity of this strange world. He became acutely aware of how stiff and sore his body was. He was still wearing his excursion suit, but his helmet had been removed. Around his wrist he wore a device he didn't recognize.

"How are you feeling?" Corbin asked.

"I hurt all over, but aren't we supposed to be dead?" Ledger asked. "The meteor."

Corbin held tight to Ledger's arm to steady him. He looked straight into Ledger's eyes with the strength of a warrior.

"What's going on? Where are we, and why do you look so different?" Ledger asked.

"We're on Orixia," Corbin replied.

"Impossible. Orixia's a dead planet," Ledger said, rubbing his forehead. The darkness of sleep still lingered.

"Not in the Ruah. We've terraformed Orixia into this," Corbin said, motioning to the beautiful landscape.

Ledger reached for his head. "I don't understand. How did we survive that meteor?" he asked, straightening himself as he recovered from whatever it was that had happened.

"At the last second, my Protector shielded us from the collision as you were fully translated into the Ruah, but your human body still felt some of the impact," Corbin explained. "My ship was waiting for us."

"Lieutenant Carvin, I'll take it from here," a majestic voice said from behind Ledger.

Ledger turned to see the same man whose words of fierce truth had pierced his mind at that tragic moment in his life when Stone Stryker had died. Behind him rested a sleek, majestic ship, the style of which Ledger had never seen before. On each side of the ramp leading up to the ship stood twelve mighty warriors in formation.

"Yes, Commander," the man Ledger had known as Corbin replied.

"Bulk up, warrior. I'll need you on Rayl in a few weeks," the Commander said.

"Gladly, Commander," he said with a sharp salute. He glanced at Ledger, offering a nod, then proceeded to walk toward the waiting ship.

Ledger was more confused than ever. "Lieutenant Carvin?" he wondered out loud as he watched his friend walk away. Ledger turned his gaze back to the majestic form of the man standing before him. A hundred questions filled his thoughts. In his innermost being, he knew the truth, but something held him back.

"Who are you?" Ledger turned to ask the Commander.

"You know who I am, Ledger. I've been watching you since birth. I've chosen you, yet even now you're fighting against my calling."

Chills flitted up and down Ledger's body. The man's eyes ignited with an eternal fire.

"It's time to choose, Ledger. I am the way, the truth, and the life. The galaxy needs a voice to deliver my hope to humanity."

Ledger began to tremble as he finally allowed himself to consider the possibility that he had been on the wrong side all along. Even though he had been lied to his whole life by Kylos, it was by Ledger's own hand that so many Jeshuans had been imprisoned and even killed. He had ignored his doubts and suppressed the call in his heart to seek the truth. It took a monumental effort to shed all the lies he'd been fed by his former father. But standing there, gazing upon the noble face of the man his friend had called *Commander*, Ledger became certain that this was someone who understood the timeless truth his former father never had. The realization settled over him at last. His strength drained away, and he surrendered himself to a new reality.

"Jeshu?" he whispered.

The man standing before him said nothing. His intense gaze warmed. Ledger fell to his knees before the man from the vision he'd seen when he touched Stone's Protector...the Merchant foretold...Jeshu, Son of Ell Yon.

"My Lord, what have you to do with me?" Ledger pleaded.

"I have much to do with you, Ledger. You will be my Navi to the galaxy. My sacrifice is offered not only to the Rayleans, but to every clan, every nation, every world. The time has come to reach the four corners of the galaxy with the truth of Sovereign Ell Yon and the hope offered to humanity through me."

Ledger bowed his head low before Jeshu, weeping for the lies he had believed, for the brother he had killed, for the family he had never known, but above all, for the blood on his hands of the followers of the very man that now stood before him.

"But I'm not worthy, my Lord." Ledger looked up through blurred eyes.

Forgiveness was waiting in the heart of Jeshu, but Ledger's self-condemnation threatened his ability to ask for it. Full restorative forgiveness cannot be offered if it is never asked for. Visions of the Ring, where Jeshu offered his life for humanity, filled Ledger's mind.

"Please forgive me, Jeshu. My hands are red with the blood of my brother—of my people," Ledger said with a trembling voice.

Jeshu reached for Ledger, pulling him up. "Not anymore. I forgive you."

There in the midst of the innumerable mass of humanity stood the forgiven one named Ledger. The goodness of Jeshu crushed Ledger beyond what his feeble heart could bear, but piece by piece, Jeshu healed him. Ledger leaned into Jeshu's chest and ached for the King of the galaxy to hold him, and so Jeshu did. Jeshu's embrace healed the broken form of young Ledger until he was able to stand on his own.

Ledger wiped away his tears, looking into the noble face of the Merchant, the one who had purchased his soul at a costly price.

"What now, my Lord?"

Jeshu reached for the Protector on his arm, and Ledger watched in wonder as the Merchant lifted this Immortal vessel of power. Ledger gawked at the incredible sight of what appeared to be an instantaneous replication of Jeshu's Protector. On his right arm, the original Protector remained, but in his left hand was another gleaming Protector. Chills flitted up and down Ledger's spine. Jeshu nodded, and Ledger held out his right arm. Ledger braced himself as Jeshu pressed the Protector downward—the synaptic connection was instantaneous. As Ledger's mind synchronized with the Protector, a galaxy of understanding flooded into his soul. When his vision cleared, the noble form of Jeshu was still standing before him.

"**Learn of me** and of my ways. Your training as my Galactic Navi begins now."

Once the Hammershot escaped from the deadly meteors that had assaulted them at the Orixian Belt, Captain Rosco set course for the nearest planet that could effect repairs on the damage they had suffered. Although battered, all the Scavenger craft had been recovered, but six excursion miners had been lost, three from Zara's crew. She remained stoic and professional in order to fulfill her obligation as a pilot during the recovery, but once that responsibility was complete, Zara retreated to her quarters. She locked the entrance portal behind her. Without removing her pilot gear, she sat down on the edge of her bed and began to shake, feeling the weight of the disaster hit her with full force. Tears tumbled down her cheeks as she replayed the events, wondering if there was anything she could have done differently—some action that could have saved the lives of her three crew members.

Her portal entrance request chimed, and she began wiping tears away.

"Enter," she called as she finished drying her wet cheeks.

The portal panels slid away, allowing Captain Rosco to enter. He stepped just inside the threshold, waiting there for a moment. He frowned.

"Are you okay?" Rosco asked.

Zara looked up at the space veteran, a man she knew had seen a dozen space tragedies not too different than what they had just experienced.

"I could have reacted faster," she said, her voice trembling. "I might have saved them."

Rosco crossed his arms. "There's nothing you could have done that would have changed what happened out there. You understand?"

Zara looked up into the weary eyes of the man. "Yeah."

Rosco took a deep breath. "I'm taking you out of the Scavenger rotation for the rest of this tour. We'll see how you're doing after that."

Zara sniffed and wiped her eyes once more. She nodded.

"Get some rest, Zara," Rosco finished.

Zara nodded again. Rosco waited a couple of seconds, then turned and left her quarters. Zara fell over onto her bed, curling her knees up to her chest. The tears returned as she thought about each of the three men who had lost their lives—Mick Allendorce, Corbin Messer, and Ledger Brandt. As she mourned them, a deeper, old, familiar pain began to swell and swallow her. Mingled with that great pain was a paralyzing fear that threatened to completely destroy her—fear that she might not ever be whole again, or even normal for that matter. Despite her careful and determined efforts to guard her wounded heart,

Ledger Brandt had infiltrated her fortress and tempted her to care.

Many hours transpired, her bed becoming wet with countless tears. In the darkness of her soul, she frantically searched for some shred of hope to keep her from being shattered, but there was no lifeline to hold to. Zara Lux faded beneath the monsters of pain and fear.

Over the course of the next three months, Ledger learned of the ways of the Navi from the Son of Ell Yon. All the knowledge, understanding, and skills that Ledger had learned in his training to become a Master Keeper was not lost but rather realigned and thus brought brilliant clarity during Jeshu's training. No other man had the access or opportunity to learn such profound things. Jeshu revealed truths in the writings of the ancient oracles that none other could understand. Jeshu honed the combat skills of an already incredibly capable warrior to higher levels than humanity had ever witnessed. Once Ledger was ready, Jeshu brought him into the forge of Immortal combat in the Ruah against the fierce enemies of Sovereign Ell Yon near the Outer Rim planets.

"Unlike the communing practiced by the other Navis—and unlike what you'll do in the future—you've been fully translated into the Ruah," Jeshu explained. "This isn't an imprint or a projection of your physical form from the human realm. Your body is wholly present here. What you experience in this place is real, complete, and permanent."

Ledger frowned. "So if I lose an eye or an arm here, I lose it in my own realm as well?"

"Yes." Jeshu hesitated before continuing. "But when you return to your realm, you'll commune with Sovereign Ell Yon as the other Navis do. I'll teach you how to commune effectively—and more, if you're able. There's a particular technique that no one has yet mastered."

Ledger was intrigued.

"Are you ready to face the legions of Dracus?" Jeshu asked.

"I am, my Lord."

In the Immortal realm of the Ruah, Ledger's mettle was tested and proved. Each Malakian warrior campaign propelled Ledger's skills to new heights, and within a few short weeks, he became renowned among Malakian and Torian warriors alike.

"I have reserved power for you, the likes of which the galaxy has not yet seen," Jeshu said on the day that Ledger's ground training in the realm of the Ruah had come to an end. "Let your mind always be guided by your Protector, and I will always be with you, even to the ends of the galaxy. But beware, Ledger—your greatest enemy lies within."

Jeshu's words were extreme in their calling and in their warning. Ledger trembled at the understanding of both.

Jeshu expanded Ledger's awareness far beyond that of mere regional conflict and warfare. He imparted a galactic understanding of the fierce battle between good and evil—Malakians and Torians— Sovereign Ell Yon and Lord C'fir Dracus. Vivid displays of force deployment and strategic initiatives illuminated a grand holographic display before them as Jeshu elevated Ledger's comprehension of the true war for the souls of humanity.

At one point, Jeshu manipulated the display, zooming in to his beloved planet of Rayl. The white and blue orb hung like a jewel in the vast sea of black space. Ledger's heart ached with longing, even though this planet had been the source of much of his past pain. Ledger glanced over at the noble face of Jeshu, seeing both great compassion and great sorrow.

"What is it, my lord?" Ledger asked.

Jeshu hesitated, his gaze resting on the gleaming, serene planet...his beloved world. "If only you had known the time of my appearance, destruction would have been spared you."

The Merchant's words hung heavy in Ledger's mind, but he dared not press further. Ledger trusted that Jeshu would reveal all that was required in time.

Despite all that Ledger had mastered, one skill remained for him to master as a Navi. Ledger stood beside Jeshu as two powerful starfighters landed just fifty paces away.

"My Lord, I know nothing about starfighter training. It was determined that I wouldn't need it in my role as a KDF agent," Ledger admitted.

"Don't worry. You'll catch on fast. It's in your blood."

Ledger cocked his head. "In my blood?"

"You're a Starlore. Your grandfather was one of the greatest starfighter pilots the galaxy has ever seen...and now you will be as well."

Over the course of the next two months, Jeshu trained Ledger in the *Starstreak*, the Malakian's premier fighter in their war against the Torians. From advanced fighter maneuvers to multi-threat space combat engagements, Ledger's skill as a pilot exceeded all who had gone before him. And when all was complete, Lethal Ledger of the KDF was transformed into the greatest Malakian weapon imaginable against the dark forces of Lord Dracus. Ledger became the first Jeshuan Galactic Navi.

When Ledger's training was complete, Jeshu called him.

"It's time to be translated back into your realm," Jeshu said. "A Rim Syndicate ship is within range of your personal transponder. Your mission lies before you. Fulfill it until the last breath you take."

Ledger knelt before the Commander of the Malakians. "I will, my Lord. I so solemnly swear."

Ledger stood, ready to don his excursion suit helmet. "I have so much to restore...so much hurt to heal. Where do I start?"

"How about with the one who was with you all along?" Jeshu offered.

"Rivet! Do you know him? Is he...safe?"

Jeshu looked at Ledger with a gleam in his eye. "Rivet is the knowledge of humanity tempered by the wisdom of Sovereign Ell Yon. He is unique, and you should make a companion of him."

Ledger took a deep breath. He felt as if scales had been lifted from his eyes. The galaxy seemed so clear now, and he felt cleansed...new...fresh. The memories of his former thoughts and words made him cringe. There was much to do...much to fix.

"And what of Arn?" Ledger asked. "He follows you with a courageous heart."

Jeshu smiled. "That's why I chose him. Find him, and you will know what to do."

Ledger thought of Zara, unsure about what their friendship meant. Had she even survived the last six months of perilous mining duty? Clearly, she didn't know nor seem inclined to follow Jeshu. He looked at Jeshu, wondering if he dared ask of her. His mission was set before him, and he couldn't see any future where his friendship with her could remain.

"Zara Lux matters," Jeshu said without any prompting from Ledger. "The whole galaxy, like her, walks in darkness, but I will be a light to them all. Bring her with you back to Rayl."

"But how?" Ledger asked.

"You'll find a way," Jeshu replied.

Echoes of past prophecies by ancient oracles came to life through the words of the one who had spoken them thousands of years ago and now stood before him. Chills flitted up and down Ledger's body as he considered his supremely unique calling.

Ledger secured his helmet on his head, then reached for the interphasal translator that had been on his wrist ever since Lieutenant Carvin placed it there. He looked once more at the regal face of Jeshu, wondering if he would ever see him again in this realm. Jeshu nodded, and Ledger removed the translator. The beauty of Orixia instantly dissolved away to reveal the dead barren world it was in the realm of humanity.

Orixia's two suns beamed down on Ledger from high in the sky. He tapped on his com band to activate his transponder. Within two minutes he received a response.

"Vessel transmitting a distress beacon on the emergency frequency. This is the transport frigate *Peersan Daub* of the Rim Syndicate. What is your status?"

"*Peersan Daub*, this is not a vessel. This is *Hammershot* excursion miner 332, Ledger Brandt. I am marooned on the surface of Orixia. Can you effect recovery?"

"Affirmative, *Hammershot* excursion miner 332. We have an extraction vessel enroute to your location. Are you injured?"

"Negative, *Peersan Daub*...thank you."

It took Ledger three days to find transports that could deliver him back to Abaria. Two weeks later, the *Hammershot* arrived at the Bria Spaceport, and Ledger arrived early to greet her. It had been six months since he disappeared. The crew of the *Hammershot* had flown an entirely new tour since the incident at the Orixian Belt. He wasn't even sure if Arn would have stayed with the crew or what Zara's status would be. If the two of them were still part of the crew, he was uncertain how to reveal himself.

Ledger watched the crew of the *Hammershot* disembark. He didn't have to wait long before he recognized the man who had followed him across the galaxy, and Ledger's heart leapt for joy at the sight of Arn. Now, with the eyes of Jeshu, Ledger saw Arn for the courageous, obedient soul he was.

Keeping out of sight, Ledger followed Arn to the Rim Syndicate depository. Once Arn completed his deposit, Ledger waited next to a group of people that stood close by Arn's path. As Arn passed, Ledger leaned his shoulder out to collide with Arn's.

"Pardon me," Arn said without looking up.

"Hey," Ledger called out. "Aren't you on the wrong side of the galaxy?"

Arn froze in his tracks, his back still to Ledger. He turned around. Once he set eyes on Ledger, his face filled with shock and disbelief, as though he were beholding a ghost.

"Ledger?" he asked, his face still contorted in a look of confused horror.

Ledger smiled. "Hey, buddy."

Ledger's voice seemed to dislodge Arn out of whatever delusion he thought he was enduring. His eyes opened wide, and a stunned but joyful grin spread across his face.

"Ledger!" Arn shouted, closing the few steps between them with arms open wide. He wrapped his arms around Ledger and lifted him up with a big laugh before setting him down and pulling back to look him in the face. "How?" he asked, not yet letting go of Ledger.

"It's good to see you, my friend," Ledger said, his eyes beaming with delight.

"I can't believe it," Arn continued. "Corbin?" Arn asked…hopeful.

"He's well, but not with me," Ledger assured. Arn looked relieved.

"But I scanned! Everyone thought you were killed. Zara…Zara!" Arn exclaimed as thoughts of her clearly flashed through his mind.

"Is she well?" Ledger asked.

"No, but she will be," Arn said, his smile not diminishing. "When you disappeared, it almost ruined her."

Ledger's heart broke as he thought of her grieving.

"We have to find her and tell her," Arn urged, looking back toward the *Hammershot*.

"We will," Ledger said. "But first, you and I must talk. We have a lot to discuss."

Arn's attention returned to Ledger, scanning him up and down, his eyes searching Ledger's face. "Yes, I can see that. You know Him, don't you?"

Ledger grabbed Arn's shoulders, a smile bursting from his lips. "Arn, you and I are going to change the galaxy!"

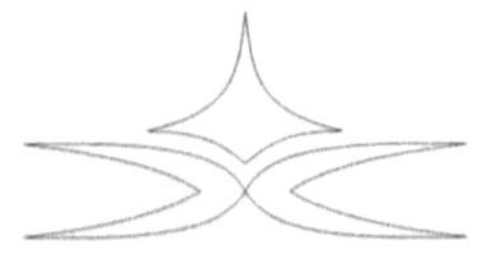

CHAPTER

5

Back from the Dead

Fasa Kylos felt his influence and control slipping away, both with the Morian Empire and with the people of Rayl. If he dwelled too long on the rising turmoil, it spawned relentless anxiety over his loss of power, and his thoughts became desperate as he schemed to regain that which had been lost. As disenchanted as Subchancellor Pylok was with Kylos and the Keeper Order, his replacement, Subchancellor Marculus, was even more so. Kylos couldn't seem to appease the man with any offering. Each time he visited Marculus, occasions that were much less frequent than with Pylok, the Subchancellor appeared increasingly annoyed and unwilling to respond to any of Kylos's petitions or recommendations. Kylos had a sense that the whole situation was becoming dire. But a new Morian First Leader had ascended to power on the Morian homeworld, and Kylos was hopeful that today might be a turning point for the Keepers and for the Rayleans as a people.

When Kylos was called into Marculus's Hall of Judgment, the cold, columned chamber felt more ominous than ever before. Marculus sat in his elevated seat like a king over his subjects, which Kylos detested. Marculus peered down on Kylos with a look of complete dominion.

"Keeper Kylos, you have been summoned one last time, for after this appearance, you will no longer be recognized as a person of authority by the Morian Empire. Your inability to effect change upon your people in regard to the rising threat of the Partisans has been judged grossly inadequate." Marculus spoke as if he were reading a court sentencing. "First Leader Chancellor Eron has established a new directive in regard to Rayl and the Raylean people."

Subchancellor Marculus tapped an icon on the arm of his chair, and a glowing electronic document appeared before him.

"'Due to an increase in hostilities directed at the Morian Empire, planet Rayl and its people will no longer be afforded the privilege of self-government. All seats of authority originated by the Raylean people are hereby abolished. Any attempts to subvert the rule of the Morian Empire will be met with swift and immediate judgment. Signed, First Leader Chancellor Eron.'"

"But Subchancellor—" Kylos began.

"There will be no response from you," Marculus interrupted. "If you attempt to address this high office of authority, you will be considered a subverter, and you will be executed. You are dismissed."

Kylos's face flushed with anger and embarrassment as he was abruptly escorted off the premises and left standing beside a busy thoroughfare.

The day he dreaded for decades had finally come.

How could this be Sovereign Ell Yon's plan for His people? he fumed. *How could His people continue under such persecution?*

Little did he know that this was just the beginning. The full fury of the Morian Empire had yet to be unleashed.

It took Arn significant cajoling to get Zara to accept an invitation to join him at an eatery near the Bria spaceport.

"She hardly leaves the ship," Arn explained as he and Ledger waited for Zara in a quaint and secluded park across from the eatery. It was a small oasis of green in an otherwise sea of dull, gray concrete and steel. "I've often wondered, if in some odd way, she blames herself for not saving you and Corbin. Since the incident, she hardly talks to anyone, including me."

Arn looked over Ledger's shoulder.

"She's here," Arn said. "Despite how tough she may seem, she's a wounded soul." Arn's brow furrowed. "I hope this goes well."

Ledger could hear footsteps behind him. He turned around, and when he did, Zara stopped ten paces away, frozen in place by the image of Ledger standing before her. For ten seconds, she didn't move. A gentle breeze rustled the branches of a nearby tree while three birds swished overhead, but Zara remained perfectly still.

"Hi, Zara," Ledger said.

His words seemed to fracture whatever it was that was holding her in place. She put her hand to her mouth, then turned away from him. Her torso heaved as she tried to suppress deep guttural cries. Ledger wasn't sure how to help her.

"Zara," he called out, taking a couple of steps toward her.

With her back still toward Ledger, she held up a hand, warning him to stay put. After a few more seconds, she took a deep breath, then turned to face him, her eyes wet with tears. She wiped them away, then carefully approached. Two steps away, she stopped.

"How?" she whispered. She tried to blink away the tears, but to no avail. She continued to wipe them away as she looked up at Ledger.

Ledger closed the distance between them. "May I hug you?" he asked.

Zara swallowed hard but didn't respond. Ledger carefully wrapped his arms around her. Zara didn't hug him back, but she turned her head and leaned into his chest. Ledger tightened his embrace.

"It's good to see you, Pilot Lux," he said quietly.

He felt her take a stuttered breath, filling her lungs with air. When he let go of her, she stepped back.

"How?" she repeated.

"That's going to take some time to explain," Ledger said.

"Where's Corbin?" Zara asked, taking a moment to look about.

"He's okay, Zara," Ledger assured her. "But he's not with me. He's returned home."

Zara set her eyes back on Ledger. Her emotions seemed to be all over the place, but more than any other emotion, anger flashed hot in her eyes.

"Why did you wait so long?"

"I was marooned...sort of." Ledger struggled. "Can we sit down? I'll do my best to explain everything."

Zara took a breath, apparently to assuage her anger, then nodded.

Inside the eatery, Arn had reserved a lone table in a secluded area so they could talk uninterrupted. Ledger waited until they had received their drinks and placed orders for their food. Zara glared at him. It seemed that no explanation was going to appease her.

"It's good to see you, Zara," Ledger began. That single statement seemed to disarm her just a bit.

"I saw that meteor hit you and Corbin at full force." She sat back, looking Ledger up and down. "You sitting here in front of me is an impossibility. I must be going insane." She reached across the table, grabbed Ledger's arm, and pinched him hard.

"Ouch!" Ledger recoiled.

Zara still didn't seem convinced he was real.

"Let me try to explain," Ledger said, rubbing the bright red mark on his arm. "The Immortals you've heard us talk about are real."

Zara snorted. "The ones in an alternate dimension?"

"Yes. A fraction of a second before the meteor hit us, an Immortal translated me into the Ruah, then used an advanced device to explode the meteor in their realm. We were also shielded with a powerful forcefield that kept us safe during the impact of the fractured meteor."

"You saw all of this happen?" Zara asked.

"Not exactly. It all happened so fast and with such force that I lost consciousness," Ledger explained.

Zara began shaking her head. "Convenient. What is this all about? Do you expect me to believe such a preposterous thing?"

Ledger leaned forward. "You saw it, Zara. By all laws of physics in our universe, I should be dead, and yet here I am talking with you. If you want the truth, you're going to have to suspend disbelief long enough for me to tell it to you."

Zara crossed her arms, still glaring at Ledger with skepticism. "Okay—continue."

Ledger regaled Zara with the full account of his time on Orixia. As wild and far-fetched as the story was, Zara remained quiet and attentive until the end. When Ledger finished, their uneaten food sat cold and untouched before them. Zara's countenance softened, and Ledger was somewhat encouraged.

"That is the most bizarre story I've ever heard," Zara said, looking down at her food. "Yet here you sit," she said, glancing back up at him. Her eyes flitted toward Arn. "I suppose you believe him?"

Arn nodded. Zara shook her head.

"You're both insane. Why did I have to get two lunatics assigned to my mining crew? And Corbin…you're saying he is one of your Immortals who posed as a lowly humanoid for months. You can't be serious! We all saw Corbin."

Ledger smiled. "You should see him now. I know how this must sound to you, but all I can do is tell you the truth."

A subtle smirk crossed her face. "I guess it doesn't matter what I believe. So, what does this mean? Are you going to rejoin the crew with Arn and me?" she asked, looking to Arn for support. Arn diverted his eyes, and Zara's gaze narrowed. "What?" she asked, looking fiercely at Ledger.

"I can't, Zara," Ledger said. "Jeshu has given me a mission that begins back on Rayl. I must return home."

Zara pursed her lips. "And you," she asked Arn. "You're leaving too?"

Arn looked Zara in the eyes. "I must, Zara. It's the whole reason I came here."

Zara's gaze fell back to her uneaten food. "That's fine. I'm sure Captain Rosco will have no problem replacing you both." She picked up a fork and lifted the first bite of food to her mouth.

"Come with us, Zara," Ledger said.

The fork in Zara's hand froze in place, then slowly fell back to the plate in front of her.

"Are you crazy?" she said, glaring back at Ledger. "Why in the galaxy would I ever consider such a thing?"

"Because we're friends, and we make a good team," Arn replied.

"That's absurd," Zara said, her voicing rising in volume. "I am not going to leave the *Hammershot* to chase some cockamamie notion about a man the Morians killed decades ago."

Ledger and Arn stayed silent, letting their suggestion ruminate in her mind. Zara fidgeted as they continued to look at her.

"Besides, I could never leave the *Hammershot.*"

"Why not?" Ledger asked.

Zara looked at him, tilting her head. "Because it's all I've ever known."

"You're stronger than that, and you're meant for more than mining asteroids. Besides, you love an adventure," Ledger rebutted.

Zara's eyes ignited.

"I just can't," Zara insisted. She seemed to struggle with a better explanation. "Captain Rosco—" she began, then stopped.

Zara stared at Ledger for a few seconds, which confused him. As he gazed into her eyes, he could see immense brokenness. She finally stood up to leave.

Ledger's Protector whispered, and he saw Zara Lux as she was without the façade of pilot bravado. Such deep pain...such loneliness...such need. She looked away, seeming to sense his perception of her vulnerability.

"I have to get back to the *Hammershot,*" she said.

"Zara, please reconsider," Arn petitioned.

Zara glared back at them. "Why should I care one bit what you two do or where you go? I have a job to do here, and that's what I'm going to do." She then turned and stormed away.

Ledger stood up, hurrying to catch up with her.

"Zara!" Ledger called out from a few feet behind her.

Zara turned around, her eyes unreadable but full of emotion. After a moment of hesitation, she marched back to him until she stopped inches from his face, her eyes ablaze with fury. "I want to hit you so badly," she said through clenched teeth.

Ledger's eyes filled with compassion. "If you must," he said gingerly.

Zara's eyes spewed darts at him. She huffed, then turned and left the eatery. Ledger stood motionless as he watched the door close behind her.

"Clearly, there's a lot more going on with her than we understand," Arn said as he came to stand next to Ledger.

"Clearly," Ledger replied.

"I think it has to do with her childhood. Remember Harcort?" Arn asked.

Ledger looked at Arn. "Yeah. The excursion miner with the most tours."

Arn nodded. "According to him, after Zara's parents were killed, it was Captain Rosco that found her, and she's been his indentured servant ever since."

"Indentured servant? Rosco?" Ledger exclaimed.

"So he says."

Ledger clenched both fists. No wonder she didn't want to explain why she couldn't come with them.

"How many credits do you have?" Ledger asked Arn.

"Nearly 2,000 in my account here. Why?"

"I'm going to have a few words with Rosco."

"Good luck with that," Arn said, slapping Ledger on his shoulder. "I'm going to finish packing."

Thirty minutes later, Ledger stood before the captain of the *Hammershot.*

Executive Officer Fraun was an extremely efficient man, which is why Captain Rosco had appointed him as his second in command. "Captain, this is one of the survivors from the Orixian Belt incident—Ledger Brandt," Fraun announced before stepping aside.

Two large and formidable armed guards stood just inside the captain's ready room. Ledger had come to understand that in this business, enemies were never far away. One of the guards scanned Ledger for any weapons. Once satisfied, he stepped back into his sentry position and nodded to Captain Rosco.

Captain Rosco looked up from his desktop, where four graphic displays were feeding a constant stream of information. On the right side of his desk, a hologram of the *Hammershot* slowly rotated with status messages that hovered and pointed to various parts of the ship.

Rosco leaned back, squinting at Ledger. "We thought you were killed at Orixia. I lost five other men that day. How did you survive?"

Ledger had prepared a response that would be acceptable to most of the crew if they asked, but he knew that Rosco was a clever and discerning man. He hoped his half-truth story would work nonetheless.

"When a large meteor impacted the asteroid I was working on, I was thrown clear. Later, a Rim Syndicate transport frigate picked me up."

Rosco's scrutinizing demeanor didn't change. "What happened to the other miner? Did he make it?"

Ledger wasn't exactly sure how to reply. "He survived, Captain, but he won't be coming back." He decided to give as few details as possible regarding the crewman of the *Hammershot* known as Corbin Messer.

"I'm not surprised," Rosco snorted. He looked toward his executive officer. "Pay him for the time worked on the tour. That's all." Rosco turned his attention back to his displays.

"That's not why I'm here, Captain," Ledger said.

Rosco frowned. "It's hazardous duty, miner. That's why we have you sign the waiver before each tour. There's no compensation for injuries, or loss of time, or frankly anything else." Rosco's gaze turned ice cold. "And don't even think about any legal claims, or you won't work in this half of the galaxy ever again!"

"I'm not here for compensation of any kind, not even the time on that tour." Ledger stepped forward. "I'm here to discuss the fate of one of your longtime crewmembers."

Rosco leaned back again, crossing his arms. "Who?"

"Zara Lux."

The room filled with a tense silence. Ledger could feel the gaze of Rosco's executive officer and the two guards behind him. Captain Rosco continued to glare at Ledger—motionless. Ten long seconds passed.

"Leave the room," Rosco ordered, motioning to the other men.

His exec and both guards exited the ready room immediately, the door swishing closed behind them.

"What about Zara?" Rosco asked.

"Thousands of light years from here, I have a mission to fulfill. Arn Naybus, one of your operators, is planning on coming with me. Miner Naybus has no commitment to the *Hammershot* beyond his last tour. During my time on the *Hammershot*, Zara and I became friends. I've invited her to come with me, but it has recently been explained to me that she has a lifelong indentured sentence on her. I'm here to negotiate on her behalf."

Ledger watched Rosco closely for some indication as to how he would respond to his request. It seemed that the relationship between Rosco and Zara was an unusual one. Did he like her? Despise her? Ledger's encounter with the thugs months ago indicated that Rosco offered some measure of protection for Zara, but why?

Rosco leaned forward, a cunning look on his face. "Is that so? And does she know that you're here on her behalf?"

"She does not," Ledger confessed.

"That's what I thought," Rosco said, allowing a sly grin to cross his lips. He drummed the top of his desk with his fingers as he thought. "Despite what she saw happen to you, she pleaded with me to stay in that meteor shower and search for you. Never seen her act like that."

Captain Rosco stood up and came around to the front of his desk to face Ledger. He eyed Ledger up and down as though evaluating him.

"What do you want with Zara, Brandt?"

Ledger was instantly offended by the insinuations Rosco was making.

"Zara is our friend," Ledger rebutted, anger flushing his cheeks. "A friend who deserves to determine her own future and make her own choices. Lifelong indentured servitude is barbaric. I don't care if we are on the Outer Rim. It should be banned, and you should be better!"

Ledger fully expected Rosco to call his henchmen guards and have him thrown off his ship, but the man hardly reacted at all. He reached behind him and pressed a com icon.

"Fraun, bring Zara to my ready room immediately."

Rosco left Ledger standing, then went to a credenza along the side wall and retrieved an ornate box. Ledger swallowed hard. He waited for some gruesome weapon to be drawn, but instead the man lifted a slender toffee-colored cylindrical item. He placed one end in his mouth and lit the opposite end with the flame of a small device on top of the credenza. Rosco inhaled deeply, then exhaled a billowy puff of white smoke that filled the room with a sweet and spicy dark aroma. He glanced toward Ledger.

"I found Zara on a remote colony in the Wheelock System," Rosco said in between puffs on his smoking stick. "Her parents were dead, the colony was in its final days of survival, and those who remained were barely alive. Out on the Rim, you survive with little help or you die." Rosco paused, his eyes seeing memories that Ledger couldn't. "Cruel people had made a slave of her. Then one day, out of nowhere, this little street urchin came running for me, clutching my leg like some beast was going to devour her." Rosco swallowed hard. "Couldn't leave her. I knew that life on board a space mining ship was no place for a little lass, but I just couldn't leave her."

Ledger was stunned. He couldn't imagine Rosco having a soft spot for anyone, especially an orphaned little girl. This wasn't the story he'd heard about Zara at all. Perhaps Rosco was just an eloquent liar.

Rosco exhaled another puff of aromatic smoke, thinking...remembering. "I intended to find someone to take her at the next spaceport, but when I tried to leave, she clung to me like her life depended on it."

Rosco's eyes reddened. "Had a little girl of my own once," he said without looking at Ledger. He shook his head. "Zara didn't need me—I needed her."

Ledger stood dumbfounded and silent, unable to conjure up a single word.

The door to the ready room swished open, and Ledger turned to see Executive Officer Fraun escorting Zara into the room. Zara's eyes opened wide in delight for one brief second, then narrowed to scorn.

"What are *you* doing here?" she asked, stopping short of him and crossing her arms. "I thought you were on your way to leave the planet."

"I was, but then—"

"But then he had the bright idea to come and barter for your release from being my indentured servant," Captain Rosco interrupted as he snuffed out the smoking stick in a shallow bowl.

He turned to glare at Zara. She was clearly flustered by both the presence of Ledger and the accusation Rosco was making.

"Is that what you are, Zara? My indentured servant?" Rosco pressed.

Ledger noticed that Fraun exited on his own, the door closing behind him.

Zara went to Rosco, her cheeks flushing. "You know I have to tell the miners a story so they don't patronize me." Zara stood straight and tall, her chin lifted slightly. "I'm as tough as any one of them and better at mining than most of them."

Rosco's hard glare softened. "Of that I am certain, and so is the rest of the *Hammershot.*"

Zara's tough persona eased for one brief moment as she looked up at Captain Rosco, almost as a daughter would her father. But as quickly as the moment came, it vanished, and she spun about, setting her sights on Ledger once more.

"So, what *are* you doing here…really?" she asked with a smug look while walking toward him, squinting as she came.

"Apparently nothing at all since you already have the freedom I was hoping to petition Captain Rosco for." Ledger met Zara's stare.

The two of them glared at each other for a few awkward moments. It was clear to Ledger that Zara truly didn't have any desire to accompany him and Arn on their mission. Realizing he had wandered into a completely different situation than what he had expected, there was only one action for him to take. Ledger turned to Captain Rosco.

"I apologize for the interruption, Captain. I bid you both farewell and will be on my way."

He bowed his head to both, catching a glimpse of Zara in his peripheral vision. The corners of her eyes seemed to drop slightly. Ledger turned to exit the ready room.

"Not so fast, mister," Rosco called out. "You don't encumber me with such a request and leave without a consequence."

Ledger stopped, turning back around. "Consequence?"

Rosco walked to Zara. Grabbing her shoulder, he turned her about so he could look straight into her eyes.

"Zara, do you want to go with this man?" Rosco asked.

"I…I can't. The ship needs me here. *You* need me here." Zara forced the words out.

Rosco put both of his large, weathered hands on her shoulders. "This is no place for one like you. It never has been, and we both know it."

"But—" Zara began.

"It's time, Zara," Rosco interrupted. "Ever since I saw you notice him two tours ago, I've been watching this guy. He's a good man, not like most of these miners that come our way. I think you should go with him, but the choice is yours."

Zara seemed to resist a moment longer, then dropped her shoulders and her chin. She turned around to look at Ledger. She bit her lower lip as she tried to sort out what to say.

"I love being a pilot."

"Lots of that where we're going," Ledger replied.

"You really want me to come?" she asked.

"Of course we do," Ledger said. "It won't be easy, but I know you're not afraid of hard."

Zara looked back at Rosco, softening to him once again. "I'll come back, Captain…I promise."

Rosco nodded, but evidently, he wasn't done. He walked to stand in front of Ledger. Being this close to the man, his looming stature was rather intimidating. He lifted his chin, looking down his nose at Ledger, eyeing him closely.

"I need some assurance that you're committed to her protection."

"I don't need protect—" Zara began, but Rosco held up his hand, and she stopped short of finishing her rebuttal.

"You have my word, Captain," Ledger said, glancing toward Zara.

"Not good enough," Rosco said bluntly. "I want legal proof."

Ledger was confused. Legal proof? He furrowed his eyebrows. "I don't understand."

"What is the strongest binding contract between two people where you come from?" Rosco demanded.

"I suppose that would be the bonding ceremony, but—"

"That will do. Here we call it a joining, but that means nothing to you. You must be bonded to Zara before she goes with you." Rosco's stern eyes left no question as to his sincerity.

Ledger's heart thumped in his chest as he swallowed hard. Captain Rosco had no idea what he was asking of him...demanding of him.

Zara stepped up to stand beside Ledger. She glared back at Rosco. "Enough!" she exclaimed. "I will not be coerced into some relational contract!"

"I've protected you from the worst of humanity, Zara," Rosco said, crossing his arms. "I'll not leave your future protection to chance. If you're to go with him, this is what I require, and it's clear to me that you want to go with him."

"Not like this!" she said, wagging her head.

"Okay," Ledger interrupted.

Zara froze, turning to look at him.

"I'll be bonded to her," Ledger finished.

"You don't have to do this," Zara said. "He won't make us do this."

"He's not wrong," Ledger said, looking to Zara. "If I'm bonded to you, there is a power in that commitment that no other contract holds. My commitment to you will be to protect you. Nothing more." Ledger looked at Captain Rosco. "Will that suffice?"

Rosco nodded. "As captain of this ship, I have the authority to enact this contract as long as I hear your verbal vows."

Ledger looked over at Zara, who was in some peculiar state of shock, her eyes confused and her mouth slightly open as she stared at Ledger.

"I, Captain Xavier Rosco, officially initiate the bonding ceremony between Zara Lux and Ledger Brandt—"

"Starlore...Ledger Starlore," Ledger corrected.

"Between Zara Lux and Ledger Starlore. Will you, Ledger Starlore, be willfully bonded to Zara Lux, promising to protect her and provide for her at all cost as long as you live?"

Ledger looked over at Zara, his heart beating rapidly. Even though neither Zara nor Rosco understood what this meant, he did, and so would every Raylean on his planet.

"I will."

"Will you, Zara Lux, be willfully bonded to Ledger Starlore, promising to abide by his side and commit to his well-being as long as you live?"

Zara just continued to stare at Ledger, apparently unable to answer.

"Now, Zara," Rosco prompted.

Zara broke her gaze from Ledger, turning a glaring eye to Rosco. "You're being ridiculous!"

Rosco didn't back down. "Will you?" he repeated forcefully.

Zara's nostrils flared as she huffed at him. "I...will."

"What higher authority do your people pledge by?" Rosco asked.

Ledger hesitated. This was transcending to a place from which he could not escape. "Sovereign Ell Yon."

"Under the eyes of Sovereign Ell Yon and by the vows you have made to each other before me and before Sovereign Ell Yon, I pronounce you bonded."

Rosco smiled. "Is there anything else that must be done to complete the ceremony?"

Zara's fierce look transformed into one of suspicion. Ledger swallowed hard.

"We must briefly interlock hands," Ledger said, holding his left palm up.

Zara pursed her lips, then gently placed her right hand on top of his. Their fingers interlocked. Ledger's heart quickened further.

"That is all that's required," Ledger said.

Zara opened her hand and let go. She walked to the door shaking her head. "I'll never forgive you for this, Rosco. Never!"

Rosco stood still...waiting. Before Zara made it to the door, she stopped, her head bowed low. Then all at once she turned about and went to Rosco, wrapping her arms around his burly torso without looking up at him. He gently returned the embrace.

"Fly hard and live long," she whispered, then turned and bolted out the door.

"She's a tough one," Rosco said. "Promise me those were more than just words you spoke."

"My word to Sovereign Ell Yon transcends any contract man could conjure up."

"Very well," Rosco said. "Fly hard and live long."

"Fly hard and live long," Ledger repeated, then exited the ready room to find Zara. His world had been flipped upside down in just 30 minutes. *What was this going to do to Zara?* he wondered. *How would he explain this to Arn?*

When Ledger finally caught up to Zara, he walked quietly beside her without saying a word. Eventually she stopped, grabbing his arm so she could directly face him.

"What just happened?" Zara asked, her eyes igniting with fury.

"I'm not exactly sure, but I—"

"Well as far as I'm concerned, nothing happened," Zara finished. She turned to strut away but immediately turned back to face Ledger, holding up a finger at him.

"Were you part of Rosco's plot?"

"No, absolutely not!" Ledger assured. "I'm as stunned by this as you."

Zara's lips shifted to the left as she considered Ledger's denial. Ledger was fairly disheartened by how she was taking this, but he fully understood it. He was just as confused and conflicted about the ad hoc bonding ceremony. He was pretty sure that when Jeshu said

Ledger would find a way to get Zara to go with him to Rayl, this was not what he'd intended.

Zara turned to go on her way, but Ledger grabbed her arm.

"Hey," he said, gently turning her back to face him. Her eyes avoided his until she finally relented and looked him full in the face.

"Regardless of what Rosco coerced us to do, we're friends. I respect you...I admire you...and I don't want anything to ruin what we had. You and Arn and I...there's a galaxy out there waiting for us. Can we start fresh?"

Ledger's words seemed to soothe Zara's resistant heart. Her eyes softened slightly, and her stiff shoulders relaxed.

"Friends? When did that happen?" Zara asked.

"When you handed me a malata drink on my deck by the beach," Ledger said with a subtle grin.

Zara's gaze fell to the ground. "I see. It's just that I don't do friends well, but I suppose that's why I missed you," she confessed, looking back up at him. "I really missed you." Zara diverted her eyes. "And Rosco's right—I need to get out of this place." She gazed past Ledger and up at the ominous form of the *Hammershot*. She fixed her eyes back on Ledger. "You're the only one Rosco has ever even considered letting me go with, so I guess there's that."

"I'm happy to hear it," Ledger said with a gentle grin. "And for what it's worth, I do promise to look out for you."

Zara nodded. "I guess we all need that from time to time. I'll look out for you too."

Ledger took a deep breath and let it out. "I'm glad." They resumed walking. "So Rosco wasn't the one you were a slave to?"

Zara shook her head, and by the look on her face, Ledger could tell he was venturing into dark memories.

"Three years," Zara muttered, lost in painful thoughts. "At 12, Rosco actually saved me from them. I owe him my life, which is why it's hard to leave."

Ledger nodded. So much about Zara now made sense. He didn't dare ask more. He glanced over at her with a twinkle in his eye.

"I think it's time we find Arn and Rivet."

"Rivet?" Zara asked.

Ledger smiled. "You're going to love Rivet."

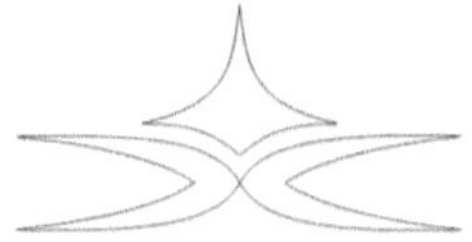

CHAPTER

10

Outworlder Haven

Ledger led Arn and Zara to the silo working platform where most of the bots were stationed. When they arrived, Ledger set his eyes on a barely recognizable jumble of metal and composites lying in the corner of the platform. One of his legs was crushed, and a panel had been torn from his torso, exposing his circuitry and inner construct. A hot surge of anger flared through Ledger.

"Rivet!" Ledger exclaimed as he came to the prone bot.

The android struggled to look Ledger's way. His movements were no longer smooth and calculated. After two tries, the android's head ratcheted to a position close enough to eye Ledger.

"Master Ledger, it...is...good...you."

"Rivet! What have they done to you? What have *I* done to you?"

"Hey!" shouted one of the mining bot chiefs responsible for silo operation. "Keep away from my bots. I'm prepping them for another mining run."

"Not this one. He belongs to me, and I've terminated his lease with the *Hammershot*."

The bot chief sneered. "Show me the termination consent."

Ledger swiped on his com band and displayed the hovering graphic of the official termination consent that Fraun had sent to him. After a quick look, the bot chief scoffed.

"Fine. There's not much left of it anyway. Ever since the accident at Orixia and the damage we took, it's been getting worse and worse. I doubt it would have made it back from this run. Get it out of here!"

Ledger positioned himself so he could look straight into Rivet's eyes. "I'm so sorry, Rivet, for everything. Can you walk?"

"Ye...ye...ye...yes."

But as Rivet tried to rise up, he faltered. Ledger and Arn each took a side of the android and helped to keep him upright.

With great effort, Ledger, Arn, and Zara were able to transport Rivet to the nearest bot repair shop. After a complete evaluation, the bot tech approached Ledger.

"Where did you get this bot?"

"It's a long story. Can you fix him?" Ledger asked hopefully.

The man scratched his chin through a scruffy beard. He slowly shook his head.

"I've never seen one like this. I may be able to fix some of his mobility joints, but his processing unit, memory modules, and analytic architecture are...well, let's just say they're not of this planet. Shucks, they're not even of this sector of the galaxy."

Zara and Arn exchanged surprised looks with each other and then with Ledger.

"I told you he was unique."

"I'm afraid I could do more damage than good if I start replacing components that aren't compatible, but it's up to you," the bot tech continued. "Whether it functions properly or not when I'm done, I still gotta charge you."

"Thanks, but no thanks. I can't risk further damage. Do you know any other bot tech that can help?"

The man frowned and shook his head.

"B...B...B...Brastryk...stryk...stryk."

"His speech is deteriorating," Zara said. "I can't even understand him."

Ledger went to Rivet. "Brae Stryker?"

Rivet closed his eyes, then opened them slowly, almost as if he were too tired to attempt speaking her name again.

Ledger took a deep breath.

"Brae Stryker. Who's that?" Zara asked.

"Every Jeshuan knows who Brae Stryker is," Arn said.

Ledger turned to face Zara. "She's my former enemy." Ledger pursed his lips. "And my mother."

Zara's brow lifted in surprise.

It took significant effort to transport Rivet to the standard passenger transport terminal at the Abaria spaceport. Ledger carefully loaded him into the bot cargo hold and had him initiate a power-down. Inside the terminal, Ledger, Zara, and Arn found an eatery to occupy their time while they waited to board their transport. It gave Zara an opportunity to find a Rim Syndicate depository station to make arrangements for her finances before leaving the planet. While she was away, Ledger figured it would be a good time to fill Arn in on the unique arrangement that Captain Rosco had instigated. When he finished, Arn sat quietly, staring at Ledger with a look of thoughtful contemplation. After a few seconds, Arn leaned back and crossed his arms.

"Bonded. Does she know what that means?"

"Not at all," Ledger replied, taking a sip of water.

Arn tilted his head to the left. "I knew that's where you'd end up, but I figured it would be two or three years, not thirty minutes."

"What do you mean, 'you knew'?"

Arn grinned. "It was obvious from the beginning there was an energy between the two of you. And when she thought you were killed...I watched her mourn you for months." Arn leaned forward. "She loves you, pal."

Ledger sputtered on the gulp of water he was drinking. "That's not even likely. She hardly acknowledges me as a friend."

Arn wasn't dissuaded. "She can say what she says, and you can think what you want, but even Rosco could see it. That's why he did it, Ledger."

Ledger sat stunned by Arn's comments. He hadn't even come to his own conclusions regarding how he felt about Zara. He shook his head.

"How's that possible? Neither she nor I have sorted out or expressed any feelings toward each other."

Arn nodded toward the entrance where Zara crossed the threshold, coming toward them. They stood up, and Arn placed a hand on Ledger's shoulder.

"Well, I'd say you don't have much choice in the matter. Your bonded is coming this way."

When Zara arrived, she crossed her arms as her left eyebrow lifted, scrutinizing the two of them.

"I see," she said. "So, he knows?"

Ledger grimaced with a smile in the affirmative.

"If we're going to pull this ruse off back on your planet, you're going to have to help me understand how two that are bonded act toward one another."

Arn glanced from Zara to Ledger then back to Zara. "There is no ruse, my dear. Under the eyes of Sovereign Ell Yon, you two are bonded until death. But don't worry, you'll figure out how to act soon enough."

Arn left the two of them standing next to each other. Ledger felt Zara's glare. He looked over at her.

"I'm sorry. I'm still trying to sort this out too," he admitted.

"I feel sorry for you," she replied.

"Why's that?"

Zara hesitated. "Because I'm getting the impression that this bonding thing is much more serious than either Rosco or I realized, and now you're stuck with a girl who's cold, unlikable, and unable to change."

Ledger smiled broadly. "You are many things, Zara, but cold and unlikable are not among them."

"Well, I disagree with Arn," Zara said, lifting her chin in defiance. "Either you're going to have to lie to your people back home and tell them we're not bonded, or we're going to have to pretend in some fashion that we are."

"In my experience observing bonded men and women, those who are the happiest are the ones that appear to be good friends," Ledger said with a smile. "How about we start with that?"

"As I told you before, that's another thing for which you will find me completely unqualified," Zara replied.

"And why is that?" Ledger asked.

Zara looked deeply into Ledger's eyes. "Because I don't trust people. They will always fail you."

"I see. Well, I will endeavor with every fiber in my being to earn your trust, and we'll work on our friendship together. In the meantime," Ledger said, holding out his hand. "Give me your hand."

Zara glanced about the bustling eatery, hesitating. Ledger leaned close to her ear. "We're no longer miners for the *Hammershot,* and you're not my boss anymore. Remember, we're just practicing our pretend bonding. Occasionally, two that are bonded hold hands. I think we should practice at least once."

Zara's eyes softened, then she placed her hand in his. Ledger looked at her. "Not so terrible, is it?"

Zara looked down at her hand, her fingers entwined with his. She seemed lost in a thought as she gazed up at him. "Wherever it is that you've been these past four months, it's changed you."

"How so?" Ledger asked.

"Before, there was darkness about you. You were lost. But now...," she said, her eyes narrowing as she seemed to peer into his soul. "Now you seem filled with purpose...and light."

"You are keenly perceptive, Zara. It is Jeshu, Son of Sovereign Ell Yon, who has made me a new creation. In his presence, darkness flees, forgiveness is given, and purpose is formed."

Zara's gaze lingered for a moment, then Ledger felt her fingers tighten their grip on his hand.

"Let's go, shall we?" Ledger said.

Not knowing if managing Rivet in his condition would be problematic, Ledger, Zara, and Arn arrived at the Bria spaceport two hours earlier than usual. They settled into a row of seats in the terminal to await their transport's boarding time. After a few minutes of waiting, a young couple with two girls took up the seats right across from them.

Ledger watched as they carefully guided the younger of the two girls to her chair, but it was obvious something was seriously wrong with her. She looked to be about ten years old, and her sister a couple of years older. Once seated, the younger sister began to rock back and forth in her chair as the rest of the family placed their bags and took seats around her. Ledger's heart filled with compassion as he watched the sweet face of the girl contort into flashes of agonizing pain. She lifted both hands to her head, her rocking increasing with each passing moment. Soon the girl began to moan, and her parents exchanged painful looks of sympathy.

The father noticed that Ledger was watching them as the mother scrambled to find a bottle of medicine. While the mother struggled with her search, the girl's moans became louder. A man standing nearby glowered at the family, clearly distracted by the noise as he was trying to concentrate on the glass tablet he was reading. After a few more seconds of fruitless searching by the mother, the little girl moaned even louder.

"Stop that incessant noise!" the man shouted.

This flustered the mother even more as she frantically searched through two different bags. When there was no resolution, the man took a couple of steps toward the family.

"This isn't the place to bring such invalids!" the man threatened.

Ledger could see Zara's eyes turn fierce. She made a move to stand, but Ledger placed a hand on her leg. She glared at him. When she was about to say something, Ledger leaned over to her.

"Don't worry. I'll take care of it," he said, standing to intercept the man.

Ledger positioned himself perfectly between the hostile man and the family, placing his right hand on the man's shoulder.

"You will take a seat and not speak another word for the rest of the day," Ledger said as he guided the man back to his chair.

The fellow's eyes ignited with fury, but oddly he complied without the slightest effort made by Ledger. The man opened his mouth to speak, but nothing came out. The fury in his eyes turned to surprise, then shock as he sat down in the chair. Ledger leaned over to the man, his hand still firmly gripping his shoulder. "Be still," Ledger whispered in the man's ear, and he became as motionless as a stone. Ledger then stood and turned back to the family.

"We're sorry," the father said, glancing about to see if his daughter was distracting others. "We have some medicine that should quiet her."

"It's alright," Ledger assured as his Protector whispered to his mind. Ledger hesitated. He had never been guided by a Protector in this manner before, but the prompting that had come clearly to his mind had not originated from his own thoughts. These new thoughts were holy...tender...powerful. Ledger yielded to the Protector as he approached the little girl.

Zara stood from her seat, glancing from the frozen man to Ledger and to the girl, wonder in her eyes.

Ledger knelt before the girl just as the mother was about to administer the medicine she had found. He looked at the father. "What's her name?"

"Tia," the mother said, hesitating as the girl seemed to calm slightly in Ledger's presence.

Ledger reached for the girl's knee. "May I?" he asked, looking to the mother.

The mother bit her lips, nodding. Ledger imagined that most people had shied away from them because of the girl's condition. He placed a gentle hand on the girl's knee.

"Hi, Tia," Ledger said softly.

The moment his hand touched her knee, the girl froze and her moaning stopped, as did her rocking motion. The mother and the father exchanged looks of surprise. The girl lowered her hands to feel for Ledger's hand. Nearly imperceptible thin wisps of blue energy shimmied up and down along the Protector on Ledger's forearm.

"She has an aggressive and inoperable fibrous brain tumor that has caused her to go blind and lose her speech," the father said with a quavering voice. "We've spent all of our money trying to find a treatment. Our last hope is with a doctor on Barook III."

The mother was still holding the medicine, waiting for another episode to grip the little girl. The older sister had left her seat to come and stand beside Ledger, clearly amazed at the calm that her little sister was experiencing.

Ledger also became aware that Zara and Arn had vacated their seats and were standing near him.

Ledger reached out his left hand to hold the girl's right hand. She blinked many times as if trying to see more clearly what stranger had come so close to her.

"Tia, Sovereign Ell Yon loves you. I'm sorry you've had to feel such pain," Ledger hesitated with his next words, for they were not his own. "But today it will end."

The words paralyzed Ledger's onlookers. He gently lifted his right hand to Tia's head. Her little hand clung to the back of Ledger's, her fingers feeling the smooth leading edge of his Protector. As soon as Ledger's hand touched the side of Tia's face, the Protector began to glow with Immortal power—the power of Sovereign Ell Yon. Both parents gasped as their little girl's face began to glow with an expression of pure joy. Five beautiful, powerful seconds lingered until at last the Protector became still. Tia's eyes closed as she pressed the left side of her face into Ledger's hand. When she opened her eyes, life had replaced death, hope had replaced sorrow, and sight had replaced blindness. She jumped out of her chair toward Ledger, wrapping her arms around his neck. Ledger embraced the girl with a deep compassion that he had never felt before.

"Thank you, sir!" Tia exclaimed.

Both parents and the girl's sister gasped in astonishment at hearing Tia's voice.

Tia released her embrace around Ledger, spinning about to welcome the exuberant hugs of her family.

"The pain is gone, and I can see, mommy!" she exclaimed. "The man has cured me!"

Ledger stood up, backing away to allow the joy of the family to fill the moment. Arn grabbed his arm.

"Ledger, Ell Yon is most certainly with you," Arn said.

Ledger glanced toward Zara. She stood frozen in place, her eyes fixed on the little girl who was dancing about and hugging her sister. The ruckus from the jubilant family began to draw the attention of many of the nearby people. Tia's father and mother began sharing what had happened, often pointing in the direction of Ledger and his two friends. Zara turned toward Ledger, her eyes filled with wonder. She reached for his hand, holding it up so she could inspect his Protector.

"What magical thing is this?" she asked.

"There's no magic involved at all, Zara," Ledger said. "This is the work of Sovereign Ell Yon."

"Sir!" a woman shouted as she turned away from Tia and her family. She came to Ledger as quickly as she could, but the limp in her leg hindered her speed. "Please...I can't afford the procedure to fix my leg."

Two minutes later, Ledger's Protector had made the woman's leg whole again. With much exuberance, she darted from person to person in the terminal, spreading the news of her healing to all who would listen. Soon hundreds of people were gathering around Ledger, Arn, and Zara to see this wonder that had spread throughout the terminal. For an hour, Ledger healed all who came, for his Protector's power seemed inexhaustible. One of the terminal managers came to try to stop the uproar since the gathering had swelled to over a thousand onlookers, causing disruptions in their normal operation, but soon he too was enamored by what he was seeing. Before long, security personnel, transport crew members, and terminal managers had all joined the mass of people to see this unworldly power that was being wielded by a man they had never seen before.

"How is this possible?" one man asked. "Where did you get the power to do such things?"

"Tell them, Ledger," Arn said, his face beaming.

Ledger stood up on a chair so that all could see him.

"People of Bria, what you have seen here is not a trick or inspired by some strange magic. You have been a witness to the power of the Immortal Sovereign Ell Yon. The galaxy has been cursed by Deitum Prime, corrupting all that is good. But Sovereign Ell Yon provided a perfect Solution through His Son, Jeshu of Rayl. He came to offer hope and life to anyone who believes and is willing to follow him. He sacrificed himself, and his spilled blood initiated a cure from the perils of Deitum Prime. But Sovereign Ell Yon raised him up from the dead, and he is alive forevermore. I am a servant of Jeshu."

Ledger lifted his arm for all to see. "This is the Protector, the minister of all that Jeshu is and teaches. I am just a man. Jeshu is the Savior of the galaxy, the One you must know to be saved from the clutches of Deitum Prime and its deadly consequences. Turn away from the evil Lord Dracus and his Deitum Prime, be sorrowful, and come to the Immortal One who can save your souls!"

"How, sir? How do we do this marvelous thing you speak of?" a man called out. "I want to know him! I want to know Jeshu!" the man said, falling to his knees.

Ledger came close to the man, seeing his repentant heart. The Protector whispered once more. Placing his left hand over his Protector, Ledger lifted a replica upward, and the crowd gasped in shock. He placed it on the arm of the man whose eyes lit up, and the revelation within his mind soon became evident to all. He stood with arms stretched upward to the stars and his face glowing with joy as he proclaimed his new life to the masses. The commotion within the Bria spaceport terminal continued to affect even the arriving and departing transports.

"This has gotten out of control," Arn said with a smile. "Our transport is scheduled to leave in 40 minutes."

"We'll reschedule," Ledger said. "Arrange to recover Rivet, and we'll leave tomorrow."

"What is happening?" Zara asked as she and Arn tried to manage all the people clamoring to reach Ledger.

"Jeshu is happening," Ledger replied.

Eventually, spaceport authorities that had neither heard nor witnessed what had happened came to shut down this outpouring of the Protector. Four hours from when Ledger first healed Tia, over 500 people had become Jeshuans.

"Gather together and encourage one another," Ledger called to them. "Sovereign Ell Yon is always near to you and will lead you. Tomorrow we'll meet to elect leaders and teach you more about your new lives as Jeshuans. Afterwards, I have to travel to Rayl, but I will return. Until then, you are the Creed Haven of Bria. Learn of Jeshu and share all that you have seen and heard today."

Despite the spaceport authorities' attempts to disperse the crowd, people continued to come and hear Ledger. Eventually, the authorities were successful, and all were dismissed. Only one stood before Ledger with a look of anticipation in her eyes.

"What I have seen here today," Zara began, "I have never seen before. This Jeshu you serve, I see how he's changed you and how he's changing hundreds of people here." She seemed to struggle to form her next words. "I want him too. Is he for me?"

Ledger guided Zara to sit beside him on a nearby bench. "Jeshu is for anyone throughout the galaxy who comes to him...and especially you, Zara."

Ledger lifted one more replica of his Protector and placed it on her arm. He never tired of seeing the elation that rose in one who became a follower of Jeshu through the power of the Protector. Zara's eyes illuminated with knowledge, understanding, and passion.

"Welcome to the world of Jeshu," Ledger said.

Zara closed her eyes. "Incredible," she whispered. Slowly she opened her eyes. "This changes everything."

Arn stepped up beside them. "Yes, it does, and this is just the beginning."

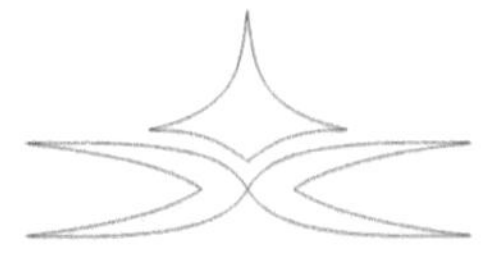

CHAPTER

11

Coming Home

Arn arranged for lodging for the three of them at a nearby temporary dwelling facility. Zara was full of questions and new feelings as she sorted out what it meant to be a Jeshuan. Their evening meal was lively and held enthusiastic retellings of the spaceport event.

That night as Zara lay on her bed in the quiet of her own room, so many thoughts swirled about her that she couldn't process them all. Her thoughts flitted from Jeshu, to healings, to leaving the *Hammershot,* and eventually to Ledger.

Zara's acceptance of Jeshu was something completely unexpected, but seeing what Ledger did at the Bria spaceport was undeniably the most profound set of events she had ever witnessed. There was, without a doubt, a power working through him that transcended human existence. As much as the stubborn part of her heart tried to deny and reject it, the evidence simply overwhelmed doubt. Seeing lives transformed was too consequential for Zara to deny. She was a logical and analytical girl, and in the end, she submitted to the truth. And when she did, something changed inside her that she couldn't deny or explain. However, her confusion about her growing friendship with Ledger didn't disappear. In fact, if anything, it magnified.

As much as she respected and admired Rosco and was forever in his debt for saving her life, she was genuinely angry with him. He had delivered her too closely to the flame that would burn her, and it had happened in a moment of weakness. Part of her heart deeply desired connection, but the emotional pain of severe loss she had experienced not once but twice had nearly ruined her. Ledger's return to life was impossible for her to emotionally process. Now she was destined to deal with this internal turmoil every day until some sort of resolution surfaced. But perhaps resolution would never come. Her carefully protected life had been derailed. Like a moth to a flame, the closer she allowed herself to be drawn to Ledger, the more fierce that pull became and the greater the potential pain. This inner turmoil amplified as she more deeply discovered who Ledger Starlore actually was. She kept searching for a reason not to be drawn to him, but it simply wasn't there. That horrendous lurking monster of pain was her only excuse.

Zara tossed and turned for over three hours as she wrestled with herself. She felt trapped between two versions of herself, and she didn't like it. One must win, but she had no idea which one that would be.

The following day, after meeting with a few of the men and women that seemed natural leaders for the new Creed Haven at Bria, Ledger, Zara, Arn, and Rivet departed Abaria to begin their journey back to Rayl. Between them, they struggled to manage the transportation and care of Rivet over the long journey, and Ledger remained greatly concerned for the android's condition. He only hoped that Brae Stryker would be able to help rebuild the bot.

Ledger could still feel the gentle touch of Brae's hand on his cheek that fateful night nearly one and a half years ago. Despite the tragedy he had wrought in their lives, he would never forget the compassion he saw in her eyes and felt in her touch. Even before he'd asked for it, forgiveness was in her loving gaze. *Is that the power of a mother?* he wondered. Such thoughts and emotions spawned strong feelings of belonging that he had never experienced as a child.

Along the journey, Zara asked every question she could about Jeshu and the Creed Havens. Ledger also began preparing Zara for their arrival on Rayl, sharing his entire past and filling her in on the intense political and military scenario that had propelled him to the Outer Rim planets. She listened intently, asking insightful questions with each chapter he revealed. Ledger was surprised at how easy it was to share the details of his scarred past with her. He was certain that his transformation as a true follower of Jeshu was a major contributing factor to his newfound transparency, but he also knew it had a lot to do with Zara. He delighted in conversing with her, and he was duly impressed by her willingness to engage in the drama of his life without shrinking back from it.

"Your world sounds as frightening as an asteroid belt with a high chaos factor," Zara said after hearing the explanation of the political nuances between the Keeper and Builder Orders and their associations with the Raylean prefect while being simultaneously occupied by the Morian Empire.

"I suppose you're right. And with characters as brutish as Lorak," Ledger added. He then realized that he needed to be careful about overwhelming Zara with her immersion into his world of turmoil. He paused for a moment, then turned to her. "Tell me, Zara, what is the most beautiful visual you've ever seen as a Scavenger pilot?"

Zara seemed lost in thought, and Ledger enjoyed just watching her think.

"I suppose I've gotten used to the incredible, being more wrapped up in getting the job done." She flashed a quick smile at Ledger. She seemed delighted to have something different to talk about. "But there was this trinary star system where every planet, moon, and asteroid were on some wild and unpredictable orbit. I could feel the chaos all around us, but in that chaos, there was such beauty."

Ledger watched as Zara's eyes sparkled from the visual memories filling her mind.

"We could hardly mine anything there," Zara continued. "But it was worth it just to see such cosmological grandeur."

After a few more seconds of tranced contemplation, Zara looked back at Ledger. "What about you?"

Over the next couple of days, many such conversations deepened Ledger's and Zara's budding friendship. Ledger discovered that he loved to hear Zara laugh, so he did his utmost to elicit laughter from her whenever he could.

After the first eight slipstream jumps, they arrived on the planet Corrigan in the Perlock System in order to change transports. This system had been outside of the realm of the Morian Empire, but not so now. In their descent from orbit, the ravages of war throughout the capital city filled the view out the port. Shattered buildings surrounded even the spaceport where they were about to land.

"What has happened here?" Arn asked.

"I don't know, but I wonder what this means for us," Ledger replied.

When they disembarked, Ledger and Arn could instantly sense that something had definitely changed since they had passed through this location on their way to the Outer Rim planets.

"Morian commandos are everywhere," Arn said quietly.

"What does that mean?" Zara asked.

"It means the Morian Empire has greatly expanded, conquering dozens more systems in the last year," Ledger explained. He looked at Zara. "I fear I may have taken you from one difficult place while delivering you to one of greater potential peril. The Morians are ruthless overlords."

Although their process to board the next transport was fraught with tense security screenings, they were able to continue on their journey without too much interruption. Three days from when they left Bria, their final transport landed at the Jalem spaceport. As they exited the ship, Ledger took a deep breath, feeling grateful, anxious, and sad. He scanned the city, remembering the words Jeshu had spoken regarding the fate of his beloved planet: *If only you had known the time of my appearance, destruction would have been spared you.*

"What is it?" Zara asked.

"There is so much to do and such little time. I see the galaxy so differently now. It's a bit overwhelming."

Before long, they had recovered Rivet and were traveling in a four-passenger speeder to the Naybus family estate.

"Going back will be difficult," Ledger said, staring out the glass canopy of the speeder as the world whizzed by.

"I get it," Arn said, placing a hand on Ledger's shoulder. "I'll be with you. *We'll* be with you," Arn offered, glancing toward Zara. "No one on Rayl knows you like we do, but soon they will."

Zara reached out and touched Ledger's arm, a rare and unusual response, but it certainly conveyed her solidarity.

Ledger became lost in thought, imagining a hundred different ways his meeting would go with those whom he had imprisoned and even tried to kill. He looked over at his friend. "There are two that I must meet first."

Arn nodded. "I know. I've already arranged it. We're to meet them at three o'clock tomorrow afternoon."

"I don't even know what I'll say. What *can* I say?" Ledger asked, emotions already threatening to ruin him.

"You're an honest man," Arn encouraged. "Just speak from your heart and let Sovereign Ell Yon do the rest."

Forty minutes later, they arrived at a beautiful estate nestled in the foothills of the Yazynan Mountains.

"Wow—you never told us you were rich!" Zara exclaimed.

"Our business in rare mineral mining has been in my family for generations. When the Morians invaded, they immediately realized the value of keeping the mine fully operational, so we've been afforded certain latitude as long as we meet their need for minerals."

As they exited the speeder, Ledger grabbed Arn's arm. "Do your parents know about me...I mean, who I was?"

"They're usually pretty consumed with trying to keep the Morians at bay and happy," Arn said. "I doubt they would recognize you, but I'll watch for anything. They're gracious people."

Arriving at the front portal, Arn, Ledger, and Zara were greeted enthusiastically by Arn's parents and his younger sister, Jemma.

"Brother!" Jemma shouted, being the first to throw her arms around Arn's neck and hug him with glee. "I feared you would never come back to us!" she said, finally releasing him. Jemma looked a couple of years younger than Arn. "When you're settled, I have some exciting news to share with you."

Arn smiled, "I can't wait to hear, little sister."

With glowing faces, Arn's parents took their turn welcoming their son home.

"Dad...Mom...Jemma, please meet my new friends, Ledger and Zara."

They exchanged brief pleasantries, after which Jemma enthusiastically shared news of her upcoming bonding to the love of her life. Arn grabbed his younger sister and gave her a long embrace. Ledger and Zara offered their congratulations as well. Soon after, the exhaustion of the journey pulled hard at Ledger and Zara, so they retreated to their rooms. Arn had given Ledger and Zara a room with an extra chamber.

"The bed is yours, Zara," Ledger said. "There's a futon in the other room I'll sleep on."

Zara nodded her appreciation, and before long they'd both settled into a deep slumber.

The next day, Ledger could hardly bear the rising anxiety as three o'clock approached. Ledger, Zara, Arn, and Rivet arrived at a remote country dwelling thirty miles south of Brohn. Arn went into the home first while Ledger and Zara waited at the speeder for a few minutes. Arn had agreed beforehand to prepare the occupants with news of Ledger's recent commitment to follow Jeshu.

After twenty minutes had passed, the time came for Ledger to make his appearance.

"Rivet, please wait here in the speeder. I'll come for you as soon as I do my best to make amends," Ledger explained.

"Under...under...understood, my...my..." Ledger put a hand on the bot's shoulder.

"It's okay, my friend. Be still." Ledger's heart still ached over the bot's condition.

As they stepped out of the speeder, Ledger found it difficult to move toward the dwelling. Zara came to stand by him.

"If Jeshu unites people that follow him, certainly a lost son coming home under any circumstance will be welcomed," Zara offered.

Ledger nodded, and they began a slow walk to the home. At the portal, Zara stood beside Ledger, waiting. She looked over at him, gently putting a hand on his back.

"I'll wait here for you," she offered.

Ledger closed his eyes, allowing her touch to strengthen him. A second later, the portal slid open to reveal Arn standing there. Ledger stepped through, offering one subtle nod to his friend as he passed by. Ledger took a deep breath, then entered the room to find a stately couple standing in the middle of a humble living space. Behind them, a large walk-through portal offered a splendid view of majestic white-capped mountains in the distance. But Ledger hardly noticed, for his eyes were fixated on the faces of Brae and Rhett Stryker, parents to their late son, Stone Stryker. Instantly, Ledger's body felt heavy. He forced his legs to continue onward, but already the deep well of raw emotions began to swell hard within him. The portal closed behind him as he approached, ever searching Brae's and Rhett's faces for some hint of their emotional condition. Stopping a couple of steps away, Ledger trembled deep in his soul. Images of Stone flashed through his mind—friend, confidante...brother. He imagined that the pain must have been magnified ten-fold for Brae and Rhett. It was too much. The corners of Ledger's lips slipped downward as he fell to his knees before them.

"Please forgive me!" he pleaded softly. Looking up into their eyes, his heart broke in two once more. "I would exchange my life for his if it were at all possible." Tears began to spill down his cheeks.

Brae Stryker's eyes also filled with tears as she stepped toward him. She carefully wrapped her arms around Ledger, embracing him. He closed his eyes, turning his head to gently rest against her abdomen and the womb that had formed him.

"My son, you are forgiven," Brae said quietly.

A strong hand fell on Ledger's shoulder.

"Welcome home," Rhett's voice quavered.

They entreated Ledger to stand and face them, and he did. He wiped his eyes, trying to get on top of his emotions and not allow the guilt to overwhelm and cripple him as it had done for months.

"Stone was the best friend I've ever had. He had the unique ability to make the people he loved better than they could be without him," Ledger said, nervously flashing a smile to help push through the things he wanted to tell Brae and Rhett.

Tears freely streamed down Brae's face, and Rhett's eyes too were red and moist.

"I am grieved to the heart for all the good I robbed from you and from all of Rayl because of Stone's death," Ledger said, examining his hands as if he could still see Stone's blood on them. "He was the best of us," Ledger whispered, tears still threatening to spill once more.

Brae took his hands, holding them tightly in hers. "We must be the good for Rayl that he once was. There is much to do for Jeshu."

Rhett once more placed a hand on Ledger's shoulder. "Stone would have it no other way than for us to take up his banner and push back the darkness of Dracus by bringing the light of Jeshu to all of Rayl."

Ledger looked up into each of their faces. He struggled to find the right words. "Your forgiveness means everything to me...thank you."

Brae pulled Ledger into another embrace, and this time, Rhett wrapped his arms around them both.

Ledger, Brae, and Rhett sat for an hour sharing memories of Stone and offering explanations where there were gaps in their understanding. With each passing moment, Ledger's shattered heart slowly began to heal in ways he couldn't believe possible. The ache of his soul was transformed into peace, his pain into joy, and his sorrow into gladness.

"There's someone I'd like you to meet," Ledger said as their parting grew close.

Ledger tapped on his com band, and after a moment, Zara entered the room. Ledger, Brae, and Rhett all stood to greet her.

"As you know, Arn has been such an anchor of friendship for me in my journey back home, but this is another friend who has become very important to me. Rhett and Brae Stryker, please meet Zara."

Zara smiled as she lifted her hand to accept Brae's. "I am pleased to meet you. I've been looking forward to this."

"Welcome, Zara," Brae said warmly.

"Where do you hail from?" Rhett asked as he took his turn shaking hands with Zara.

"I'm from Abaria, one of the Outer Rim planets," Zara returned.

"We welcome you to Rayl," Brae said with a smile. "Have you known each other long?"

"Zara and I—" Ledger began.

"—are bonded," Zara finished.

Ledger gawked at Zara, stunned that she would speak so boldly of their coerced arrangement. Brae's and Rhett's eyes lifted in surprise.

"Oh...well...congratulations," Brae offered, glancing up at Ledger.

"How long have you been bonded?" Rhett asked.

"Only just," Ledger said, glancing toward Rhett then back to Zara. She seemed to sense the awkwardness of the moment.

"Captain Rosco on the *Hammershot* performed the ceremony," she continued.

There was an embarrassing pause.

"I just thought you should know," Zara finished, her cheeks slightly flushed.

"Yes, of course," Brae said. "I'm glad you told us. And again, congratulations."

Ledger decided to change the subject. "Before we leave, there's one more offense that I am heavy of heart to share and must ask forgiveness for."

Brae and Rhett glanced at one another.

"Go on," Rhett said.

"Rivet," Ledger said. As soon as he spoke the words, Brae's countenance fell. "He's functional but severely damaged," Ledger confessed. "He insisted on coming with me on the mining vessel. I tried multiple times to dissuade him but—"

"Is he here?" Brae interrupted.

"In the speeder," Ledger replied.

Brae bolted out the front portal, leading the rest of them. Arn met them at the speeder where Rivet was leaning against the side of his seat.

"Oh, Rivet!" Brae exclaimed.

"La...la...lady Brae," Rivet replied.

"There was a critical accident on one of our mining runs, and the silos he was working on were severely damaged, along with many of the bots working on them," Zara explained.

"Can you help him?" Ledger asked as they worked to get Rivet out of the speeder.

Brae was already conducting a quick damage inspection of the android.

"I think so. Help me get him to our shop," Brae said.

Once Rivet was positioned on Brae's workbench, she became lost in her analysis of his damage.

"She's the best mechtech in the galaxy," Rhett said. "She'll fix him."

Ledger nodded then turned to Rhett. "May I have a word with you, sir?"

Zara glanced toward Arn. "We should see if Brae can use our help," she said, spinning off with Arn to assist Brae. Along the way, Arn received a holo message that he had to attend to, leaving Zara alone to help Brae with Rivet.

"Come," Rhett said, pointing for Ledger to follow him out of the shop.

It took Ledger a few paces before he had formed a beginning to this unusual conversation.

"We are in a peculiar situation," Ledger began.

Rhett looked over at Ledger. "Yes...like none I've ever heard of before."

They fell quiet as Rhett led them to a wooden fence that bordered their property. "This is my thinking fence," Rhett said with a slight grin. "The mountains give me something to fix my eyes on, and the fence holds me up so I can think."

Rhett took up his thinking position, putting a foot on the lower rail and his elbows on the top rail. Ledger followed suit. Shoulder to shoulder, Ledger instantly acknowledged the truth of Rhett's words. He took a breath of the crisp country air. Exhaling, he tried starting once more.

"I spent 23 years of my life thinking I was Ledger Kylos, son of Fasa Kylos. Then on the day Stone died, I discovered I was the son of Rhett and Brae Stryker—your son. In my confusion, I fled to the far side of the galaxy, trying to sort out who I was. That's where Jeshu met me."

Ledger glanced over to see Rhett looking at him with patient eyes. Rhett turned slightly to face him.

"My feelings about this are still a mess," Ledger confessed. "I know who I am as a follower of Jeshu, but I'm still trying to sort out who I am as your son and as a citizen of Rayl."

Rhett nodded. "Our feelings are a bit tangled too, Ledger. I think it's going to take some time to figure this out."

"Agreed. I don't understand why Jeshu chose me for what's to come, but during my training, he called me a Starlore," Ledger said, hoping Rhett would understand what he was getting at.

Rhett's gaze drifted to the beautiful white-capped mountains in the distance. "I'm honored by this conversation, Ledger." He turned to look Ledger straight in the eye. "I can't think of a better name to have, son. Bear it well."

Ledger breathed a sigh of relief. The last thing he wanted to do was start his relationship with Rhett by offending him.

Rhett stuck out his hand for Ledger to take, and Ledger's heart warmed. In his first real conversation with Rhett, he felt more fatherly love than he had in 23 years with Kylos. *Is this what it's supposed to feel like?* he wondered.

"Rhett, I don't understand...why would Jeshu call me a Starlore? That was his name, wasn't it?"

Rhett seemed lost in memories for a moment.

"Yes, Jeshu chose that name when he was just a boy."

Ledger shifted his feet. "I studied our early history that spoke often of the great Daeson Starlore, one of the first Navis, but he also mentioned a grandfather being a great star fighter pilot. I must be missing something. Can you help me?"

"You're right. You are missing something...a lot, actually. There are things you should know about your family history, and it's your mother who should tell you."

"Okay," Ledger replied.

"But let's give her time to put Rivet back together first," Rhett suggested.

"Sure...I can wait."

As a new follower of Jeshu, Zara had entered into a whole new existence, and it was thrilling, but the struggle within herself continued in the worst sort of ways. Her feelings regarding Ledger and their bonding contract were becoming extremely disorienting, and she was becoming more and more uneasy about it all.

Zara did her best to assist Brae as she began to work on Rivet, but clearly Brae Stryker's tech skills were so advanced that Zara essentially became a tool-bearing assistant. Every now and then, Brae attempted to start some nuanced conversation, but the work required to repair Rivet looked incredibly difficult, requiring all of Brae's attention. After some time had passed, Zara risked interrupting Brae's intense focus.

"Brae, may I ask you a question?"

"Of course," Brae said, her hands buried into Rivet's chest.

"I feel ill-prepared for the thing your people call bonded."

Brae instantly stopped working, turning to look at Zara. "I see," Brae replied, looking Zara full in the face.

"Could I visit with you in private when you have a few minutes?" Zara asked.

"Of course," Brae said, glancing toward Rivet. "The repairs I have to do on Rivet are rather time critical. Perhaps we could meet three days from now?"

"Yes," Zara replied. "I would be so grateful."

The ride back to Arn's home was quiet. It seemed as though each of them was preoccupied with thoughts of their own.

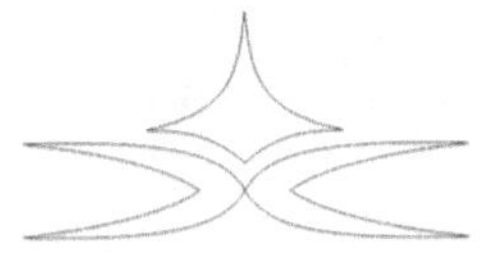

CHAPTER

12

Dissolving

When they arrived back at Arn's home a couple of hours later, Ledger came to Zara in their room.

"I was a little surprised you told them so hastily about us being bonded," Ledger said.

"Are we bonded or not?" she asked.

"We are, but—"

"Then don't you think it would be even more awkward to pretend we're not?"

A slight smirk flashed across Ledger's face. Zara turned away to place her coat in the closet.

"Fair enough, but I don't think you fully understand what being bonded means to our people," Ledger said.

Zara twisted about to face Ledger. "Then tell me. What does it mean to your people?" she asked, tilting her head slightly.

"Well, it means that a man and a woman have agreed to be committed to each other for life, to watch over and protect one another," he began.

Zara crossed her arms, nodding. "Mm-hmm. Just like we vowed."

Ledger ran his hand through his hair. "But it's more than that. They're committed to caring for each other. It's a vow that is deep and unbroken, made before Sovereign Ell Yon."

Zara continued to nod. "Go on. What else?"

Ledger's eyes darted everywhere except Zara's face as he rubbed the back of his neck. He finally stopped fidgeting and looked her right in the eye.

"They love each other," Ledger said, not shying away from her gaze.

"Love...that elusive, mysterious thing called love," Zara said, taking a step toward Ledger. "That's difficult to pretend, isn't it?" she asked, now just a few inches away from him. His stomach began to flutter. "I don't know what love is, Ledger, so I doubt I'll be convincing in that regard."

Ledger's gaze fell to every beautiful detail of Zara's face. He struggled within himself, not wanting to jeopardize their understanding.

"Are you messing with me, Pilot Lux? Trying to see if I'll stick to our agreement?"

Zara lifted an eyebrow, and Ledger couldn't decide what that meant. He decided to play it safe. "There are a lot of people to meet and there's some intense business ahead for us. Please don't make this harder than it needs to be."

Zara stepped back, exchanging her tender eyes for the serious look Ledger was used to.

"Now that I know a little more about what bonding means, I'll be better prepared for our next encounter with your people," she replied with her command voice.

Whether she was messing with Ledger or not, he felt messed up, and he didn't like it. Too much responsibility lay ahead of him to be distracted further. A chime alerted them to an approaching visitor, and they were interrupted by an invitation to the Naybus supper meal.

As they walked down to supper, Arn informed Ledger that the next meeting of the Jeshuan Council would be held in two weeks in Jalem. Together they decided that it would be best to wait to inform the leaders about Ledger's transformed life until he could present himself in person. Therefore, Arn simply let the Council know that he would be presenting some important information critical to the mission of the Jeshuans.

Arn's parents were gracious hosts and offered Ledger and Zara an invitation to continue to stay at their spacious home until things had settled down and they could find a place of their own. This gave Ledger the opportunity to make arrangements for one more significant plea for forgiveness.

"Who's next on your list?" Zara asked, sitting in a chair opposite Ledger in their room.

"A young woman named Ayla," Ledger replied. "She and Stone were close. This will be even more difficult since she has no reason whatsoever to believe me or to offer forgiveness."

Zara thought for a moment, then looked up at Ledger. "Were they bonded…Ayla and Stone?"

Ledger shook his head. "But I'm sure such a thing was in their near future." Ledger wrung his hands together as he thought of them. "He loved that girl, and from how he talked about her, she must be amazing and have keen discernment. She loved him too."

"I see," Zara replied.

It was Brae and Rhett who made the arrangements for Ledger and Ayla to meet. Three days later, Ledger and Zara arrived at the Stryker country home. Ledger shut down the engine to the speeder and sat still, trying to conjure up the courage once more to do what he needed to do. Zara sat quietly next to him.

"Hey…I saw you take out three Soren raiders. You've got this," Zara encouraged.

Ledger shook his head. "This will be harder. Will you come with me this time?"

"If you think that's best, I'll be with you," Zara replied. "Friends take care of each other, right?"

Ledger nodded. "Thanks."

When they arrived at Rhett and Brae's door, Rhett met them. He placed a hand on Ledger's shoulder.

"Be patient with her," Rhett advised before ushering them into the living room where Ayla sat beside Brae, her trembling hands folded.

Ledger and Zara sat down on a couch opposite them. Ledger glanced at Ayla, sorrow still etched deep in every aspect of her beautiful face. Her brow furrowed slightly at her first glimpse of Ledger.

"Ayla, this is Zara. She's a friend," Brae introduced.

Zara offered a faint smile, nodding her head. Ayla acknowledged Zara, then fixed her eyes back on Ledger. Brae motioned for Ledger to begin.

Ledger rubbed his hands together, being careful to look Ayla straight in the eye as much as he could muster.

"Thank you for allowing me a chance to speak with you," Ledger began, struggling to keep a steady voice. "I don't deserve your forgiveness, nor anyone's, for my crimes against you, Rhett and Brae, and thousands of Jeshuans are heinous. I'm sorry beyond what words can express. I was lied to and fashioned into a weapon to be used by Lord Dracus to persecute and kill Jeshuans, but now, by the power of Jeshu, I am renewed. He has given me understanding and a mission to fulfill for his name."

Ledger paused to fill his lungs and reset his shaky voice.

"Stone was the best part of my life, but please believe me when I tell you that the darkness that surrounded me then as a KDF agent is what I now fight against. I will spend every remaining minute of my life honoring Stone and his mission to serve Jeshu. I know I cannot repay my debt...only Jeshu can do that, and he did so when he died for me on the Ring. I belong to him," Ledger finished, pulling back the sleeve on his right arm to reveal his Protector.

Ayla's eyes were difficult to read as she absorbed the words Ledger had spoken. A painful silence saturated the room as everyone waited for Ayla to respond. She took a breath, exhaled, then glared at Ledger.

"I told Stone you were dangerous when I first met you. I warned him that very night," she said, barely more than a whisper. Her gaze dropped to her hands then back to Ledger, tears filling her eyes. "You robbed me of my future with the man I loved. Looking at you sitting across from me frightens me more than you will ever know," Ayla continued with a trembling voice. "The Protector you wear could be a clever fake. I fear that your apparent sincerity may be a ruse, and I fear what that will mean for all Jeshuans. You were dangerous then, but if by some nefarious scheme this is a deception to infiltrate the Creed Havens, you will be a thousand times more dangerous than when you were overtly working to kill us. I'm not as trusting as Stone was, nor will most other Jeshuans be."

Ayla's words cut Ledger to the heart as he watched her look to Brae and Rhett for some shred of proof that Ledger's confession and new heart were real. Ledger's head dropped low. When he lifted his eyes back to her, they brimmed with tears.

"Ayla, I don't deserve for you or any other Jeshuan on Rayl to trust me. The truth is, I have nothing to prove you wrong in your suspicions."

Zara scooted forward to the edge of the couch.

"Ayla, I've been a mining pilot on the Outer Rim planets for many years, and I've seen thousands of men come and go. In that world, you learn to discern the dark souls that pass through." Zara shook her head. "It's hard...nearly impossible for me to imagine Ledger to be the man you describe, but by his own mouth and by what I have seen since coming to Rayl, I believe it to be true," Zara offered, looking at Ayla with tender eyes of compassion. "I can testify that when he returned to me after having encountered Jeshu, his darkness had utterly vanished. I travelled across the galaxy because..." Zara paused, looking up at Ledger. "...because his good heart has drawn me here. For what it's worth, I don't believe this man is capable of the deception you fear."

Ayla bit her lip, her eyes focused on Zara. She then turned her gaze back to Ledger.

"I don't have the capacity to offer you forgiveness here and now...perhaps not ever. The truth is, I'm trying hard not to continue to hate you." Ayla hesitated, staring long at Ledger. "So I need to know...what do you plan to do?"

Ledger was a little surprised by the question. He took a minute to formulate his answer.

"Jeshu has given me a specific mission that will likely disrupt the status quo of our current vision for the Creed Havens." With that announcement, Ayla, Brae, and Rhett all looked concerned. "I am to take the message of hope given by Jeshu to all people throughout the galaxy. The time of the Outworlders as foretold by Ezias is here."

"How?" Brae asked.

"I can't do it without the support of the Jalem Creed Haven Council. So, to answer your question, Ayla, Arn Naybus is going to present me at the Jalem Creed Haven Council meeting in a few days. I must win their approval and support."

Ayla was quiet as she contemplated Ledger's answer to her question. Finally, she looked up at him with resolve in her eyes.

"Then I will go with you," Ayla insisted.

"But I thought you feared what I might be or do," Ledger said.

"That's true, but I learned from my father that the best way to defeat your fear is to face it. I must see with my own eyes whether or not you are truly a follower of Jeshu."

Ledger took a deep breath. "Very well. Arn will contact you with the details of our departure."

The meeting ended quietly and silently as Ayla stood and left Rhett and Brae's home without another word.

"Thank you for hosting this difficult meeting," Ledger said. "I don't expect Ayla to ever offer forgiveness to me, but I had to try. This was as difficult as I expected it to be, and there is still much more to come." He turned to Zara. "Thank you for your good words."

Zara nodded.

"Perhaps I can offer a bit of encouragement," Brae said. "There's someone who would like to see you."

Just then, a fully functional Rivet stepped through the rear portal and into the room.

"Master Ledger, it is good to see you."

"Rivet!" Ledger exclaimed, going to the android. He inspected the repair work that Brae had completed, unable to see a single fault. He then grabbed Rivet and hugged him. "Are you truly all right?" Ledger asked, stepping back to look at the android's flawless form once again.

"Lady Brae has fully restored me to my former functionality. Would you like me to demonstrate?" Rivet said, taking a defensive posture while raising his right hand in Ledger's direction. There was an audible energy buildup in Rivet's forearm.

"Whoa!" Ledger exclaimed, holding up his hands to protect himself as the entire room shrank back. "No, Rivet...stand down!"

Rivet held his position for a few seconds, then lowered his hand. "Unfortunately, I do not have a mouth that can smile, nor do I have the capacity to laugh. Consider us even for attempting to abandon me at the spaceport many months ago."

Ledger glared at Rivet, shocked. One glance toward Brae and Rhett told him that they too were stunned by what Rivet had just done. Zara walked up to Rivet with an ear-to-ear grin on her face. She leaned in close to Rivet, apparently trying to look into his electronic eyes. She then burst out laughing.

"I love this android!" Zara's mirth seemed to diffuse the tension in the room.

Ledger looked at Brae. "Humor…have you ever—?" he began but stopped when Brae shook her head.

"Rivet, are you sure you've been properly restored?" Brae asked.

Rivet looked at Brae. "Lady Brae, do not be concerned. I have been studying the human capacity to trick someone to create humor. Did I accomplish that?"

"That was a little too intense, Rivet," Ledger said. "Please don't do that again."

"As you wish," Rivet replied.

"Who does he serve?" Rhett asked.

Ledger and Brae exchanged glances. It was a fair question. He had been with Brae since her birth and then also with Ledger since his birth.

"I defer to you," Ledger offered.

"Why don't we ask Rivet?" Brae said. "I discovered that he has a special connection with Sovereign Ell Yon that we may never fully understand."

They all turned to look at Rivet. "Well, Rivet…who are you to serve?" Rhett asked.

Rivet walked to face Brae directly. "Lady Brae, it has been my honor to serve you during much of your life, but I am afraid that young Ledger Starlore will find himself in many precarious situations as he fulfills his mission to Jeshu. But more importantly, I like Ledger's choice of companion much more than I do yours," he finished, turning to look at Rhett.

After a second of silence, the entire room burst into uncontrollable laughter. After everyone had recovered, Ledger came to Brae.

"Are you sure he's the same?" he asked.

"I guess you're going to find out soon enough," Brae replied with a grin.

Ledger noticed that Rivet made it a point to seek Rhett out and speak with him.

"Rhett Stryker, I do hope you know that I hold you in the highest regard. Brae was my charge since her birth, and there is no other human on Rayl that I would rather have turned my charge over to than you. You have done well in protecting her. Thank you."

"You always surprise me, Rivet," Rhett replied. "I ask in return that you protect my son as your charge with just as much commitment."

Rivet bowed his head slightly. "I shall endeavor to do so, good sir."

"Zara and I have something we must attend to," Brae said as she nodded for Zara to follow her. "We'll return in a bit."

Brae led Zara on a walk through a large grove of trees at the edge of their property. It was a delightful place with low growing wildflowers decorating the pathway on each side and streams of sunlight dancing through the openings in the trees above.

"This place reminds me of my home as a little girl," Brae said, gazing longingly at the beauty of the natural surroundings. She glanced over at Zara. "You wanted to speak to me about being bonded," Brae started. "Is everything okay?"

Zara wasn't sure how to begin.

"On the Outer Rim planets, rarely does a man and a woman make a lifelong commitment to each other, at least not like it seems they do here on Rayl," Zara tried to explain. She felt a little flustered as she searched for the proper words.

"Ledger tried to explain it to me—what bonded meant to your people—but I'm still perplexed by it," Zara said as they stopped beneath a large sprawling tree.

"Our people hold the bonded relationship between a man and a woman in the highest regard," Brae explained. "We believe that Sovereign Ell Yon ordained the bonding ceremony many millennia ago. It's sacred to us. The two become one flesh...their souls are knit together."

Zara had never heard of such a thing on the Outer Rim planets. It sounded wonderful but frightening at the same time. "And you and Rhett have this kind of bonding relationship?"

Brae smiled. "We do."

Zara fidgeted, looking up to a limb where a squirrel was busy eating a nut. "Ledger and I don't have that."

"Why not?" Brae asked.

Zara struggled, not sure if Ledger would feel betrayed by where this conversation was going. "Life was extremely difficult for me from when I lost my parents to when Captain Rosco found me. At 12 years old, the Captain took me onto his ship and began to train me. He protected me, knowing that life on a mining ship could be perilous in many ways, especially to a young girl. He was kind to me, always watching out for me."

Zara stopped to look up at Brae. "I tell you this because it has always been Captain Rosco's goal to deliver me to a better place...with good people. When Ledger came along, Rosco immediately recognized what an honorable man he was. He had heard the story about Ledger taking on three vicious raiders to protect me. So when Ledger came to Rosco to ask if I could come with him back to Rayl—" Zara paused here, looking into Brae's eyes for some courage to continue. "Well, Rosco insisted that Ledger and I be bonded so that Ledger would be obligated to protect me."

"You two were forced to be bonded?" Brae asked.

"Coerced is a better word," Zara corrected. "Rosco knew this was my best chance at a better life, and so he demanded Ledger make an oath to Sovereign Ell Yon before he would let me go."

Brae encouraged Zara to resume their walk as Zara's story made its full impact.

Zara's head dropped. "It's not right...I know that. Especially after understanding what being bonded means to your people. Ledger shouldn't be bound by such a thing just out of an obligation to offer me protection."

Brae turned to search Zara's eyes. "Do you love each other?" she asked.

Zara bit her lip. "I've never known love, Brae. Ledger is the best friend I've ever had, but what is love? Since coming to Rayl, my heart and my mind have never been so misaligned."

"Oh dear..." Brae whispered.

"I know," Zara said. "I will not compel Ledger to be trapped in a commitment that was forced on him...one that was never intended or understood."

In that moment, Zara knew what must be done, even though her heart rebelled against it. "What I need to know is how two people can be released from a bonded relationship."

Brae's eyes opened wide as she stopped to look at Zara. "You want to dissolve the bonded relationship with Ledger?"

"We were never truly bonded to begin with," Zara said. "If Ledger doesn't love me, he will come to despise me, and I won't do that to him. Being coerced into a bonded relationship is cruel."

Brae stared at Zara for a long time.

Zara buried her head in her hands. "I'm so sorry," she muttered.

Brae put an arm around Zara. "You are one of the wisest and most mature young women I have ever met. There is a bonded dissolving decree that can be invoked under certain circumstances, and this would certainly qualify."

"I see," Zara said, raising her head.

"I would recommend you give this some time and think this completely through, Zara," Brae advised. "Neither bonding nor dissolving should be taken lightly. When you've come to a decision, let me know. I know a wise man who can help you through this."

Zara nodded. "Please don't say a word to anyone."

"Of course," Brae replied. "Shall we go back? I have a story I need to tell Ledger."

Zara smiled. "If it's okay, I think I'd like to stay a while. You've given me a lot to think on, and this seems like the perfect place for it."

Brae gave Zara a quick hug. "Come back when you're ready."

"Thank you," Zara whispered.

When Brae returned to their home without Zara, Ledger grew concerned. "Is she alright?" he asked.

"She asked to spend some time in the tree grove. It's my favorite place to think," Brae replied. "Rhett told me you have questions about your heritage," Brae began, leading them to their sitting room. Rivet joined them as they all took seats facing one another.

"Yes, Jeshu mentioned a grandfather, and it seems to me it could be useful if I knew about him."

Rhett looked at Ledger with a sly grin. "Prepare yourself. What you're about to hear will take the wind out of your chest."

Seems a little melodramatic coming from Rhett, Ledger thought.

Brae and Rhett exchanged looks. "What I'm about to share with you is hardly known outside of our family, and I think it's wise to keep it that way."

And mysterious, Ledger added.

Over the course of the next hour and a half, Brae regaled Ledger with the utterly profound story that ultimately explained how Daeson Starlore was Brae's father and therefore Ledger's grandfather. Each time Brae spoke of the instrumental role that an android played, Ledger couldn't help but glance over at Rivet. The story Brae told seemed so preposterous, yet Ledger's Protector affirmed every word of it as truth. Ledger's world began to open up in a way he had never imagined, but as it did, the pieces of his life seemed to fall in place, and his destiny became inevitable. The power of his history propelled him forward with unimaginable force. The Aurora Galaxy was waiting.

When Brae was finished, Zara entered the room and took a seat next to Ledger. Only then did he realize that he had been leaning forward on the edge of his seat the entire time. He finally relaxed, sitting back against the couch.

"Did I miss anything important?" Zara asked.

Ledger looked at her and smiled. "They were filling me in on my family history. I'll share some of it with you later."

Zara seemed okay with that.

A few days later in the evening after supper at Arn's home, Zara quietly disappeared. Ledger searched and found her standing alone on the deck outside their room, gazing at the beauty of the distant snow-peaked mountains. The air was crisp but not so cool as to be unpleasant. Ledger came to stand beside her, not sure if she was willing to have him invade her peaceful respite. Lately, Zara seemed more distant than usual, which troubled him.

"You doing okay?" he asked, glancing over at her.

She continued to look to the horizon for a moment, then lowered her head. She sighed. "Not really."

"Is it something I can help with?" Ledger asked, turning to face her.

Zara turned her head toward him, her eyes affirming his doubts. "This isn't right, Ledger," she began.

Ledger tilted his head, wondering which one of a thousand possibilities she was referring to.

"You and me," Zara continued. "This whole bonded situation isn't right, and we both know it."

Ledger swallowed hard—another difficult conversation. He decided to remain quiet and just listen, but inside it felt like pieces of him were starting to crumble.

"I spoke with Brae a few days ago. After seeing what she and Rhett have, it was clear to me that you were right...I didn't fully understand what being bonded meant. Where I come from, such a thing is rare and certainly not as defined as your people have established. I see the strength of it...the power of it." Zara looked deeply into Ledger's eyes. "That's not this," she said, waving a hand between them. "This was forced on both of us, and it's not right."

The sadness Ledger had seen in Zara's eyes now invaded his heart as something precious began to slip between his fingers.

"But Zara, we're friends...more than friends," Ledger began, searching for a way to express his feelings more explicitly than he had ever dared.

"Perhaps, but we're not bonded, are we? Not really."

Ledger took a deep breath as his gaze dropped to the floorboards of the deck. "No," he confessed.

"We must dissolve our bonded status," Zara said. "Brae explained that a dissolving decree can be performed that will release you from your obligation to be bonded to me."

Ledger wanted to reach for her, but she seemed so sure, and any feelings that he had hoped she might have for him were clearly absent.

"Zara, I promised Rosco—" he began.

Zara's eyes turned cold. "You were coerced into this, Ledger, and so was I. Answer me honestly. If Rosco hadn't forced you to be bonded to me, would we be bonded today?"

Ledger gazed into Zara's fierce beautiful eyes, his lips silent and still.

"That should tell you exactly why we must dissolve our bonded relationship. Tomorrow at Brae and Rhett's home, a Jeshuan officiant will meet with us to initiate the dissolving decree," Zara said with finality.

Ledger had no words to describe how broken...how shattered his heart felt as he came to realize how strong his silent but unreciprocated feelings for Zara had become. He gazed into her pale-blue eyes.

"What does this mean, Zara? Are you leaving Rayl?" Ledger asked, hoping that wasn't what she intended.

Zara paused. "No. My life as a follower of Jeshu is just beginning, and I have so much more to learn. I'm already hearing the Protector call me into service. This is where I must be for a time. And although we won't be bonded, I still want to join in the mission to take the hope of Jeshu to other worlds. Are you okay with that?"

The hurt inside Ledger eased slightly. He nodded. "I'm relieved to hear it. And I want you to know that whether we are bonded or not, I will watch out for you and protect you as though we are."

Zara's brows furrowed ever so slightly. She almost looked as though she were experiencing pain. But her eyes softened. She leaned in toward Ledger, placing her cheek against his.

"I believe you," she whispered into his ear, then kissed his cheek. She turned away and left Ledger on the deck, alone and profoundly confused.

Ledger reached up and touched the place where she had kissed him. His skin was still tingling from that one tender moment.

The next day, Ledger and Zara traveled to Brae and Rhett's home. When they arrived, Ledger landed the speeder and shut down the engine. As Zara started to exit the speeder, Ledger reached for her arm.

"Are you sure about this, Zara?" Ledger asked.

Zara paused, taking a second look into Ledger's eyes. "Is it right for two people to be bonded the way we were bonded?" she asked, searching his eyes.

Ledger hated that she asked that question. He could not deny that he had strong feelings for Zara—but strong enough to ask to be bonded? She was right, of course, but he hated what it meant. He felt foolish for how strong she was...how disciplined she was. Without offering a reply, Zara broke from her gaze with him and exited the speeder.

Brae and Rhett greeted them at the door and invited them into their sitting room, where a distinguished-looking man with streaks of silver and dark hair at his temples waited. As they entered, the man stood up to greet them, and Ledger experienced a vague sense of recognition.

"Ledger...Zara...this is Joshat Sephner," Brae introduced. "He was one of the few Keepers that stood against the execution of Jeshu."

Ledger then remembered seeing images of Sephner. Fasa Kylos had spoken disparagingly of him and two others, claiming that they had initiated dissent among the Keepers when they needed unity most of all.

Ledger reached to accept the man's hand. "I'm honored to meet you, sir."

"And I you, young Ledger," Sephner said warmly. "Rhett and Brae have shared some of your story with me." The man's eyes held a gleam of wisdom, and his voice was warm but confident. He turned to greet Zara. "And I am pleased to meet you too, Zara. Let's sit down."

Once seated, Sephner folded his hands in front of him.

"The first thing I want to say is that dissolving a bonded relationship is a grave consideration," Sephner began, his countenance growing solemn. "According to our mandates given from Sovereign Ell Yon, there are few circumstances under which this is allowed. Are you in contention with one another?"

Ledger looked over at Zara, wondering if perhaps she had shared something with Brae that he wasn't aware of. She looked back at him with the same concern written on her face.

"No," Zara exclaimed.

"Absolutely not," Ledger agreed.

"I see," Sephner said, looking a bit concerned. "I understand then that you were essentially coerced into a bonded relationship that neither of you wanted."

Ledger looked at Zara once again, but she kept her eyes on Sephner.

"More like neither of us expected," Ledger said, looking for some affirmation from Zara, but she kept staring ahead at Sephner.

"Neither I nor the officiant of the ceremony understood what bonding truly meant, at least not as defined by the Raylean people," Zara explained. "There was no expression of love."

Zara's last comment cut like a knife. Ledger looked to Sephner to see what his response would be. The gentleman lifted a hand to his close-cropped salt-and-pepper beard. His gaze switched from Zara to Ledger.

"If you are sure you want to move forward to dissolve this bonded relationship, there is a mandatory six-month abatement period that must be observed," Sephner said.

"What does that mean?" Zara asked.

"You will still be officially bonded, but it's recommended that you separate and live as though you are not bonded. The purpose of this six-month time span is to allow both the man and woman an opportunity to confirm that this is the right thing to do and is not simply an emotional reaction to a particular circumstance," Sephner explained.

Zara nodded. "I see."

"At the end of the six-month abatement period, if you are still convinced you want the bonded relationship to end, I will officially dissolve it." Sephner leaned forward to gain both Zara's and Ledger's attention. "I'm sympathetic to your situation. You both belong to Jeshu, and the voice of Ell Yon speaks to you through your Protectors. Be careful and listen closely."

Ledger looked over at Zara. She glanced his direction, then back to Sephner.

"Thank you, sir. I understand," Zara said, remaining pragmatic and formal to the end of the meeting. Brae and Rhett seemed sympathetic but supportive of their decision. Rhett offered to speak with Ledger, but Ledger realized he needed time to process before he could verbalize any of his emotions.

The ride back to Arn's estate was silent for over half of the way.

"Arn is your friend," Zara finally said, breaking the silence. "I'll find a place to stay."

"No, Zara. Rhett and Brae have offered me a room for a while. You stay at the Naybus estate."

"That's kind of you," Zara said, looking relieved. "I don't want this to affect our work for Jeshu," she said, her voice softening. "I have a lot to learn from you. Can we make that work?"

Ledger glanced over at this amazing woman, his heart aching in a way he couldn't explain. "Of course, Zara. This is just a return to normal, right? To before Rosco messed us all up."

"Yes...normal," Zara replied.

When they arrived back at the Naybus estate, Ledger landed the speeder.

"It's going to be hard going back to being just friends with you," Ledger said.

"Friends are all we ever were," Zara replied. "I think we'll handle it just fine."

Ledger didn't think there was anything left in his heart to break, but the finality of her comment extinguished the remaining embers in his heart.

So be it, he thought. *There's much work to be done. I must focus on that,* he told himself.

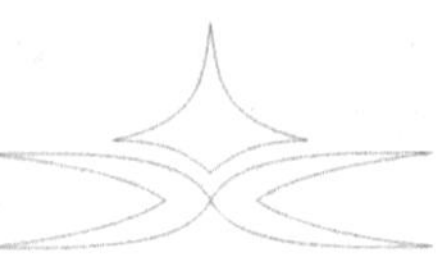

CHAPTER

13

Facing the Fire

"If only you had known the time of my appearance, destruction would have been spared you, but alas, you will not stand. Fleets of your enemies shall surround you and lay waste to the beauty of your cities." – Jeshu, Son of Ell Yon

The following week, Rhett piloted an eight-passenger transport carrying Ledger, Arn, Zara, Brae, Ayla, and Rivet to Jalem for the Creed Haven Council meeting. Ledger learned that it had been a few months since either Brae or Rhett had attended a Jalem Council meeting.

"How vicious have the Keeper Defense Force agents been in their attacks on the Creed Havens?" Ledger asked as they neared the meeting location on the eastern edge of Jalem.

"When you left, there was a brutish rash of raids, but in the last few months, they have all but stopped," Brae said.

"Why is that, do you suppose?" Zara asked.

"No one's quite sure," Rhett replied. "But the Morian commandos have more than taken up the slack with their own version of persecution. With each month that passes, we have to be more and more on our guard. They've already imposed a complete weapons ban on all Raylean citizens."

"That's disturbing news," Ledger said. "The KDF has limited resources, but the Morian Empire…that's another story."

It was a sobering possibility to consider, and Ledger's comment seemed to sit heavy on the entire group.

"Many of the original sectators of Jeshu should be at the meeting tonight," Arn said to lift the mood. Rhett and Brae both smiled.

"Jaym currently leads the Jalem Council," Brae added.

Ledger reached forward to touch Brae's shoulder. "Thank you for being here with me tonight."

Brae reached up and touched Ledger's hand. Having both Brae and Rhett stand up for Ledger would carry a lot of influence with the Council.

When they arrived, Arn recommended that Ledger stay incognito until the time of his announcement so that Arn could properly prepare the Council for what was sure to be an eventful evening. That was fairly easy to accomplish since citizens of Jalem often wore hoods or coverings to keep the Morians from identifying them too easily.

The hall that was hosting the meeting was large, with many alcoves and pillars affording ample opportunity for Ledger to remain in the shadows, unrecognized. Ledger was eager for his announcement to be done with since he knew the evening would be fraught with strong emotions from many people. With his hood covering in place, Ledger found the perfect secluded spot behind a large pillar, where he could watch the entire hall and its occupants without being discovered. The Council members greeted Brae and Rhett with great joy, as did many of the attending Jeshuans. Ledger noticed that Arn was also greeted with polite bows of respect and warm welcomes. Arn introduced Zara and Ayla to many of the attending Jeshuans, and although Rivet garnered some attention, the android sat stoically on the far right of the gallery closest to Ledger's hideout behind the pillar.

Minutes before the meeting began, the 12 appointed Council members gathered to sit at a large table in the front of the hall with all members seated facing the gallery section. The gallery seating was for esteemed guests or for any Jeshuan that had been vetted by someone of known loyalty. Three Jeshuan scitechs launched a dozen small security drones to search out the hall to confirm there were no surveillance devices. The scitechs evaluated their glass tablet displays as the drones scanned every inch of the hall. They signaled an "all clear" sign to the Council.

"This Creed Haven Council meeting is called to order," Jaym declared. His seasoned confidence made him a natural choice for this important position. "Before we begin, we have been asked to consider the words of the leader of an organization you are all familiar with. Although there is some risk in allowing this, considering the recent activity of the Morian Empire in regard to their diminishing tolerance of our efforts, we feel it is worth the risk."

From the back of the gallery, two men and a woman walked forward, their cloaks billowing in the wake of their strong strides. Ledger caught glimpses of blasters and talons on their belts. He instantly recognized their personae as those of warriors. They stopped before the Council table, offering a slight bow of their heads, then turned about to address the gallery where 200 prominent Jeshuans were seated. The leader stepped forward, lowering the hood from his head. The man was a solid veteran of combat.

"Fellow Rayleans, I am Cornellius, First Chief of the Partisans."

A wave of audible concern swept through the hall. The man let the rumble subside before continuing.

"We are here before you this night because the Morian Empire is continuing to aggressively remove our freedoms. The new Morian First Leader has been ruthless, and we have every reason to believe that it is his intention to utterly subjugate the entire planet of Rayl, ravaging our world of its resources and enslaving our people."

As the man talked, the intensity of his dialogue increased, rousing the people of the hall.

"For years the Partisans have stood boldly against this tyranny—against this heinous violation of our rights as Rayleans. We must unify to defeat this evil empire. You Jeshuans have a network of hundreds of thousands throughout the planet. Together we can fight them. Now is the time to rise up, for if we do not join together, we will not survive. There will be no tomorrow for Rayl!"

The impassioned words of Cornellius had a stirring effect on the Jeshuans. Many people in the gallery were nodding their approval of the man's proposal. Ledger couldn't deny the pull on the heart of every Raylean with any measure of national pride. As a man of combat himself, Cornellius's words beckoned to Ledger, but in his heart, he knew this was not the way of Jeshu.

Cries of allegiance began to ring out from many in the gallery. Jaym stood, trying to calm the hall. Arn left his seat to come stand by Ledger.

"This is not what I was expecting," Arn said quietly.

"We are not called to take up arms against the Morian Empire!" Jaym declared.

Cornellius turned about to glare at Jaym with a fierce countenance.

"You do not have the luxury of choosing pacifism!" Cornellius shouted. "The Morian Empire has chosen war *for* you. They will kill you—steal your children, ravage your lands. How can you say you will not fight against them?" Cornellius turned about to address the whole hall. "Do not betray your people...your world. Join us, and we will stand strong together!"

Brae and Rhett stood up and tried to address the people.

"Jaym is right!" Brae declared. "Our fight is not with the Morians. It's with Lord Dracus!"

This exchange ignited a tumultuous response from everyone in the hall. People began shouting at the Partisans, at Brae, at the Council, and at each other. Jaym attempted to regain control, but Cornellius and his two comrades continued to stir up the people. As Ledger watched, his Protector began to call him to action. He felt a strong sense that this would be a defining moment in the history of the Navis.

"This is not good," Arn said just as Ayla appeared at his side.

"What's happening, Arn?" she asked.

"It's time," Ledger said, moving to step out from behind the alcove.

Arn grabbed Ledger's arm. "What are you doing?" he asked, his face etched with concern.

"The Protector calls," Ledger replied as he walked on toward the three Partisans in front of the Council, his hood still in place. Arn and Ayla followed behind for a few steps, then stopped. Rivet stood up as Ledger passed him. The entire hall seemed to sense that something significant was happening as the cacophony of voices diminished to silence.

"Fellow Jeshuans," Ledger called out. "You must not be compelled by the passionate words of this man to take up arms against the Morian Empire. This is not the way of Jeshu!"

Ledger's words settled over everyone, momentarily diffusing the rising tension.

Cornellius fumed with rage. "Who is this coward that will not defend our brothers and sisters?"

Still twenty paces away from the Council table, Ledger removed his hood to reveal to all who he was. Cornellius's face transformed from anger to one of great alarm. He and the other two Partisans instantly drew their blasters as every person in the hall jumped out of their seats, including all 12 Navis at the Council table.

"What have you done?" Cornellius shouted to the Council while fixing his eyes on Ledger. "You've brought this butcher and betrayer into your hall."

"He's the leader of the KDF!" one of the other Partisans shouted.

"Not anymore!" Arn shouted from behind Ledger. "Fellow Jeshuans, this man has become a follower of Jeshu."

"He's responsible for killing hundreds of our people!" Cornellius shouted back. "He is in league with the Morian Empire!"

"Traitor!" one of Cornellius's comrades shouted, then squeezed the trigger on his blaster, intent on killing the one who had been an instrument of death and destruction on many fellow Rayleans.

Rivet jumped 15 feet to land in front of Ledger as Cornellius and his comrades released a volley of deadly plasma shots directly at Ledger. In perfect combat position, Rivet shot forth a protective energy shield as Arn threw himself against Ledger to push him out of the way of the deadly fire. Rivet's energy shield absorbed each shot fired…all except for the first. Five microseconds too late, one plasma round ripped past Rivet's head, through the space where Ledger had been standing, and exploded into Ayla's abdomen who was standing behind them all. Arn and Ledger crashed to the floor in front of the Council table. Once the Partisans could see that their blasters were ineffective against Rivet's shield, they ceased fire.

"You fools! You've betrayed us all!" Cornellius shouted.

A fourth Partisan burst into the hall from the main entrance. "Morian Commandos are coming!" he shouted. "We have to leave now!"

Chaos ensued as people shouted and scrambled in every direction. Rhett, Brae, and Zara rushed to Ayla as Ledger and Arn regained their feet.

"No!" Arn cried out, seeing the charred wound in Ayla's abdomen.

Members of the Council rushed to see Ayla's condition as others tried to calm the people.

Zara touched Ayla's neck, checking her pulse. "She's dead," she said solemnly.

"Why?" Jaym said, looking to Brae and Rhett for some explanation. "Why did you bring this killer to this place? Is he in league with the Morians?"

Ledger knelt down beside Ayla, his heart crushed once more by the consequences of his mere existence. He lifted her limp hand in his as tears brimmed his eyes. Sorrow seemed a constant companion to his heart now.

But then, the whisper came. Ledger looked up at Jaym's accusing glare and the cold, harsh stares of the other Council members. Without saying a word, he placed his hand on Ayla's abdomen, and his Protector illuminated with a radiance that filled the entire hall with the powerful blue flames of Sovereign Ell Yon. Every soul remaining in the hall hushed to silence as Immortal energy saturated the space. A few seconds later, the surge subsided, and a quiet calm fell on all. Ledger placed his hand behind Ayla's neck.

"Sister...rise up!"

At Ledger's words, Ayla opened her eyes, and the world beheld the full power of Sovereign Ell Yon through the one named Ledger Starlore. Every onlooker gasped.

Ayla's face filled with confusion as she looked up to all the faces staring at her.

"What happened?" she asked. Then her eyes widened. "The Partisans...is everyone all right?"

Ledger smiled. "Everyone's all right. Can you stand?" Ledger asked, lifting her to a sitting position.

"Yes, of course," she replied as Ledger guided her carefully.

"Jaym, the Morians are indeed coming from multiple directions," one of the scitechs reported. "Our sentinels indicate there's no escape from here."

"What of the Partisans?" Jaym asked.

"They were able to flee and join their squad. There's a firefight a few blocks from here," the man replied.

Everyone gave space as Ledger helped Ayla to her feet. He turned to face the members of the Council that had gathered about them.

"If ever you doubted the forgiving power of Jeshu, I stand before you as a testimony, for I am the greatest of offenders. Jeshu has redeemed me."

Jaym eyed Brae and Rhett.

"He's ours," Brae said. "Now a true follower of Jeshu."

"Clearly, the power of Ell Yon is with you," Jaym said, offering his hand to Ledger.

As Ledger took Jaym's hand, the eyes of all who remained in the hall fastened on the new Navi. Ledger turned to address them as the distant sound of combat echoed through the night and into the hall.

"My fellow Navis, we must understand that this attack is from Lord Dracus. Such battles are not won in this world but in the realm of the Ruah. Put on the armor of Jeshu and do battle with the forces of the Scourge, for the Morians are not your true enemy! We must take our battle to the true enemy of Jeshu. We need to commune with Sovereign Ell Yon."

"He's right," Jaym affirmed, bending to one knee and resting his left forearm there. He placed his right fist firmly on the ground. Everyone in the hall followed suit.

After assuring himself that Ayla was truly whole, Ledger guided Zara in how to commune since this was the first time she would fully awaken in the realm of the Ruah.

When she opened her eyes and rose up from her body, she stood amazed and bewildered at what she saw, as did every other Jeshuan who entered the Ruah at that moment. A full tactical forward operating base was set up in the hall with over 60 Malakian warriors giving and receiving orders as they prepared for a full-on, incoming Torian assault. The sound of plasma and laser fire echoed throughout the hall as explosions shook the ground beneath their feet.

"Here is where the true battle for humanity is fought," Ledger said as dozens of massive Malakian warriors moved toward them, ready to equip and brief the new arrivals.

Zara watched as one hundred new arrivals who had knelt down as unarmed Navis now rose up as warriors for Jeshu. Each of them began donning combat gear that the battle-seasoned Malakian warriors handed out.

"How can this be?" Zara asked, gawking at all she saw.

Ledger finished securing his body armor and weapons belt, then helped Zara with hers. She seemed taken with his daunting size and form when compared to her own. Ledger glanced toward Ayla to see what her reaction was to the intense atmosphere of the hall. She seemed confident and well-versed in equipping herself with her combat gear. They exchanged glances.

"You need to be careful here, Zara," Ledger warned. "Stay safe and observe only. You have no training, and this realm can be vicious."

Though clearly still overwhelmed by her abrupt introduction to the Ruah and this world of war, she eyed Ledger with narrow eyes.

"You know me better than that. I'm not one to stand in the background. Teach me."

Ledger glanced at the gathering leaders around the table where the Council had been sitting. "There's no time. You're an incredibly skilled pilot, but you have no combat training. Believe me, you'll be a warrior here sooner than later." A friendly smirk spread across his face. "And by the way, if you thought the Scavenger was awesome, wait until you fly the Starstreak!"

Ledger glanced over at Ayla, not knowing fully what her state or condition might be, having just been revived from the dead. "Will you stay with Zara and start her training?"

Ayla stepped up beside Ledger. "Your android is here, but we're going to need guards for our bodies anyway."

"I'd be grateful," Ledger returned. "Start with the Emuna shield and the plasma rifle. We can leave the introduction of the rest of her combat gear for a later time."

Ayla nodded. "Let's listen in on the brief first," she said, pointing to the Malakian and Navi leaders gathering around the Council table. Rivet walked toward them and took up a protective position over the communing Navi.

"If our warriors look like that," Zara said, nodding to the powerful Malakian combat warriors, "then what does the enemy look like?"

Ledger shook his head as he snapped a power module into his plasma rifle and charged the weapon.

Brae and Rhett approached Ledger in his full combat gear, scrutinizing him.

"Considering your form here in the Ruah, you clearly have combat experience," Rhett commented. "How much?"

"Enough," Ledger replied just as the leader of the Malakian forces stepped forward to address the Navis. The rest of his Malakian warriors continued to coordinate and communicate with their squads who were battling the Torian forces nearby. Four combat-ready warriors stood at the hall's portals, each protecting one of the entrances.

"I'm Major Tarsk. Torian forces are in the process of initiating a major assault by manipulating the Morians to take out your assembly," the major said as he positioned a sophisticated holo-puck in the center Council table. He activated the holo-puck, and a perfect three-dimensional representation of their sector of the city appeared with a montage of strategic data indicating Malakian and Torian force strength and positions. Each Navi gasped at the sight.

"I've never seen such a magnitude of Torian forces like this before," Brae murmured as she scanned the 3D display.

Ledger's visor filled with additional information as he and his enhanced combat suit assimilated all of the data. A quick analysis verified Brae's assessment—the Torians had indeed initiated a massive assault force, and they were advancing toward the hall. He located the Malakian tactical command center a mile north of their current position.

"The Torians are bolstered by the new Morian First Leader who is under the complete control of Dracus. The Scourge understand that this event tonight is a decisive moment for the future of the Creed Havens."

"Why, Major?" Jaym asked.

Major Tarsk glanced at Ledger then to Jaym. "Because after tonight the Creed Havens and your mission for Jeshu will never be the same. They're coming for him," Tarsk said, returning an expectant gaze to Ledger.

Everyone around the table fixed their eyes on Ledger. He was surrounded by dozens of seasoned Navi Ruah combat veterans, not to mention Malakian warriors with centuries of warfare experience. What could he possibly offer that they would care to hear?

Yet Jeshu had prepared him for this moment.

In his frail humanity, Ledger hesitated, but the Protector nudged him forward. He stepped out from the rest of the Navis to address the whole group. Ledger caught Brae's and Rhett's concerned looks. From their perspective, he was still a greenhorn in the world of Ruah warfare. However, he had the rare privilege of being trained by Jeshu himself, and his training had been intense. No one in the realm of humanity knew this yet, but soon they would see what those fierce battles with Torian warriors in the Outer Rim planets had taught him.

Brae watched as Ledger stood tall before the Council and the other gathered Navi comrades. The journey from Stone's death to this moment had cut deeply to her heart, and she knew that Rhett felt every bit of that pain as well...perhaps even more so. But the transformation in Ledger was indescribable, and because of it, her heart swelled with joy. It was in this moment, as she watched Ledger rise up to be a man of the Merchant, that Jeshu's cherished words came back to her.

Your joy will sustain you, and your sorrow will be the catalyst to save millions. Stay true and strong.

Sorrow had indeed come. *Is Ledger the catalyst to save millions?* she wondered. *Or will he add to the sorrow I have already endured?*

A new anxiety ignited within her bosom as her love for Ledger fully ripened. Ledger was her *son*. She glanced over at Rhett, seeing the pride of a father once more in his gaze. Could she be strong enough to watch another son endure the call of such Immortal extremes? She fastened her eyes back on Ledger as he rallied himself to speak.

"What I'm going to say will be difficult to hear, for we are on the precipice of a new calling as Navis for Jeshu. The people of Rayl have rejected Jeshu as the Son of Ell Yon."

His fellow Navis' eyes opened wide.

"You have all sensed this for some time, and if you listen closely to the Protector, you know it to be true. Jeshu didn't come here to save Rayleans only...he came to save the galaxy. I've been sent by Jeshu to initiate the age of the Outworlders. We belong to a kingdom bigger than our clans...bigger than Rayl. The kingdom of Sovereign Ell Yon is vast, reaching to the four corners of the galaxy. No longer are we Navis of Rayl—we must become Galactic Navis!"

Major Tarsk nodded. "Dracus is desperate to keep the truth of Jeshu contained to this planet so that he can use the Morian Empire to eradicate the Navis completely."

"If the Creed Havens spread to other planets, there will be an explosion of truth and hope into the galaxy that Dracus will never be able to contain," Ledger added, focusing on the holo tactical display before them. "Major, this is not a time to retreat and escape. This is a time to advance and conquer."

Major Tarsk's eyes narrowed. "I like the way you think, Starlore. What do you have in mind?"

Brae watched as Ledger manipulated the 3D holo display with speed and finesse, as if he had done so a hundred times. He zoomed into one section of the city that highlighted a concentration of Torian forces.

"The Torian tactical command center?" he asked, looking at Major Tarsk for confirmation. Tarsk nodded, eyeing Ledger closely.

Ledger continued. "It's time we stop defending and start attacking. The Torians are expecting us to fight just long enough and hard enough to make our escape in the realm of humanity. We will feign that as our goal, but instead we'll execute an assault on their tactical command and control center by assisting the Partisans in their fight against the Morians. This will hinder the Torians' ability to influence the Morians' true objective of taking out our Jeshuan assembly. With a hundred skilled

Navis assisting your Malakian squads, we have a good chance of turning the tables on them."

Tarsk eyed the display closely, evaluating Ledger's plan. "I don't think the Partisan conflict will be enough to draw the Torians' focus away from this hall."

Ledger zoomed the display out and then back in to focus on the location of the Partisan resistance effort. More Partisan squads were joining in the escalating battle.

"It will if the Torians know I'm there," Ledger said.

Brae's heart failed her. She felt Rhett's hand firmly grip her own.

Please, Ell Yon...not again! she pleaded.

Ledger scanned the warriors standing about the table, his gaze landing momentarily on Brae. Lines of worry etched across her brow. He discerned the angst in her eyes but couldn't fully understand why. Raised without a mother and with a false father, such concern was foreign to him. Ledger's comment about using himself as bait seemed to stun the major and most of the other attending Navis as well. Tarsk opened his mouth to protest, but Ledger continued.

"This isn't about saving me—it's about saving this Creed Haven and all the leaders here so that our galactic mission survives. I must be the bait. Meanwhile, we will have two assault squads flank the Torian forces here and here." Ledger pointed to two positions in the projected display. "When all is in place, we'll attack the command and control center. If we're successful, we should have plenty of time to detour the Morian commandos from their search." Ledger nodded at Tarsk. "Do we have Starstreak support?"

The major frowned, rubbing his chin as he thought through Ledger's plan. "Yes. A squadron of Starstreaks are tasked to provide close air support at my call."

"Any orbital craft we need to be concerned about?" Rhett asked.

"Admiral Kalem has assured me that he can keep them at bay for the next two hours," Tarsk replied. The major took a deep breath and released it. "The plan is risky but a good one," he said, shifting his gaze from the 3D holo display to Ledger. He looked out over the attentive Navis. "Prepare yourselves. Colonel Graydox is one of the most ruthless Torian commanders I've encountered. His tactics are unorthodox, so be prepared for anything. We'll split into four squads and exit the hall's portals. If I call for retreat, fall back to this location, and we'll get as many of you out as we can."

"If we support the Partisans, even from within the Ruah, this will accelerate the demise of Rayl. The Morians will unleash everything they have on our planet," Brae said.

Ledger nodded, scanning the assembly. "By the words of the oracle, Micaba...it must be so."

In that moment, the burden of the call of Ell Yon sat heavy on the hearts of everyone in the room, including the Malakian warriors. Embracing the reality of the end of the Raylean homeworld was a bitter medicine to swallow. A heritage of generations was about to dissolve away from the pages of galactic history. Many other worlds had faded into obscurity, legacies lost forever. Would that be the outcome of the Raylean people too? Would it truly go that far? It was difficult to believe so.

Major Tarsk split the Navis into four groups, each under the command of one of the Malakian warriors. The four squads separated, taking up positions at one of the four hall portals. Ledger stayed back with Zara in front of the Council table where their physical bodies were gathered together in communing positions.

Ledger faced Zara, her eyes laced with apprehension. "If things go sideways and it looks like we're going to lose this hall, return to your body. For now, just guard us," he said, motioning toward the communing forms waiting in the realm of humanity.

Zara grabbed his arm. "Ledger...where did you learn to fight in this realm?"

"On Orixia, from Jeshu." He put a hand on Zara's shoulder. "I'll be back."

Then the most peculiar thing happened. Rivet turned his head toward Ledger, almost as if he could see his represented body in the Ruah.

"I will stand by her, my liege," Rivet said.

"Rivet...you can see into the Ruah?" Ledger asked, taking a step toward the android.

Rivet cocked his head slightly. "I cannot see or hear all things, but I do have a sense as to what is happening there. I can tell you are concerned for Lady Zara. I will remain here with her."

Ledger stared at the bot, completely amazed once again. "Thank you, my metal friend," he said, then activated his surge anti-grav engine and took a fifty-foot jump across the room to land beside Rhett, Brae, Arn, and 18 other Navis, including three Council members along with a number of Malakian warriors. Major Tarsk was their squad leader. Ledger's headset beeped with the major's stern voice.

"Squad leaders...move out!"

Zara stood dumbfounded by what she was witnessing. Alternate dimensions, fierce warriors fighting for and against humanity, Immortal beings with powers and technology she hadn't dreamed existed—she had awakened to a new reality that was fierce and terrifying. And in the center of it all stood the man that had plucked her out of the corner of the galaxy to join him. What she had seen Ledger do at the Bria spaceport had opened her eyes to the unique man that Ledger had become, but now, even in this realm of brutal warfare, he seemed to be at the forefront of some great galactic significance.

The more Zara learned about Ledger, the more emotional turmoil she experienced. In just the few days since their meeting with Sephner and Ledger's subsequent move to Rhett and Brae's estate, she missed him. It was hard to be near him and even harder to be away from him, even though she knew dissolving their bond was the right thing to do.

If only he would quit being so...prodigious, she thought. *Surely there's nothing left to discover about him.*

"Wow!" Ayla's voice startled Zara from behind.

Zara turned to see Ayla gazing Ledger's way as they exited the south hall portal.

"Even the Malakians seem taken with him," Ayla said.

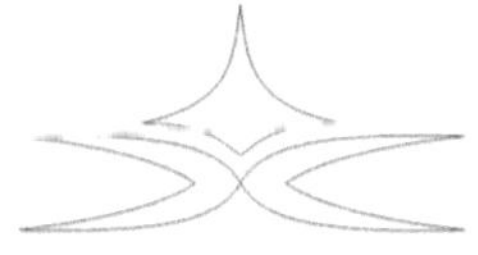

CHAPTER

14

Power Revealed

Ledger found himself in an awkward position. Introduced to the Jalem Creed Haven Council only minutes earlier, he was already burdened with expectations of leadership and performance. Though no one had seen him fight in the Ruah, his stature there and the deference shown by the Malakian warriors marked him as a Navi to be taken seriously. Despite this, Ledger chose to submit to the experience of the other Navis, especially Brae and Rhett, as simply another member of Major Tarsk's squad.

As soon as the group exited their hall portal, a world at war exploded around them. Fierce battles raged less than a mile away. Ledger had to admit that the intensity of conflict here exceeded that of any battle he had participated in while under Jeshu's training. Clearly, Rayl was the epicenter of the galactic Immortal battle.

Major Tarsk's squad included 10 Malakian warriors and 22 Navis. In the skies above them, dozens of Starstreaks and Torian fighters engaged in fierce air combat warfare. Before them, just two city blocks away, both realms raged with the vicious sights and sounds of ferocious combat. Overhead, a Torian troop transport descended under the guard of two fighters to resupply their forces. Major Tarsk positioned their squad for an entry into the conflict from the northeast. They were now close enough to see Partisans and Morian commandos exchanging rapid-fire plasma salvos while the Ruah battle grew many times more intense. Five minutes later, Ledger and the rest of his squad joined hundreds of Malakian warriors on the front line of the battle, paralleling the Partisan-Morian fight. Tarsk directed his squad to gather behind an abutment, just out of the Torian line of fire. Plasma bursts and laser fire flashed all around them.

"The strength of the Torian forces is one click west of here," Tarsk radioed, pointing at a projected display from the device on his forearm. "We have the fourth battalion there holding the line." Tarsk turned his head Ledger's way. "What's your plan to divert them here, Starlore?"

"First I need to meet with your commanding officer," Ledger said. "If we are to take out the Torian command center, we'll need our entire force on board."

Tarsk nodded. "This way."

The Malakian tactical command center could hardly be recognized as such, except for the battle-hardened colonel in the middle making snap decisions for hundreds of warriors spread across 17 city blocks.

"Colonel Ruger," Major Tarsk announced. "This is Navi Bravo squad."

Ruger turned to see the Navis with Tarsk. A crooked smile flashed across his lips when he noticed Brae and Rhett.

"Glad to have you join us, Navis," Ruger said. "We have a massive assault happening because of your Council gathering." Ruger eyed the group for a second. "Which one is he?"

"This is Ledger Starlore, Colonel," Tarsk said, nodding his way. "He's got something you should hear."

"Hmm," Colonel Ruger grunted, eyeing Ledger closely. "I made the mistake of underestimating a Starlore twenty years ago," he said, glancing at Brae. "I'll not do that again. Tell me what you have in mind."

"We need to take out the Torian command center," Ledger said boldly.

Ruger's eyebrows lifted in surprise. He ran his hand through his jet-black hair. "I heard that about you—bold for one so young. What do you have?"

Ledger took the next five minutes to explain his plan. When he was through, Ruger's eyes narrowed, hesitating. Ledger pulled the colonel aside before he asked certain questions that would make Ledger's intentions difficult. After a couple more minutes of private conversation, Colonel Ruger approved the plan. Rhett and Brae came to Ledger.

"We're not used to being kept in the dark. What's going on?" Rhett asked Ledger.

Ledger struggled with an answer.

"When I was training with Jeshu, he taught me that our influence in the Ruah can be greater than we ever believed. I can't explain everything right now, so I must ask you to trust me."

Rhett and Brae hesitated, glancing at each other, then nodded. Before long, Navi Bravo squad was pushing hard up to the battlefront. Major Tarsk led them to an intense part of the fight where a ferocious exchange of laser bursts and plasma fire streaked across the plaza in a relentless flow.

Ledger's moment had come. Deep inside his soul, an understanding formed that nothing would be the same after this. Fear gripped him in the worst of ways. A part of him wished he could be an obscure, ignorant man consumed with pursuing the simple pleasures of life back on one of the Outer Rim planets, but he knew that was not his destiny…it could never be his destiny after having tasted the purifying power of Sovereign Ell Yon and his quest to save humanity from darkness. But did he have the courage to step into his true destiny? His frail humanity pleaded for him to run, but the still, quiet whisper of Sovereign Ell Yon began to resonate inside his being like the power of a sun. Ledger took a deep breath and stepped forward.

Major Tarsk hesitated. "You sure about this?"

Ledger nodded, pointing to one of the buildings where the Torians appeared to be spearheading their assaults. "As soon as they focus on me, follow hard with everything you've got until I reach that building, then retreat."

Tarsk's eyes opened wide. Brae, Rhett, and most of the other Navis shook their heads.

"Ledger," Arn said, grabbing his arm. "This is suicide!"

Ledger's gaze was locked on his destination. Visions of billions of souls destroyed by the work of Dracus filled his mind…worlds lost…children abused…death robbing life. The mind of Ell Yon consumed him. Without a word, Ledger stepped forward and into the battle zone between Immortal forces.

Ledger charged headlong into the torrent of energy weapons illuminating the night sky. He sprinted and leapt the first 100 yards with little resistance. Then the fires of Gehenna unleashed on him. Over the com link, Ledger heard Major Tarsk's command to engage as he deflected, dodged, and evaded what seemed an impossible onslaught of firepower. His Emuna shield ratcheted to zero percent with too little time to recharge between assaults, so he was left to submit completely to the promptings of his Protector and his tactical combat suit's neural connection.

With perfect prediction, Ledger maneuvered in between each blast with the precision of a medtech surgeon. Some of the Torian forces were forced to focus on the Malakians and Navis charging behind him, which helped immensely, but the final 75 feet to the Torian command center facility threatened to be unbearable and impossible to survive. At one point, Ledger leapt into the air with his plasma rifle blasting multiple Torian warriors with extreme accuracy. Thirty feet up, his Protector unleashed an expanding energy burst that instantly obliterated multiple plasma cannon emplacements at once. This momentarily stunned the Torian forces, allowing him to land and make entrance into the building.

This would be the beginning of his end.

Inside the facility, Ledger stepped into a grand entrance where he eliminated multiple Torian warriors with such skill and speed that those remaining seemed hesitant to engage. Seconds later, Torian reinforcements arrived, sealing off the entrance through which he had come.

"I'm the one you're after...I surrender!" Ledger shouted from behind a large pillar.

Three more plasma bursts slammed into the pillar and the wall behind him, but then an eerie silence filled the space. Dust, smoke, and remnant fires billowed through the room. Ledger waited until he was certain they wouldn't fire on him, then he threw his plasma rifle to the ground and stepped out from behind his cover with his arms in the air. Within seconds, five massive Torian warriors fell on him. As the firefight continued outside, the warriors briskly ushered Ledger out the back portal of the facility and into a troop carrier under heavy escort. Ten minutes later, they delivered Ledger to a facility three blocks further behind enemy lines. Once inside, the Torian squad commander grabbed the back of Ledger's neck and shoved him hard. It was impossible for Ledger to catch himself with his hands fastened securely behind his back. He turned slightly to keep his face from smacking the ground first. His right shoulder took the brunt of the fall, and pain shot through his right side as he collided with the floor. Before he could reposition, a large steel combat boot smashed into his abdomen with the force of a hammer. He vomited from the pain, but that was only the beginning. A second boot hit him full in the face, ripping skin and breaking teeth. Two more blows and Ledger teetered on the edge of unconsciousness.

"Keep him conscious. The commander's going to want to see this," the company commander ordered.

Ledger rolled just enough to see through bloodied and blurred vision, a commanding Torian warrior glaring down at him. The warrior tapped on his com band.

"General Graydox, this is Colonel Mallock—we've got him. Yes sir, we have a Protector suppressor on him." Ledger couldn't understand the muffled response. "Yes, I understand."

The colonel nodded, and two massive warriors gruffly hoisted Ledger to his feet, only to throw him into a chair. Mallock grabbed Ledger by his hair, yanking his head back.

"The general wants to see this...if you survive the ten minutes it'll take for him to get here," Mallock sneered. He released Ledger, then turned to walk away as his two warriors took turns delivering blows into his stomach and face, breaking ribs and tearing more flesh. Ledger could hardly bear the pain, and it threatened to push him into the abyss of unconsciousness, but he forced himself to stay present. Despite his form in the Ruah being translated, his five senses were heightened, adding to the excruciating pain of their torture.

"That's enough. Leave something for General Graydox," Colonel Mallock commanded.

The reprieve wasn't comforting. It only allowed millions of neurons time to transmit the magnitude of his damaged body to his brain, each one firing in urgency, begging him to make the pain stop. Muffled noises from the furious battle outside bled through the walls as warm blood trickled down both sides of his beaten face. Three minutes later, a large commanding warrior entered the facility with three more Torians in tow. The markings on the man's uniform identified him as one of Dracus's commanding officers. General Graydox walked up to Ledger, and as he did so, two of his warriors gruffly lifted Ledger to his feet. Graydox's gaze narrowed as he examined Ledger, a subtle scowl forming on his face.

"So this is the Navi I've heard about from the Outer Rim planets." Graydox eyed Ledger's right forearm, where his Protector was encased in a crisscrossed energy webbing. The general's eyes diverted back up to Ledger's face. "You Navis are hard to kill in the Ruah...much easier in your own realm." Graydox smirked. "Rest assured, we're about to kill the whole lot of you, but I'm going to enjoy watching you die in both realms."

Graydox hesitated, scrutinizing Ledger up and down as if trying to understand what was so important about this particular human. He scoffed.

"You don't seem any more worthy than the rest of them," Graydox said, drawing the vilest Talon weapon Ledger had ever seen. The edges of the freshly assembled metal composite blade gleamed in the murky light of the torture chamber.

Ledger turned his head to the side to spit blood out of his mouth so he could speak. "I'm not."

"Then no wonder this is so easy," Graydox replied with a condescending grin.

Ledger gathered enough strength for a final message. "Do you really think that Sovereign Ell Yon is so limited in his power that killing me will advantage your cause in even the smallest of ways?"

Graydox recoiled, ready to end Ledger, but Ledger smiled in return. "For an Immortal, you're not very bright."

Graydox turned red with rage. He came at Ledger, his free hand gripping Ledger's throat.

"I will cut your tongue out and dismember you piece by piece before I let you die," Graydox growled.

Ledger tried to talk, but his air was completely cut off. Graydox released his grip slightly. "Your insults will now turn to pleas for death."

"Colonel Ruger, are you ready?" Ledger said.

Graydox's face contorted in confusion.

"We're in position and ready, Navi Starlore," the colonel radioed through the micro QED transmitter placed in his ear.

"Now!" Ledger commanded.

Graydox's eyes opened wide. He swiftly backed away, gripping his Talon with both hands and lifting it high above him in preparation for a body-slicing death blow. Ledger closed his eyes as Graydox's Talon reached the pinnacle of its striking position.

Then Ledger opened his eyes at the final moment. "In the name of Jeshu...we're coming for you!" he declared.

Graydox swung, but before his Talon blade could reach Ledger's vulnerable body, something remarkable happened. Ledger initiated the self-dissolution technique Jeshu had taught him, forcing his Ruah body to dissolve away in an instant. Graydox's Talon sliced through the empty chair without restraint.

"NO!" Graydox screamed.

Zara paced back and forth between the Council table and their kneeling bodies, desperate to know more about the battle she heard happening outside the walls of the Navi hall. The radio chatter gave some insight, but it wasn't enough. Were her new friends okay? *Is Ledger okay?* Everything that came through the radio indicated that he was at the forefront of the most intense fighting. The demon of fear and deep emotional pain taunted her from her past, and she could hardly bear it. Somehow, she had to protect herself. But before she could stop it, memories of watching her parents die as a little girl flooded into her mind, gripping her heart once again with emotional trauma so deep and so severe that she physically recoiled.

"They're all good fighters," Ayla said, trying to calm Zara.

"You've never seen Ledger fight," Zara replied with a quaking voice. "What if he doesn't make it?"

"You're right, I've never seen him fight, but by the way that Malakian officer addressed him, I have to believe Ledger knows exactly what he's doing," Ayla returned. "Anyone who's trained with Jeshu incites fear into the hearts of the Scourge."

Zara wasn't convinced. She looked at the kneeling forms as she passed by them once more. That's when she saw Ledger's body move. She ran to him.

"Ledger!"

In the realm of humanity, Ledger collapsed from his kneeling position to all fours. He clutched his stomach with one hand as he rolled onto his side.

"Ledger!" Zara cried again as Ayla joined her, shock on her face.

"He can't hear you. Somehow, he's returned to his body without physically coming back."

Zara glanced at Ayla as a sudden terror filled her eyes.

"Unless they've killed him!"

All of Zara's pain fully ripened into another chapter of unbearable anguish. She watched helplessly as Ledger rolled onto his side, clutching his stomach. Shockingly, he was still breathing.

"We have to return and help him," Zara said, preparing to reunite with her own body.

"I'm...okay," Ledger groaned in the realm of humanity, apparently understanding what they might be thinking.

With Zara on one side and Ayla on his other, they stared as Ledger took deeper breaths, then determinedly regained his kneeling position. A final breath and exhale, and a moment later Ledger returned to the Ruah, rising up renewed and whole. With eyes closed, he slowly stood, gathering strength as he did so. He opened his eyes. Zara restrained herself from reaching for him. It was her first step toward protecting her heart.

"How?" Ayla asked, shaking her head. "It's impossible!"

"I don't have time to explain," Ledger said as a Malakian warrior carrying a combat bag and jetpack entered the hall through one of the portals.

"For you, Navi Starlore," the warrior said, then exited as fast as he entered.

Zara tried to find words as Ledger donned the new gear.

"Did they kill you?" Zara asked, trying not to sound overly anxious. After witnessing Ayla come back from the dead only a few moments ago, Zara no longer knew what was possible.

Ledger glanced her way just as he donned the helmet. "Not quite. And I have a lot more to do. Continue guarding our bodies. If all goes well, we should return within the next half hour."

Ledger positioned the jetpack on his back, and his suit seamlessly merged with the structure of the propulsion system. Zara and Ayla followed him to the nearest portal. He stepped through, then launched upward with the speed of a missile.

Zara turned to see Ayla looking up as Ledger disappeared into the night sky. She saw deep admiration in Ayla's eyes.

Zara's heart stumbled at the thought of Ledger rushing back into the throes of such intense battle...sacrificing himself to the brink of death. A flash of memory of seeing Ledger pulverized by a meteor filled her mind, and the deep pain of loss fully revived within her. Zara quietly resolved to reaffirm the decision she had made at twelve years old—love no one like she had loved her parents.

As soon as Ledger had positioned the jetpack, his suit instantly acknowledged its new functionality, displaying an entirely new set of data fields and graphics.

"Set coordinates for Bravo sector 3 Lima," Ledger commanded as his powerful jetpack rocketed him upward at dizzying speeds.

Instantly the coordinates displayed on his visor along with an enhanced and magnified graphical display of the location—the Torian Tactical Command Center. Ledger changed his trajectory to a low-level profile, taking a wide berth around the intensity of the front line of conflict between the Torians and Malakians battling below him. His display showed divisions of both Malakian and Navi forces pushing deep into Torian territory, pinching in on the Torian tactical command center. He smiled as he imagined General Graydox's expression after receiving communication that his command center was under attack.

The path now lay clear for Ledger to make a direct flight to the southern attacking division. The fighting had grown fiercest in that quadrant, so that was where he needed to be. He approached fast so that the Torians would have a difficult time locking onto his position with their class-3 plasma cannons. Dodging and maneuvering between energy bursts with incredible skill and finesse, Ledger made a brilliant landing just inside the Torian defense line. In a fraction of a second, he shed the jetpack and took out six Torian warriors with his rapid-fire blaster, eliminating a significant portion of the opposition to his Malakian force advancement.

MALAKIAN JETPACK

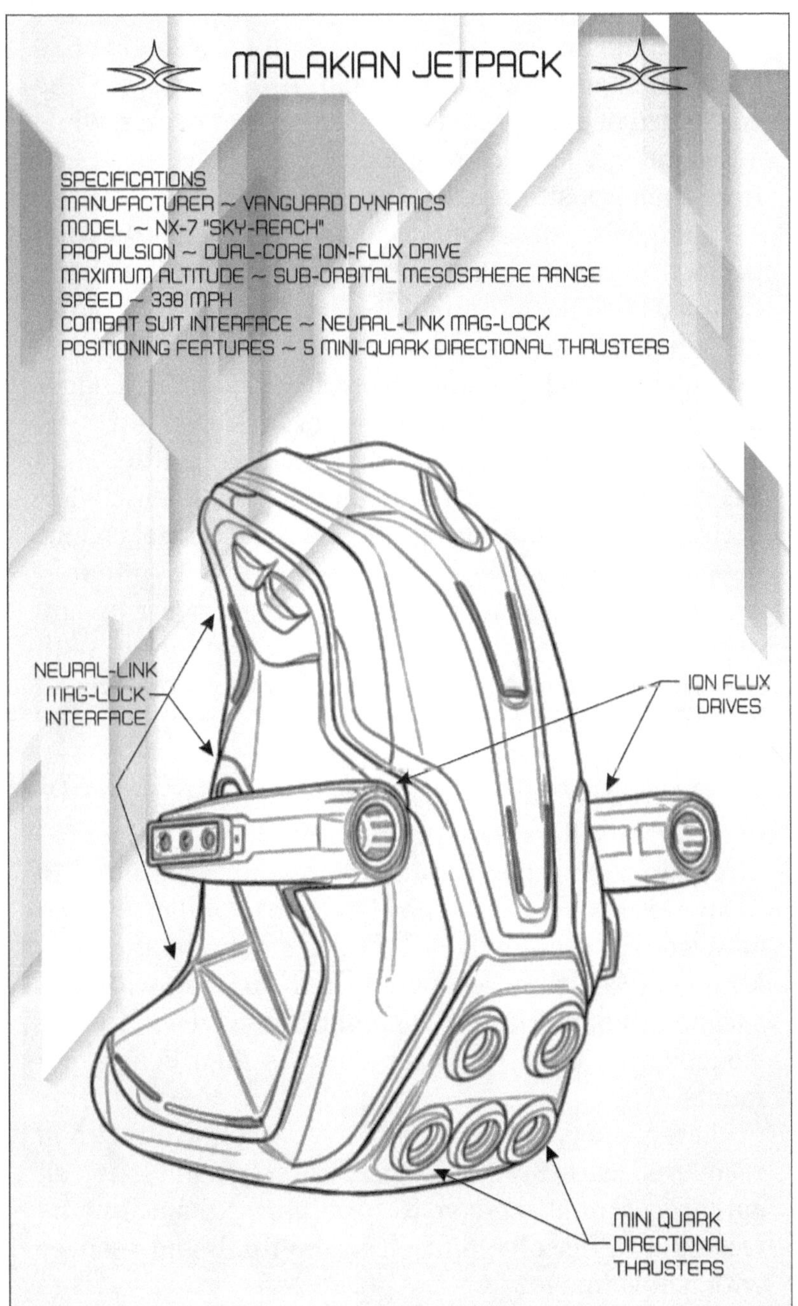

With the line breached, Ledger rallied a squad of 30 Malakians and Navis in a charge directly into the courtyard of the Torian tactical command center, while a second division of Malakians and Navis advanced from the opposite side.

Ledger's situational awareness was beyond perfection as his mind entered a combat flow-state. Coupled with the continual stream of tactical data from his tactical combat suit and second-by-second promptings and guidance from his Protector, Ledger dominated every single Torian warrior he encountered. It was magical to watch. Brae, Rhett, and the rest of the Navis also fought with fierce efficiency, their newfound courage ignited by the first real chance in years to overpower the Scourge. Within 15 minutes, the entire command center had been overrun and destroyed by the joint Malakian and Navi forces. With no command center, the Torians found themselves in utter disarray, scrambling to retreat and recover what remaining forces they had.

The forces of Ell Yon had won the day, a victory long overdue. Without Torian Immortal influences directing them, the Morian commandos continued to focus exclusively on the Partisan conflict, which allowed all the Navis to return safely to the hall. Minutes later, they recovered their human forms and escaped unharmed into the night, a new vision for the galactic mission of Jeshu set firmly in their hearts and minds.

Later, once Ledger, Arn, Zara, Ayla, and Rivet had recovered with Brae and Rhett to their home, they all gathered around Ledger to hear him explain how he was able to dissolve himself in the Ruah and recover with a new image.

"I remembered Jeshu saying that such a thing was possible, but that it was difficult to do," Rhett mused.

"If we and other Navis can learn it, it could change everything!" Brae added.

Ledger nodded. "It took me months to master. I'm not sure I can even teach anyone to do it, but I'm willing to try." He scanned the eager faces looking at him. "The truth is you have to be willing to die. There's a moment when it feels like you actually do."

Ledger's answer sobered the excitement among his fellow Navis.

"The next time we gather, I'll do my best to teach as many as are willing to try."

Admirals Yelrod and Kyrsa were summoned on board Dracus's flagship, *Apollyon*, to give a briefing on the progress of the Raylean Eradication objective.

"Another Starlore has arrived, my lord," Admiral Yelrod said. "The power he wields against our warriors is like nothing we've seen before. It rivals that of Ell Yon's son. He single-handedly destroyed Colonel Graydox's forces."

Dracus scowled as he considered Yelrod's words. He glared at Admiral Kyrsa.

"When will your Morian pawn be ready?" he asked.

"I'm still maneuvering assets under First Leader Eron," Kyrsa explained. "He's as ruthless as we need him to be, but because of such, he's proving more difficult than I expected. I'll have everything in place in eight months, my lord. We're strengthening the Partisans while simultaneously building the Morian Empire's fleet to world-crushing proportions. Soon we will decimate the planet."

Dracus's eyes narrowed, his jaw clenching in frustration. "Admiral Kyrsa, every day we delay, another Jeshuan slips out from under us. Accelerate your efforts, or this will be the last command you ever see."

Kyrsa swallowed hard. "Yes, my lord."

CHAPTER

15

Confessions of the Heart

Over the course of the next six months, Ledger and Arn worked tirelessly to organize and lead missions to neighboring worlds, sharing the truth of Jeshu with all who would listen. Oftentimes, Ayla and Zara joined in the work to establish new Creed Havens. Some of the Outworlders accepted their glad news with joyful hearts, but others rejected them with vehemence, even threatening violence at times. In between missions, Ledger attempted to train numerous Navis in the art of bodily dissolution in the Ruah, but it seemed that he alone had this unique ability, at least for now.

Ledger and Arn grew inseparable as co-laborers for Jeshu, coordinating with the Jalem Creed Haven Council for support to fund the mission to take Jeshu to the Outworlders. Rivet became indispensable to Ledger in fulfilling these missions. His uncanny ability to sense danger and protect them proved invaluable. He also helped organize logistics and resource support for the newly established Creed havens. Ledger came to trust the android implicitly.

During this time, Ledger and Zara carefully observed Sephner's direction to live as though they were not bonded. At first, Ledger struggled to see the point in such a thing, but as the months passed by, it became evident to him that such a practice was designed to manifest and magnify the true feelings of the heart. However, it also seemed to magnify his confusion regarding his relationship with Zara. Contrarily, Zara seemed to bear the burden of the abatement with stoic professionalism.

Being true to his promise, Ledger trained Zara in Ruah combat, which he discovered she had a tremendous aptitude for. He enjoyed thinking about the day he introduced her to the Starstreak. After her first mission, Zara couldn't stop smiling.

"That was the most thrilling experience I've ever had," Zara said as they returned to their communing bodies.

"Even better than dodging asteroids?" Ledger asked.

Zara looked over at him as they prepared to return to the realm of humanity, her grin as big as he'd ever seen. "Way better," she said with a gleam in her eye.

Seeing Zara this exuberant warmed Ledger's heart and weakened his resolve to honor the abatement. Once they'd returned from the Ruah, however, Zara's stoic persona returned, which in turn disheartened Ledger. For reasons he couldn't explain, he loved seeing Zara happy, and this abatement seemed to rob them both of any lasting joy.

On their missions, Ayla proved to be as remarkable a young woman as Stone had described her to be. Ledger was careful to give her space, knowing that she was still working through her feelings of resentment toward him for the great loss Ledger had caused. And yet he discovered a part of him that needed her friendship and her forgiveness. When she smiled or even occasionally laughed, Ledger discovered that his heart delighted in it. He found himself looking forward to time spent with her, and she seemed to reciprocate. A bond of true friendship slowly forged over the passing months.

The assaults by the KDF continued to diminish as the Morian Empire flexed its power over the people of Rayl with increasing intensity throughout each passing month. The newly appointed First Leader of the Morian Empire held no sympathy for the worlds he had conquered, especially Rayl. As the oppression intensified, the Partisans gained members and assets to strengthen their rebellion. The skirmishes between Morian commandos and Partisan combatants became more frequent and more intense. Raids by the Empire became a daily occurrence in every major city as they searched out Partisan strongholds. Sometimes the raids occurred without impunity on innocent Rayleans. As would be expected, tensions continued to rise between the occupying Morians and the Rayleans. Ledger and the rest of the Navi leaders wondered when a tipping point for the Morian Empire would occur and what that would ultimately mean for fellow Rayleans across the planet.

The dark cloud of the Morian Empire's presence hung over the Raylean people like a never-ending night, for the oppression continued to increase day by day. Rarely did they have anything to be hopeful about, but the bonding ceremony of Arn's younger sister, Jemma, and her chosen, Brayson Mern, was a sliver of joy worth celebrating. Arn's parents reserved the elaborate Zenith Lux Hall in the eastern district of Jalem. The celebration gave them all an opportunity to forget their woes for an evening and share in the joy of two young Rayleans joining lives.

With Jemma being Arn's only sister, his parents held nothing back to give her the bonding ceremony of her dreams—a ceremony that rivaled that of a royal ball. Ledger and Arn returned from their off-world mission three days in advance of the ceremony to ensure they could help with the final preparations.

"You seem rather morose," Arn observed as he and Ledger checked on the final arrangements for the venue. "Does it have anything to do with your approaching dissolving ceremony?" Arn pressed.

Ledger frowned, wondering why Arn would remember that the day he and Zara were supposed to end their official bonding status through a dissolving decree was the day after Jemma's bonding ceremony. Ledger didn't respond. His friend had become incredibly discerning—a useful trait when dealing with challenging or hurting people, but rather annoying when it came to himself.

As they entered Zenith Lux Hall, Ledger was taken with the splendor of the structure. The entrance level was a marbled court with a lofty glass ceiling and gold-rimmed rails that ran along each side of the hall. A grand staircase led down onto the ballroom floor that gleamed as the centerpiece of the luxurious and elegant building. Two exquisite, colossal chandeliers dominated the center of the ballroom, with smaller ornate chandeliers suspended beneath the balconies and lining either side. The entire hall blazed in white marble and gold trim. It was one of the most beautiful structures Ledger had ever laid eyes on. Being surrounded by such beauty only amplified the solemn state of Ledger's soul. He tried to shake it off and assist Arn in his duty to ensure all preparations for the venue were in place.

"The Partisans made a bold assault on one of the Morian command stations just outside of Jalem," Arn said as they finished their confirmations with the Hall administration office.

"Yes...I've heard," Ledger replied. "The Morians will respond with even more ferocity. I hope Jemma's bonding ceremony won't be affected."

Arn grimaced. "That would be most unfortunate."

Two days later, amidst a calm in the ensuing turmoil that much of Rayl was experiencing, Zenith Lux Hall was filled with the most well-known and prestigious Raylean officials on the planet, as well as hundreds of lesser-known friends of the Naybus family, including Ledger, Ayla, Brae, Rhett, and Zara. When Jemma appeared at the top of the stairway in her beautiful ceremonial gown, the entire audience smiled with delight, and the ceremony began. As the officiant recited the vows for Jemma and Brayson to repeat, Ledger stole a glance toward Zara. Their eyes met briefly in a moment of shared sorrow.

Once the bonding ceremony was complete, the celebration festivities began. Food was served, toasts were made, and music filled the hall as traditional Raylean dances began. Ledger mingled and chatted with dozens of men and women, but he intently searched the ballroom for one person in particular. A hand tapped his right shoulder, and when he turned around, there stood the stunning and beautiful Ayla.

"There you are," she said with a smile. "I've been looking for you."

"Really? What have I done now?" Ledger asked, returning the smile.

"Well, for starters, you haven't asked me to dance," Ayla said, pushing her auburn hair over her shoulder.

"I must remedy such an offense immediately. Ayla, may I have this dance?" Ledger held out his hand.

"I'd be delighted," Ayla said with a curtsey, taking his hand.

When they took the floor, Ledger led Ayla in a dance that allowed them to face one another for long enough periods of time to exchange a few words.

"You look beautiful this evening," Ledger said. He couldn't help thinking about Stone as he watched the smooth and rhythmic motions of this incredible young woman. Ayla was intelligent, driven, and full of passion for serving Jeshu. She deserved someone who would love her like Stone did.

"By the way," Ayla said, looking delightfully up at Ledger, but suddenly her countenance became still and serious. "I want you to know that I respect the work you are doing for Jeshu and the Creed Havens. You are indeed a changed man...a worthy man."

Ledger swallowed hard, unprepared for how Ayla's words affected him. He was grateful that she approved and, more importantly, believed him.

"And I also want you to know that I forgive you," she said as tears filled her eyes.

Their dance slowed as Ledger felt the full force of her forgiveness. It soothed and healed his soul in a way he couldn't have imagined. His eyes reddened.

"Thank you, Ayla," he whispered as he leaned into her and embraced her. She held on to him for a minute.

"We both needed this," she said softly.

Ledger nodded.

Zara smiled as she accepted Arn's offer to dance, relieved for the distraction. The irony of attending a bonding ceremony the day before her bonded status to Ledger was to be dissolved was not lost on her, and the weight of it was hard to bear. Although dissolving their bonded status was intended to officially set them free from obligations to one another, she didn't feel free at all.

"You look stunning tonight," Arn said with a smile as he and Zara participated in a couple's dance. "But the festive charm of your attire doesn't match the heaviness of your heart."

Zara glared at Arn. "I'm sure I have no idea what you're talking about," she countered as she glanced across the floor to see Ledger and Ayla dancing elegantly together.

"Your eyes betray you, Zara," Arn said, following her gaze. "I flew beside you in that Scavenger for over a year. You're one of the most courageous people I know. Why are you so afraid to tell him how you feel?"

Zara's eyes flashed with anger, then softened. "I'm not sure myself how I feel."

"Really?" Arn said, eyebrows raised. "It seems to me that you and Ledger are the only ones who don't know how you feel about each other. If you ask me, you're both being rather stupid."

Zara stopped the dance with a huff. "It's not that easy. Our bonding never should have happened, and you know it. Ledger told me months ago that we wouldn't be bonded if it weren't for Captain Rosco. That's the whole reason I asked to dissolve our bonded commitment."

"But Zara, things aren't as they seem—"

"I'm not going to force Ledger into a coerced bonding commitment," Zara cut in. "Besides, Ayla is much more suited to a man like Ledger, and if you don't believe me, just take a look."

Zara nodded across the room to where Ledger and Ayla were dancing. Seeing them embrace was all the evidence she needed to prove her point. Although Zara and Ayla had become friends while working side by side on various missions for Jeshu, seeing Ayla with Ledger hurt more than Zara wanted to admit.

"I have to go," Zara said. She turned to look at Arn. "You're a good friend, Arn, and I appreciate your concern, but I can't do this anymore. After tomorrow's dissolving ceremony, I'm going home. I choose to be happy...for both of them."

Zara turned and began making her way to the grand staircase. She needed to get away from this celebration... away from Rayl. It would take some time to get her head straight, but she was determined to do so. Surely, she could serve Jeshu well at the Creed Haven on her homeworld.

When Ledger and Ayla parted, Ayla seemed fully at peace for the first time since he had returned.

"There's another matter I wish to discuss with you," Ayla said as they resumed their dance. "A matter of the heart."

Ledger lifted an eyebrow. "Okay."

"It seems to me that you're conflicted regarding a romantic interest, and I am hoping I can help resolve that for you," Ayla said, tilting her head slightly.

Ledger was intrigued. Ayla was a beautiful and amazing girl, but at the forefront of his mind was the duty to honor Stone. He decided to play ignorant.

"I'm not entirely sure what you're referring to," Ledger prodded.

"Really? Are you sure?" Ayla egged. "Because Arn and I have been talking, and we think that you and Zara are, quite frankly, being stupid."

Ledger stepped back. "I...you...what?"

"Come on, Ledger. For two brilliant people, you seem to be purposefully ignorant about how you both feel for one another, and it makes no sense," Ayla scolded. "You'd better go and get her before you blow it for good. Tonight is your last chance!" Ayla said, pointing to Zara, who was beginning to walk up the grand staircase to exit the hall.

Still reeling from Ayla's chastisement, Ledger watched Zara ascend the staircase.

"Where's she going?" he asked.

"She's leaving, buddy," Arn said, stepping up to stand beside Ayla. "She's going back to Abaria."

"Abaria? Why?" A part of his soul ached as though it might die, and in that moment his heart awakened to his deep feelings for Zara. The thought of losing her to the opposite end of the galaxy was like a punch to his stomach. The abatement had given him a relational safety net, but that was about to end.

"Because you haven't given her a reason to stay," Arn replied.

"You love her, Ledger. Don't be a fool!" Ayla added.

Ayla's words unlocked his heart. He turned to face both of them.

"She's actually leaving for Abaria?" he asked.

Arn nodded, the corners of his mouth pulled down slightly.

"I can't let her go! What am I doing?" he asked, a sense of urgency filling his soul.

"Go!" Ayla ordered.

Ledger darted through the throng of dancers, arriving at the bottom of the stairs just as Zara reached the top of the staircase.

"Zara!" he called out.

Zara turned around to look down at Ledger. She had never appeared more beautiful to him than she did at that moment.

"Please wait," he called, scaling the steps two at a time to reach her.

Creases lined her beautiful brow as frustrated anger flashed across her face. She crossed her arms as he ascended the last few steps.

"What?" she asked tersely.

"We haven't had a chance to dance. Will you dance with me?"

She hesitated, glancing toward the exit, then back to Ledger. "I don't think so, Ledger. I've decided that it's time for me to go home. Once our dissolving ceremony is over tomorrow, I'm leaving for Abaria."

Ledger stepped closer to her. "Please...just one dance."

Zara's eyes furrowed in sorrow. "Please go away. This is almost over, and then you'll be free to move on."

She turned to leave, but Ledger reached for her hand. She hesitated, glancing down at his hand holding hers, but then she pulled back. Ledger desperately searched for words to change her mind.

"I don't want to be free. Please, Zara, just one dance with me. Then, if you wish, I'll let you go."

He took another step to close the distance between them, but she held up her hand to stop him.

"You don't understand," she began, her eyes fierce with resolve. "I can't do this. You hurt so much. I have to make it stop. Just go away. Besides...you belong with Ayla."

Zara's eyes momentarily softened, betraying her stoic composure.

He reached for her outstretched hand once more.

"I won't hurt you anymore. Five minutes...that's all I ask."

Zara closed her eyes.

"One dance," she whispered. "Then I leave."

"One dance," Ledger repeated.

He held her hand as he escorted her back down the grand staircase. To Ledger, this skilled, tough Scavenger pilot looked more like a princess at this moment. Once they stepped onto the dance floor, ancient music associated with a traditional Raylean dance filled the air. Ledger and Zara positioned themselves shoulder to shoulder facing opposite directions, their right arms lifted above them. They turned their wrists so that the backs of their hands touched. Ledger's stomach fluttered.

If there was a climax to the confusion in Zara's heart, this was it. As hard as she had tried to dismiss her affections for Ledger, she had utterly failed in the attempt. The mounting turmoil had only left one way of escape—flee. But now, he was forcing her to face this tortuous inner conflict in a final episode of emotional pain.

Zara felt Ledger's firm but tender hold on her hand. Even this touch caused her heart to stumble. As they took the dance floor and stood shoulder to shoulder, each facing the opposite direction, the representation was stark. They had always been facing opposite directions, never quite daring to turn and face each other...to hold each other. As the dance began, frustration and bitterness swirled through her. She had seen how Ayla and Ledger looked at each other with great admiration. Logically, Zara understood why he would be drawn to Ayla. Ayla was fabulous in every way—it just hurt every time she saw them together. It was in no small part the reason she had to leave.

The notes of the music forced the couple into motion, and Zara chanced looking up at Ledger. His eyes beckoned to her soul in a way she had never seen before. Something had changed, and it enticed her heart with that same deep longing she was trying to kill. The movements punctuated her fall. He seemed to welcome her in a way she could hardly refuse. *Dare I try? Dare I risk love one last time?* she wondered...yearned.

Ledger boldly set his gaze on Zara, and she seemed surprised by it. As they turned and stepped in rhythmic synchronicity, the music lifted the cares of the world away from them until all Ledger could see was her. Through each movement of the dance, Zara's countenance slowly warmed with a glow of hope until her eyes held a gleam that he had never noticed before. The pain of losing her to pragmatism was the catalyst that revealed just how much he cared for her.

The song continued in powerful but distant movements, always bringing them back to one another with the touch of the back of their hands. And each time, Ledger fell deeper in love with Zara. Though not a single word was spoken, the bonding of their hearts was unleashed by the melody of this ancient song.

As the final notes of the song swelled to a climatic end, Ledger and Zara each made a final turn, placing their hands palm to palm. When the last note faded away, Ledger interlocked his fingers with Zara's, pulling her close to him—face to face. He looked deeply into her eyes, now just inches apart. He could feel the warmth of her returning gaze.

"It took me months to understand why you wanted to dissolve our bonded union, and I respect you for your courage more than you will ever know. But now that I'm about to lose you, I can't bear the thought of my life without you. I see now what I could not see before. I want you to know that I have loved you since the first time I saw you. You're brave…you're beautiful…and you have so captured my heart that I can think of little else other than I want to spend the rest of my life side by side with you."

Zara's eyes glowed with affection as Ledger watched her lips form a response.

"Is this real?" she asked, her eyes searching Ledger's. "I've tried to deny my feelings for you a thousand times but couldn't. Please don't tease me…is this real?"

Ledger held both of Zara's hands in his. "We're bonded, Zara, and I've wasted six months of our lives pretending we weren't. I want to spend the rest of my life earning those days back. My love for you is more real than anything I've ever felt. I need to know if you feel the same."

Zara bit her lower lip, her fingers curling into the fabric at his chest. She hesitated, then looked up into his eyes. "I didn't realize how much you meant to me until I watched you die on that asteroid. The best part of me died with you that day, and when you returned, my life revived. That's when I knew I wanted to be with you. That's when I knew I loved you. I just wasn't brave enough to try."

Ledger leaned in until their foreheads touched. "You love me?" Ledger whispered.

"Yes, I love you."

Ledger touched her cheek. "You've healed my heart, Zara. I need you."

She drew back just enough to see his face, her hand slipping from his chest as fear crept into her eyes. "I'm scared, Ledger. Terrified of loving you and losing you." Her voice broke. "I can't—"

Ledger caught her hand before it could fall away. "I'm not going anywhere." Ledger stroked her cheek with his hand. "Please—take this risk with me. Let me love you for the rest of our lives."

Zara's eyes brimmed with tears, then she nodded.

"Zara Starlore, will you stay bonded to me for life?" Ledger asked.

Zara closed her eyes, filling her lungs with new life. "Yes, I will stay bonded to you."

Ledger gently stroked Zara's cheek, oblivious to the hundreds of people around them and the change of music happening in the hall.

"Do you remember when Rosco asked if there was anything else that was needed to seal our bonding ceremony?" Ledger asked.

Zara nodded.

"I lied."

Zara's brows furrowed.

"Interlocking hands is only one of two acts that must be accomplished," Ledger confessed.

"What's the other?" Zara asked.

"A kiss, but I was too intimidated to say so. May I kiss you now?"

"Only if it's the first of many," she said with a coy smile.

Ledger moved closer to Zara and kissed her, sealing forever the bond of love between them.

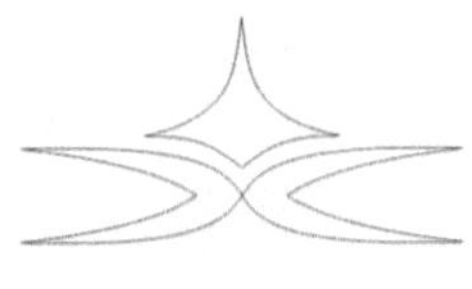

CHAPTER

15

The Empire's Wrath

Oh, my precious Rayl and her inhabitants, you have rejected my calling and scorned the voice of my Merchant. I will therefore give your inheritance to the Outworlders, and you shall have a home no more. You will be scattered among the stars and be forgotten. And when the age of the Outworlders is fulfilled, I will remember you and gather you unto me from the four corners of Aurora and establish Rayl once more. I will be your Sovereign, and you will be my people forevermore. – Micaba, Oracle of Ell Yon

Jemma's and Brayson's celebration continued late into the evening. Ledger and Zara, their hearts renewed by their mutual confession of love, were inseparable for the remainder of the evening. At one point, Ledger and Zara gathered beside Rhett, Brae, Arn, and Ayla to say goodbye to Jemma and Brayson and to wish them well. Even Rivet, his gold and white body shimmering under the gleaming chandelier, participated in congratulating the newly bonded couple. A satisfying expression of delight lingered on the faces of everyone standing in their circle.

"Thank you all for making our celebration such a joy," Jemma said, clinging to Brayson's arm.

"We're so grateful to each of you," Brayson added, his hand covering Jemma's.

"There was much to celebrate," Arn said with a broad grin and wink toward Ledger.

With a sheepish grin, Zara leaned into Ledger's side as he wrapped an arm around her. Ayla glanced her way, smiling.

Ledger's com band vibrated. He pulled up the lower portion of his sleeve to see an encrypted and urgent message. Arn lifted his wrist too, evidently having received the same message.

"Excuse us for a minute," Ledger said, stepping away from the group. "I'll be right back," he whispered to Zara.

Ledger and Arn retreated to a window beneath one of the balconies.

"It's from our secure QEC," Arn stated. "Have you authenticated?"

"Yes," Ledger replied. "Let's see what's going on."

The communication was in message form only—no audio, no video.

"URGENT. PRIORITY ALPHA ONE. IMMEDIATE RENDEVOUS REQUIRED AT JORN, 47.3495N, 113.0796W. SOLE PRESENCE. END SECURE TRANSMISSION."

Ledger looked up at Arn, comparing the destination planet and coordinates.

Arn confirmed the same destination on his com band and nodded. Ledger frowned. He scanned the rest of the hall. Brae and Rhett were still chatting with Zara, Ayla, Jemma, and Brayson. Many high-level Navis had come tonight.

"Why just us?" Arn asked.

Ledger shook his head. "Must have to do with the Outworlder missions. The new Creed Haven on planet Jorn must be in trouble."

"Agreed. There's a Spacehawk in Jalem reserved for emergencies. Brae and Rhett would know where," Arn suggested. "But I haven't ever piloted it."

"That won't be a problem," Ledger said.

"Oh, yeah…I forgot. You're an ace pilot too."

Ledger smirked. "We'd better let them know."

By the time Ledger and Arn had returned, Jemma and Brayson had been pulled away by some other prominent guests.

"What's up?" Rhett asked with a discerning eye.

"We've been called away," Ledger replied.

"When?" Zara asked, grabbing Ledger's hand.

"Immediately, I'm afraid. Alpha One priority," he added, eyeing Brae.

Brae's brow furrowed. "Must be serious, but we didn't receive an alert," she said, glancing toward Rhett.

"Is a Spacehawk available?" Arn asked.

"Yes. I'll coordinate with Jaym for you," Rhett said.

"Be careful," Brae warned. "We all know how devious the Morians have become. If it weren't for it being an authenticated QEC transmission, I'd be suspicious."

"We will," Ledger said, pulling Zara away for a personal conversation.

"I don't want you to go." Lines of worry etched Zara's face, her courage with love now being tested so quickly.

He stroked the side of her face. "I won't be long," he assured. "Then we can start our new life together."

Zara leaned her head into his hand and closed her eyes. She wrapped an arm around his waist. "I'm looking forward to that."

Ledger kissed her once more, then glanced toward Arn. Ayla was speaking a few encouraging words to him.

"Shall I join you on the mission?" Rivet asked as he approached Ledger and Zara.

"No, Rivet. Please stay with Zara until I return," Ledger replied.

"As you wish, my liege."

Ledger turned to leave Zara, but she held tight to his hand.

"Fly hard and live long," she said, a gentle smile on her lips. Ledger turned back to her, holding her closely once more.

"Fly hard and live long, my love," he whispered to her ear. He kissed her cheek then forced himself to step away from her.

To Ledger's dismay, it took Jaym a full thirty minutes to arrange for Arn and Ledger to be shuttled to the Jalem Creed Haven spacecraft, but twenty minutes after that, they were strapped in one of the surviving Spacehawks that Jeshu himself had designed. Ledger launched the craft up and away from a private spaceport 60 miles outside of Jalem's city limits. The Morian Empire had taken control of every slipstream conduit so that not even a cloaked ship like the Spacehawk could clear the gateway without being tracked to some degree. Besides this, the Navis were careful not to reveal that their Spacehawks had cloaking ability, so extreme caution was required. To their knowledge, Jeshu's Spacehawk design was the only spacecraft to have such technology.

"Thank you," Ledger said over the com as he thought of how Arn and Ayla had worked together to help him and Zara. Ledger accelerated the Spacehawk to break Rayl's orbit and set course for the short slipstream jump to the neighboring planet of Jorn in the Kayn System. Although all slipstream conduits in this region of space were monitored and controlled, for now there was little restriction in their use.

"You're welcome," Arn returned. "But Ayla deserves equal credit. She and I sat down and opened up with each other about you two. We came to the same conclusion and decided to smack you both in the head."

Ledger laughed. "I guess that's what it took." Then Ledger had a pleasant thought. "You and Ayla, huh?"

"Don't even," Arn replied. "This is all about you and Zara...that's it."

"Okay, buddy...whatever you say. Hopefully you've learned something from our debacle," Ledger finished.

A few minutes later they had entered and exited the slipstream conduit connecting Rayl and Jorn. Ledger was careful to stay well clear of any Morian battleships, although the Jorn Planetary Defense Forces could also be threatening. At first radio contact, Ledger provided the minimal clearance information typically required, and there was no pushback from their control ports.

"That seemed a bit too easy," Arn said as they began their descent into Jorn's atmosphere.

Ledger had the advanced sensor array on the Spacehawk scanning for anything that could pose a threat.

"The coordinates are near the Creed Haven, so we need to set down at the Terra Vin spaceport and take a speeder the rest of the way," Ledger said. "We can't risk exposing the actual location of the Haven to the Jorn authorities—and certainly not to the Morians."

"Copy that," Arn replied.

Ledger received landing clearance from the Terra Vin spaceport control.

"Hawk Victor 34, proceed to landing pad Four Alpha."

"Copy, proceeding to Four Alpha," Ledger repeated.

Ledger began shutting down his Omegeon-assisted long-range scanner array as he made his final approach to the landing pad. His finger hovered over the 'OFF' icon on his glass instrument panel. As his finger moved forward, the sensor suddenly alarmed, signaling that two security craft were less than one mile away. This wasn't unusual—except that the sensor also indicated that both ships had armed weapons systems and were locked on to their Spacehawk. Normal sensors would have never picked up the status of the patrols' weapons systems.

"I've got two Morian patrol craft with weapons hot and locked on," Ledger radioed to Arn.

"What? Why?"

A mere 50 feet from touching down, Ledger paused his descent.

"Hawk Victor 34, continue your landing approach immediately," control radioed.

Ledger scrambled for a response. If they landed and the patrols were intent on firing on them, they would be sitting ducks.

"Control, we're showing a landing strut malfunction. Stand by."

Ledger tuned the sensor array to get a clear reading on the patrols. The warning system indicated that the patrols were positioned behind one of the massive spaceport facilities as if poised for an ambush.

A few heated seconds passed as Ledger and Arn considered their options. Was this a false alarm, or had some nefarious action been planned?

"Hawk Victor 34, land immediately. We need to clear that airspace for other craft," control ordered.

Ledger's headset crackled with an open airwave transmission from an unknown source.

"Communication compromised. Morian commandos at the spaceport. Do not—" the radio transmission was interrupted by the sound of multiple plasma rounds exploding near whoever had been courageous enough to warn them, and in that moment, mayhem was unleashed.

Two dozen Morian commandos exited the spaceport firing class two plasma rifles at their Spacehawk just as the two lurking patrols crested the top of the far facility with engines ablaze. Ledger retracted his landing struts and punched his engines to full throttle while banking away from the approaching patrols. The patrols immediately began firing plasma rounds. Ledger activated the Spacehawk's Tri-delta energy shield just in the nick of time as two rounds found their mark. The Spacehawk ratcheted from the concussion, but the shields protected them. They were now out of range of the ground commandos, but the Morian patrols hounded them in hot pursuit.

"They were hoping to take us into custody," Arn said.

"Not anymore," Ledger replied. "They're out to kill."

"But why?" Arn asked.

Another radio transmission on an open channel blared in their headsets.

"QEC transmissions compromised," it began. Ledger recognized Rhett's voice. He wondered why Rhett would be sending an emergency transmission all the way to Jorn from Rayl. The answer quickly followed.

"Planet-wide Morian assault on Rayl. Flee the planet if you can. Do not return!"

Ledger didn't have time to even process Rhett's message as the Morian patrols barreled down on them. Ledger juked left and right to avoid another hit, then flipped on his cloak and executed a vertical reversal maneuver that positioned the Spacehawk in a head-to-head position with a high-speed closing vector. Ledger hoped the patrols wouldn't be astute enough to track their heat signature.

Swish! Ledger's Spacehawk flew over the patrols in a fraction of a second. The patrols turned left and right, apparently unable to track them. Ledger went pure vertical and rocketed the Spacehawk up to orbit.

"What's going on, Ledge?" Arn radioed. "Rayl under attack? Was the transmission real?"

"That was Rhett's voice," Ledger replied. "This was obviously a trap. I think they singled us out to capture us because we've been leading the off-world missions."

"To get intel on outworld Creed Havens?" Arn asked.

"It's the only thing that makes sense. We've got to get back to Rayl." Ledger's first desperate thoughts were for Zara.

I'm not there to protect her, he anguished within himself.

"Agreed," Arn responded.

Once in orbit, the Spacehawk's sensor array flooded with indications of hundreds of Morian ships entering the Kayn System from the Moria gateway. Long-range scanners revealed that every one of the arriving warships was en route to Rayl.

Ledger kept the Spacehawk cloaked as he and Arn tried to navigate back to Rayl, but the traffic in this sector of the system was absolutely chaotic. At the slipstream gateway, Ledger managed to bypass the Morian monitoring station and slip in between two other jumping craft undetected. Once they exited near Rayl, the chaos that the sensor array had warned them about became reality.

"Ledger! What is happening?" Arn exclaimed.

Ships were flying everywhere, many of them Morian military craft, including multiple battleships, dozens of frigates, and hundreds of fighters, along with more troop landing craft than Ledger could count. Thousands of smaller spacecraft were fleeing the planet in every direction, trying desperately to make it to one of a dozen gateways positioned around the planet. For any craft that had weapons or looked even remotely military in nature, the Morian armada eradicated them without mercy. The scene was surreal, unlike anything Ledger had ever witnessed. The sight was crushing—everything he had grown to love stood on the brink of total destruction.

"This is a full invasion!" Ledger radioed. "The Partisans have pushed the Morians to the tipping point. This is the beginning of the end of Rayl."

Ledger's statement framed the horrific visual with a simple, dreadful truth.

It was impossible to maintain an effective cloak through the atmosphere, simply because of the massive heat signature and contrails produced, but with the space around Rayl in total chaos, Ledger hoped they could descend fast enough to avoid detection. He chose an entry vector over one of the larger oceans where activity was minimal. Once through, Ledger descended to 2,000 feet and accelerated toward Jalem.

"Jalem's going to be impossible. It will be the Empire's primary target," Arn said over their com.

"I know, but what choice do we have? That's where our people are," Ledger replied.

As they flew over the coastline and approached the outer limits of Jalem, Ledger's heart failed him. The capital city of Rayl was ablaze from bombardments and ground troop assaults in hundreds of locations. This ancient city that had stood as a beacon of Sovereign Ell Yon's presence in the realm of humanity was being systematically destroyed by the relentless fist of the Morian Empire. Columns of black smoke rose up throughout the city, heralding the end of a legacy.

"Ledger...is this the end of us?" Arn asked.

Ledger found the words difficult to form. "Yes. I'm afraid it is, at least for a long time to come."

Ledger carefully navigated through the city, zigzagging to miss the hundreds of active firefights and skirmishes. It took twenty long minutes, but finally they arrived at the Zenith Lux Hall. The magnificent structure lay in ruin with only fragments of its former glory still intact. The glass ceiling lay shattered across the entire hall, its remnants still smoldering from recent, heavy plasma fire. Entire sections of the hall's walls had crumbled to burning heaps.

No! Ledger screamed in his mind. *Please, Sovereign Ell Yon, save our people...save Zara.*

Ledger set their Spacehawk down in the middle of a thoroughfare right next to the hall. They sprinted to one of the entrances and climbed through rubble to enter what was left of the once magnificent facility. Already they could see the evil handiwork of the Morian commandos. A dozen bodies were strewn throughout the rubble. At the top of the grand staircase, Ledger and Arn looked down on the ashes of what was once beautiful. Just a few hours earlier, Ledger had stood at this very spot convincing Zara to stay and dance with him. Now he wished he could go back in time and let her go, for perhaps then she would have escaped this snare of death. Arn's countenance was filled with dread. Ledger's heart pounded against his chest as a sense of panic threatened to overwhelm him. His eyes darted to every corner and every piece of rubble as he searched for his love.

Part of the staircase had collapsed, so they had to be careful navigating down its remaining structure. At the bottom lay dozens more bodies, but not as many as the number of people in attendance when they left. It gave Ledger the slightest glimmer of hope. Ledger and Arn split up, checking for life in each prone body, but so far, the commandos had executed their mission with deadly precision. Some they recognized—many they did not.

"Ledger!" Arn called out. He was bent low over a body.

Ledger rushed to his side to see Rhett lying on his stomach, blood and plasma burns across his back and shoulders. They moved some of the rubble aside and carefully turned him onto his back. A horrible black burn ravaged half of Rhett's face, from his left eye clear down to his neck. Ledger checked and discovered a weak pulse.

"Rhett!" Ledger pleaded.

Rhett wheezed, too weak to cough. His eyes opened, wincing in extreme pain.

"Ledge—"

"We'll get you help," Ledger said, his voice trembling. In the short span of knowing Rhett, he had come to love him as his father. Now Ledger was perilously close to losing the one man who had soothed the pain of a life of betrayal from Fasa Kylos.

"No—" Rhett wheezed. "Morians...took them. Find—"

Those few words were Rhett's last...words of concern for the people he loved. He had no strength left to even close his eyes. Ledger hung his head as sorrow ravaged his heart, and he wept. Arn closed Rhett's eyes with his hand.

"I'm so sorry, Ledger," Arn said.

Ledger lifted his head, despair and anger mingling deep in his soul.

"I will not rest until we find them," Ledger pledged.

"Together," Arn said.

Carefully, Ledger and Arn climbed out of the rubble of the once magnificent hall to look upon the smoldering city of Jalem and beyond. They gazed across the devastation the Morian Empire had wrought upon the Raylean homeworld, the deafening sound of continued battle filling the night air.

"I will give your inheritance to the Outworlders, and you shall have a home no more. You will be scattered among the stars and be forgotten," Ledger said, remembering the ancient words of the oracle Micaba.

"What does that mean for us?" Arn asked.

"It means our mission will not be easy, and it starts with finding our people."

"But how?" Arn asked.

Ledger's com band vibrated to let him know a message had arrived. He glanced at the display, then back to Arn.

"Rivet!"

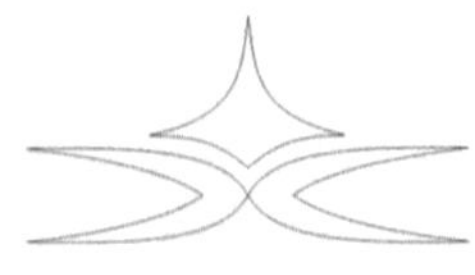

ABOUT THE AUTHOR

Chuck Black graduated from North Dakota State University with a degree in Electrical and Electronic Engineering. After traveling the world as a tactical combat communications engineer for the United States Air Force, he was accepted into pilot training and served the nation as an F-16 fighter pilot. He is the author of twenty-four novels, including the popular *Kingdom Series*, *The Knights of Arrethtrae* series, the *Wars of the Realm* series, *The Starlore Legacy* series, and *Call to Arms: The Guts and Glory of Courageous Fatherhood*. *Kingdom's Dawn* was on CBA's top ten best sellers list twice in 2008 for all Christian Youth Literature.

Chuck is also an entrepreneur with sixteen patents and is currently the president and general manager for FlowCore Systems, a chemical injection automation company in the oil and gas industry located in Williston, North Dakota.

Chuck is a believer in Jesus Christ as Lord and Savior and in the Holy-Spirit-inspired, infallible Word of God. He is devoted to his wife, Andrea, their six children and spouses, and numerous grandchildren. It is his desire to inspire people of all ages to follow the Lord with zeal and to equip parents, pastors, and youth leaders to accomplish the same through his allegorical and Scripture-based novels, seminars, podcast, and published articles.

MORE BOOKS BY CHUCK BLACK

THE STARLORE LEGACY
SCIENCE FICTION BIBLICAL ALLEGORY

THE KINGDOM SERIES
A MEDIEVAL ADVENTURE ALLEGORY OF THE ENTIRE BIBLE

THE KNIGHTS SERIES
LEGENDARY TALES OF HEROIC VALOR

WARS OF THE REALM
MODERN DAY SPIRITUAL WARFARE

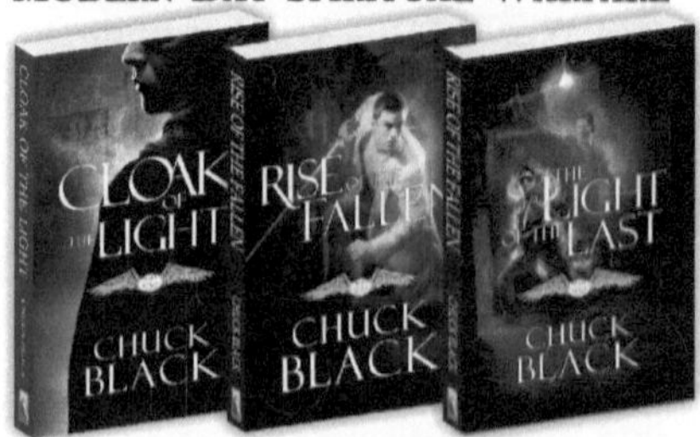

DRAMATIZED AUDIOBOOKS
AVAILABLE FOR EVERY TITLE

www.ChuckBlack.com

CHUCK BLACK
THE STARLORE LEGACY
NOVA
EPISODE ONE

THE STARLORE LEGACY
NOVA
A mighty empire. A lowly slave. A galaxy to save.
Will a hero rise?
Daeson Lockridge was born of royal blood, and all of his plans are falling into place now that his performance flying the legendary Starcraft at the academy places him as the second ranking cadet in his class. Only his cousin, Prince Linden Lockridge ranks higher. But a chance encounter with a lowly Starcraft mechanic shatters his perfect plan. The mysterious Raviel intersects his life and everything he thought he knew about himself, his family, his planet, and his galaxy seems a lie. Exposed as a fraud and with no one to trust he must flee the mighty Jyptonian fleet and search for the truth... a truth that will change his life and the future of the galaxy forever, for the Immortals are watching.
Published by
Perfect Praise Publishing
Williston, ND
ALL RIGHTS RESERVED
PERFECT PRAISE PUBLISHING

CHUCK BLACK

THE STARLORE LEGACY

FLIGHT

EPISODE **TWO**

THE STARLORE LEGACY
FLIGHT

Ancient prophecies promise a future of hope, but who dares face the wrath of a powerful tyrant?

Daeson seeks the counsel of the oracle that propelled him into a life of ruin and terrifying adventure. But the ruthless Chancellor Lockridge offers no quarter to his life-long friend turned traitor. Lockridge's thirst for revenge spills the blood of thousands of innocent Rayleans, and Daeson bears the burden of global calamity. Rejected by all except the spirited Raviel, Daeson struggles to carry on. When the whispers of the Immortal Ell Yon beckon Daeson to a remote moon of the planet Mesos, he must find the courage to face his deepest fears. Can Daeson trust the words of an ancient Immortal and inspire the slaves of Jypton to rise up? Not only does the future of his people hang in the balance, but the entire galaxy as well!

Published by
Perfect Praise Publishing
Williston, ND

PERFECT PRAISE
PUBLISHING

ALL RIGHTS RESERVED

CHUCK BLACK
THE STARLORE LEGACY
LORE
EPISODE THREE

THE STARLORE LEGACY
LORE
The Raylean people teeter on the edge of annihilation.
Can Daeson lead the quest for their promised homeworld?
Daeson finds himself a prisoner in a tribal world where the law of survival rules. Gone is the hope of the promised homeworld given by the mighty Immortal, Ell Yon. Daeson must fight to restore a future to the Raylean people, but to succeed he must overcome the marauders of cruel worlds, the tragedy of quantum peril, and the arch-enemy of the Sovereign Ell Yon, Lord Dracus. The odds are mounting against him. The relentless loyalty of his friend, Tig, sustains him as he rediscovers the power of the Protector. Can he lead the Rayleans to freedom once more?
Published by
Perfect Praise Publishing
Williston, ND
PERFECT PRAISE
PUBLISHING
ALL RIGHTS RESERVED

www.ingramcontent.com/pod-product-compliance
Lightning Source LLC
Chambersburg PA
CBHW030904060726
47591CB00005B/1405